Escape from the Mad Tribe

Stel ran, walked, and felt his way through the night, faintly hearing a chant over and over. How the Roti followed him, he couldn't tell. Finally, coming to a stream, Stel plunged in, allowing the current to spin him downstream. Much later, Stel pulled himself to the bank and, astonished, watched as the Roti, mindlessly staring straight ahead, paddled a long log past him.

But in the ensuing days, though Stel eluded the killers repeatedly, they reappeared, always preceded by their narcotic chant. Stel found himself picking up the rhythm, traveling, as they did, in time with it. He shook the chant out of his mind—but it returned and so did the trackers.

Stel had to escape. For in this far-future world, the Roti wanted to kill him—just because he had gray eyes.

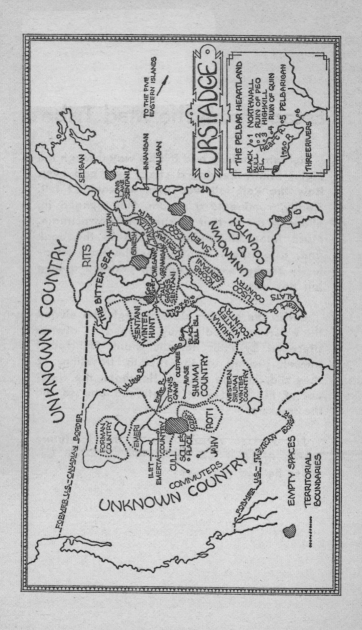

The Ends of
the Circle

Paul O. Williams

A Del Rey Book

BALLANTINE BOOKS • NEW YORK

To Anne and Evan

A Del Rey Book
Published by Ballantine Books

Copyright © 1981 by Paul O. Williams

Library of Congress Catalog Card Number: 80-69733

ISBN 0-345-29551-X

Manufactured in the United States of America

First Ballantine Books Edition: April 1981

Cover art by Ralph Brillhart

Map by Chris Barbieri

FROM the west wall of the Rive Tower in the city of Pelbarigan on the Heart, a young guardsman leaned out and yawned in the glare of the winter sun, now toward the west and glancing off the snowfields beyond the river. Far out on the river, a party of Pelbar was cutting ice, leaving large squares of dark water in the gray and moving the blocks toward shore, where they would be brought to the caves under the city for storage against the coming summer heat.

"Ahroe, you don't watch," said the guardsman. "Your husband has fallen four times now. He is tired. The Dahmens are too hard on him. He will never bend. I know him. He is a good man, but incredibly stubborn."

Ahroe said nothing. She resolutely looked upriver toward where a thin haze of woodsmoke had climbed above the trees on the bluff and lay like gauze on the still air.

"Ahroe," said Erasse. She didn't turn. He shrugged and looked away.

Far out on the ice, Stel, Ahroe's husband of twelve weeks, was talking softly with Ruudi, his cousin. "It's not a new world for me, even though we have peace with the outside tribes," he said. "It could scarcely be worse." He hooked the iron clip on the last dripping ice block and, heaving against it, sent it gliding and spinning toward shore.

"Never mind that. We're here to cut ice. Look. The thaw has already darkened the ice over the channel. You will survive."

Stel laughed in his throat. "You get to sleep at night.

And in a bed. With a little sleep, I could cut ice beside the worst Tantal that ever grew horns."

"You knew what would happen if you married a Dahmen. You made your own bed. Too bad you don't get to lie in it." Ruudi chuckled.

"Well, there's no use talking about it, Ruudi. I will never be as subservient as they want. It isn't in me. I have tried —speaking of the Dahmens, here comes one." Both men looked up as Aparet, who was directing the ice-cutting, came closer. She was a short woman, with graying hair, the beginnings of creases by her eyes, and well-defined wrinkles by her mouth.

"Let's bend to it," she began. "The thaw has begun early this year. Stel, go out to the edge of the dark ice and start a new cut. We want to get this close ice before it melts away from underneath. Work it right back and it will be a shorter drag to the gate."

Both men stopped. "It is already dangerous out there, Aparet Dahmen," said Stel. "You can even see air moving under the ice. It is eating it from underneath. I am afraid I might go through."

"Resisting again? This is a clear enough request, Stel. You aren't as weighty as you suppose. In fact you are rather light. You will find—"

"True enough. I am light with my present diet. But not light-headed. I'd sooner work the light ice than swim the dark channel."

"Go. That is more than a request. It is now a command. You are in a new family now, and—"

"Don't remind me. That I remember. All right, I will go. You come, too, and show me the place you mean."

"I am serious, Stel. I am about to recommend you for exclusion from Pelbarigan. All the Dahmens know discipline."

Stel hesitated. The habit of obedience was strong in him, being something that all the Pelbar are raised to, especially the males, who traditionally and by law subserved the commands of the women. Aparet said nothing more. Stel picked up a spud and an ice saw and started out toward the dark ice, sliding his feet, holding the long spud crosswise.

"Aparet, wait . . ." Ruudi began, but she raised her hand and shot him a hard look.

Stel stopped and set the spud to the ice. "Here?" he called.

"You know not. About fifteen more spans."

Stel stood still a moment. Then he turned and continued out, but as he neared the darker ice, it cracked and gave way with nearly no warning, plunging him into the water. The spud kept him from going under the ice. He scrambled quickly up, heaving his weight forward, but the ice gave way again. He had thrashed well out onto the dark band of ice, and the current in the channel welled and flowed up around him, spilling out across the ice as he struggled up, each time the ice breaking under him. Ruudi had gone for a rope, but running, shouting, and looking, he could find none where the ropes ought to have been. Stel kept heaving forward, plunging and struggling. Aparet stood watching. Finally he reached across to thicker ice, set the spud into it, and rolled himself up onto it, rolling again and again out toward the farther shore.

Aparet called to him. "Stel. You went too far. Go upriver and come back across."

Stel stood, shivering and dancing. "I can't. It won't hold. You know it. I'm going across to the fish shed and get dry." He turned and trotted toward the west bank.

"Come back," Aparet shouted.

"Hurry up, Stel," Ruudi yelled from beside her. "We will rig up an ice spanner." Aparet turned to him, but eight men were already there, looking at her.

"You'd better go, Aparet. Report to your precious family. We don't want you here," said Quid, an older man in a ragged tunic.

"What? Wait now," she began, but he picked up an ice hook, and she saw clearly enough that Pelbar courtesy had given way to a surging anger in them all. She turned and started for shore. "I will get the guard," she called back. "Make your ice spanner." Four men ran for shore.

The river was nearly a thousand arms wide, and at Pelbarigan the channel ran near the eastern shore. Stel had a long run. He could feel his feet going numb, and his hands, as he worked with short, quick steps to keep going in the cutting wind. He thought he could make it to the shed, but that was a makeshift structure, and he hoped a chert-and-steel fire set that the Sentani had not used still lay tucked in some corner of it. The shed seemed to stay far and small as he ran, but eventually he drew close to it and burst in the door. In the oak chest, fire makings lay in their pouch. He took them quickly out, fumbling with his hands to undo the knot on the pouch. It didn't work. He couldn't feel, nor make his fingers move. He stood and stamped as he worked, finally setting his teeth to the knot and tearing at it.

The shed held no place for a fire. It was generally used in summer and fall, so he had to kick aside snow by the door, set down the opened pouch, gather what tinder he could, and kindling. It wasn't going to work, he thought. He beat his hands on his thighs but couldn't even feel pain. A glance toward the eastern shore showed at least a dozen Pelbar, including four guardsmen, standing on the far side of the dark ice. No one was assembling an ice spanner, a very large trellis of poles, with floats, used to cross thin ice in emergencies. They were shouting to him, but he was too far away to hear them.

A glance up under the eaves showed him a phoebe's nest. He reached for it, and in his clumsiness, showered it down on the snow around him. Carefully, watching his hands, working them like two stumps, he gathered what he could, then stumbled around the shed looking for another nest. There were none. He ran inside and rummaged as well as he could in the chest. The cold seemed to be creeping up his legs. He knew to move continually. Under the chest he found a mouse nest, lifted it carefully, put it in his tinder, packed the charcoal flecks laboriously and slowly into it, and tried to strike a spark. He couldn't grip the big chert lump. He put it between his knees, but then found it impossible to strike. Inching forward, he placed his knees right over the tinder, struck down with both hands, again and again, carefully, but a little frantically, and caught a spark. Not trusting his hands to pick it up, he bent down, curled tinder over the glowing charcoal, and blinked away tears, but kept blowing. The smoke increased. He knew he would have to watch his hands because if they started to burn, he would not feel it. Finally a flame burst.

He added the phoebe's nest, piece by piece, quickly, laid on the woven fire pouch itself, then ran for twigs from nearby brush. Finally he had a small fire, and by running and adding to it, built it up until he was sure he wouldn't freeze. Rather than running for larger wood, he tore at pieces from the fishing shed, building the fire with the window hood, the door gutter, then the door itself, two stools inside, then part of the near wall he kicked out. I will fix it for them next summer, he thought.

Feeling began to come back into his hands, and with it needles of sharp pain. His body trembled violently, but he started to take off his clothes to dry them. Looking back across the river, he saw that the west-bank trees already laid their shadows all the way across the river to the eastern shore. He could see Ruudi still standing on the ice, stamping and beating his arms, and so he waved. Walking to the edge of the river, he told his cousin, with both arms, to go back to the city. Ruudi held both arms out, palms up, in resignation, then shouted something. Stel made the same gesture and ran back to the fire, busying himself with his clothes. He saw clearly enough that he would be out there all night, and so had work to do.

Dark came quickly, and with a return of his warmth, so did fatigue. He heard some shouting from the river and, once dressed, walked out onto the ice. It was Ruudi again. He had a large bag of food and a sleepsack. Swinging them round and round his head, he finally slung them across the thin ice to Stel. A guardsman stood with him, but it was not Ahroe. He could see the Dahmen patch on the man's sleeve. It was Ight, middle-aged now, used usually only for inside work, meek and as pliant as a green reed.

Ruudi said nothing of significance, so Stel knew that he felt he couldn't. He knew too that the incident had caused tensions. Trouble lay ahead. Stel took the bag, waved, and walked back to his fire. The sack was heavy.

As he surmised, it contained, among other things, a note, but he was surprised to find it was from his mother, Sagan. He took it out and read it in the firelight, the sleepsack across his shoulders for warmth:

Stel, my son, I will not trouble you with your mistake. You knew all along my feeling about the Dahmens, the archtraditionalists, but lovers are not listeners. However, it is our distinct feeling—not mine only but that of the Southcounsel and the family—that having been deprived of exclusion by the peace, the Dahmens have already given up on you and that Aparet's actions were deliberate. I do not write this lightly. No ropes were available in the prescribed locations, and the materials of the ice spanner had been cut up recently for firewood. The gate guards were Dahmens. We found that the usual roster had been altered to make this so—six days ago. You will find in this sack enough provisions to get you going, should you choose to do so, to Northwall, to appeal there to the Protector. I know that is desperate, but I fear for you, and we have all agreed to bear the shame. Do not concern yourself about Ahroe. She is one of them, and it is our opinion that she has consented to your death, though we may be wrong. But we are going to leave that relationship to you. I am glad you made it across the thin ice, and we watched your fire grow with great relief. Rutch laughed to see you in the distance kicking the side of the shed out. He and I send you all our love. This will be resolved. You have much of the night to think it all out —all night should you choose to come back to the city. I do not want to lose seeing you, but I fear deeply that should you stay, I would lose you forever. We all send our support, but since you married a Dahmen, you are now a Dahmen yourself. The Ardena says she stands with us. But there will be shame.

Stel read the letter several times, pondering it as he chewed on dried meat and fruit and ate half a small loaf of tough bread from the sack. He looked now across the river at Pelbarigan, looming black and square, with Gagen and Rive towers jutting up like two blunt horns, a small light on each seeming to blot away too many stars. He sighed and rubbed his hands in the new fur mittens he had taken from the sack.

He was sure his mother was wrong about Ahroe. She could not have been party to any conspiracy against him.

He was sure that his exclusion from her bed, then her room, to sleep in the hall—when they let him sleep—was just the nature of the Dahmens. She would not be allowed to break their decisions regarding him, and he saw that she held strictly to them, but with a grim mouth. He was sure she was not happy. But then her whole conduct puzzled him.

He had been wrong. As he thought about her, the shape of her body seemed to fill his hands again. He felt her soft breath, and the wisps of hair that escaped their rolls and blew across her face. He felt her ardor for him and the rising and choking strength of their loving. That was enough reason to submit himself to her, but now he saw, to his sudden astonishment, that the submission he had felt in himself was a part of the act of loving Ahroe, and not at all a general attitude. He had no desire to give the other Dahmen women any more than the usual respect that Pelbar males by rule and habit showed to all women.

Now he saw that their strict rules calling for what seemed to him an abject personal surrender had revolted him because he had seen in it a sexual element that was not in their thought at all. He had entrapped himself. He pondered his own emotional nature with a startling new insight. Could he change it? He didn't see how. He didn't see himself kneeling and groveling, either actually or symbolically, to that gang of crones, stern-faced tyrants, and haughty girls. Ahroe, yes. For her, anything. And yet, why had she not been out on the ice? What part had she in this?

Stel's thought in such matters was still largely shaped by his society, the thousand individuals in this one walled city in the middle of a vast wasteland and wilderness inhabited only by a few transients of the Sentani and Shumai, both roving groups which passed through, the Shumai with their families, the Sentani generally only in hunting and trading parties. Everything had changed after the fight at Northwall two falls ago—except that Pelbarigan had not accepted as much change as the northern Pelbar city, and the Dahmens, who had been conservatives before, now had not moved a span from their former position, in fact seemed to stiffen and grow more rigid than ever.

Stel chewed the other half of the small loaf, dipping it
into his cooling tea, sucking its tough crust, thinking over
his problem again and again, seeing with alarm that the
running man in the stars had begun to slide down westward. He stood up and dusted his hands, threw another
board on the fire, then walked down to the river's edge.
He looked toward the black wall of Pelbarigan, yearning
for Ahroe, but feeling tangled more and more in the net
that he felt was pulling him under. Then, as if his yearning thought were a mallard, splashing off the river, wheeling, and flying out toward her, only to be brought down
suddenly by a hunter's arrow, he felt something inside him
fail and drop. He felt the cold river surge up around him
again. He could not go back. It would not work. But he
could not well go to Northwall, either.

However, he would go. Somewhere. Tired as he was, he
turned back to the shed, tore off further boards, and
quickly, with his deft builder's hands, began to shape the
snow sliders Jestak had taught them of. He swept all the
shavings into the fire. His muscles ached, but his fatigue
focused him in on the methodical work of his preparations. He had been in no condition that evening at all to
think clearly, but having made up his mind, he simply set
about his flight from Pelbarigan.

High on Rive Tower, Ahroe leaned on the wall. She
was crying with her eyes, but stifling sobs with a hard-set
jaw. She saw Stel's fire across the river, and occasionally
she saw his shadow pass in front of it. She knew there was
more trouble in the city than merely their personal trouble. Stel's family was a small one, but Sagan was a well-
respected designer and the family a well-ordered one, if
somewhat too democratic. The Dahmens had trouble at-
tracting men from other families, but Stel had seemed to
her to fit in—at least into her arms and thought. They fit
in every way. That is, they would have, she thought, were
it not for her family. Her anger toward Stel rose further
every time he declined courtesy to them. But they demanded so much. She came to hate the sight of him, even
when she loved his jokes, his smile, the toss of his head.
Even now she seemed to see his gray eyes, as they must
have been, narrow and troubled, staring into the fire,

smarting as hers were, wondering what would happen when he returned to the city the next day.

She tried not to believe that her family had planned his death. It had been an accident, a bit of stupidity. But then the ropes were not in place. The ice spanner was not leaning in its usual place. She knew the deep anger and resentment swelling up in her family toward Stel. She saw it grow. She even shared it, while hating sharing it. Initially she assented willingly enough to their disciplines on him, thinking he would bend, then finally accept them. He seemed so gentle. But as they grew more rigid, so did he. As they heaped more duties on him, he accepted them more grimly, performed them more meticulously, and would not yield, either to their scorn or their demands for courtesy and submission. She had almost rebelled herself when he was finally excluded from their room, but by that time he seemed so unreasonable that she also wanted to strike out at him. Yet she saw his fatigue and pain and yearned to comfort him.

Now that he sat huddled across the river, his small fire showing in the general blackness, and the deep purple of the snow, she was more confused. She had missed her last period, too. What if she was pregnant? She had said nothing, but her life would be unbearable if she had a child without Stel there. The whole Southcouncil would shun her. Perhaps the west would as well. Anger at his stubbornness rose and mingled with fear, pity, and general misery in her thought the way the smoke of several nearby fires will rise and mingle into one drifting gray vagueness. She saw Stel's fire grow more bright. Finally she felt along the wall for the stairs.

II

BEFORE morning the guardsmen on the towers could see Stel's fire flicker down and die out. They watched it idly since it was the only object of much interest, speculating on Stel's future. With early light they could see Ruudi, Oleg, and Rutch, with four guardsmen, putting together a large, stretching ice spanner and gliding it out onto the surface of the river. Ruudi lay on it and worked his way across the dark ribbon of the channel. They saw him stop on the far side, looking at tracks, then looking at the trough in the ice where Stel had gone through. They saw him stoop and pick something up, then race for the fishing shed without sliding the ice spanner back across the channel for the guardsmen.

Ruudi swung wide of the line of tracks leading back to the ice, running hard, yelling for Stel. No answer came. When he reached the shore, he saw the burnt-out fire, the wreckage of the shed wall, a wisp of smoke from the fire curling up into the early sun. Then he saw a message in the snow, written deep and large. Panting, he shaded his eyes to read it:

Good-bye, Dahmens. You must play your games with others. I have taken what is called the coward's route. Good-bye to all the Arden, and to you, Ardena, whom I salute. May you all prosper, as is proper. Ahroe, you are free. I take all the shame upon myself.

A large arrow pointed out to the river, and Stel's tracks began from the tip of it, moving directly toward the hole in the ice.

"Great Aven," Ruudi choked, then turned again and raced out onto the ice, shouting.

It was not long after quarter sun that the whole council met, with Jestana, the Protector, presiding. The council room was full of tension. Rago, the Dahmena, Northcounsel this cycle again, was surrounded by a small knot of whispering family members. Ahroe was there, looking grim and empty. She was deeply shamed, but forced to be present at this review of the suicide of Stel. Across the room, the Southcounsel, Ardena, sat with Sagan and Rutch, and a small cluster of others. They were grim and silent, also shamed by Stel's act. Ahroe noticed that Sagan, though, was curiously composed. She had nothing to say.

Ruudi was asked to recount all the events of the previous afternoon, and of the morning. The Protector allowed no accusations, only evidence. When Rago remarked that Ahroe had married beneath herself, she commanded the Northcounsel to silence for the rest of the hearing. Nothing could be proved. It was claimed that Sentani, camping outside, had cut up the ice spanner for firewood. Others disagreed. No one knew surely. The Protector was careful not to let the session disintegrate into a wrangle.

It was near high sun when she raised her hand and called for silence in the council room for fifteen sun spans. It was a time, she said, for prayer to Aven, for reconciliation, for sorrow. Most of the people, though, neither shut their eyes nor bowed their heads, but watched the dust swim in the shafts of light streaming in the long windows on the south side of the chamber. The Jestana, though, sat perfectly still, eyes shut, hands in her lap. No one dared stir very much.

Finally she opened her eyes. "Now, listen to me," she began. "I have reviewed the testimony in my mind. It is my feeling that Aparet was endangering the life of Stel with premeditation, and that she was aided by her family in doing so. And yet there is no proof of this; therefore, it is not legally a reality." A stir from the Northcounsel caused her to raise her hand. "On the other side, without question Stel had given the Dahmens severe provocation, because by law he was now a Dahmen, hence subject to their family rules. He knew the severity of the family before he married. It is my judgment also that Ahroe should have no blame and receive no shame. I know that in practice, though, this will not be so, and it seems very likely that she will live the rest of her life here without a husband, so strong is the feeling from the south and west quadrants. Perhaps, Ahroe, you will find a husband in some far branch of your own family.

"What is more serious, in my judgment, is the increase of tensions caused by this incident. As an enclosed city— and this is still what we are, although there is some movement toward opening—we must cohere. But with the removal of outside threat, our differences are becoming more apparent. We will have to guard against this, for it will have severe repercussions. Just because we are open to the outside tribes, we have not changed our social order. The Dahmens have the right to interpret that severely. Other families have the right to read the word of Pell in other ways." Again she had to hold up her hand for attention.

"And yet there is one whole aspect of this situation that puzzles me. The message of Stel, left in the snow, is a curious one. It expresses regret, but not desperation. It jokes. It was written by a man who had just, by valiant effort, saved his life from the river. He was being asked by the Dahmens to violate his own basic nature. I don't understand how he agreed to his marriage in the first place, but having done that, his doom was, as it were, already signed.

"This occurs to me. Are we sure he went under the ice? We have no body. We have also the fact that Ruudi took him a sack of food and a sleepsack last night. Did Stel take that into the river with him? It was not found.

"Now I direct that this matter be not fully adjudged at this point. I direct that the guard send upriver to the Shumai camp for a hunter to come and examine all the evidence on the west bank, that is, if the curious have not wholly trampled it out. We should have this information by sunset, and I direct that we will meet here once more then." She held up both hands for silence again.

"Until then, I command that the families in contention in this issue have no words with one another about this or any other matter. Now, guard, send as I have directed. This council stands recessed."

A strangely long moment of silence hung in the chamber before anyone moved. The Protector was known to be a wise woman, through long experience, but no one else had thought of the possibility that Stel was not dead. What if he had fled, perhaps to Northwall? Slowly the murmur of voices grew as they left the room.

Not only did a guardsman immediately begin the short run northward to the Shumai winter camp, but six more crossed the ice spanner to prevent any further interference with the remaining tracks left by Stel. The scene moiled in confusion, though. A number of people had been across the river that morning, and tracks crossed tracks in a bewildering array of footprints. The ice on the river was partly snow-covered, partly blown free. As far as Ruudi could remember, Stel had crossed several snow-free places, his tracks resuming again in the tongues of snow beyond them.

The sun had not passed one-eighth of its way toward setting when the guardsman reappeared with three Shumai, trotting easily along the free ice near the shore, then swinging out and crossing the ice spanner. Hagen, the oldest, a thin man with long light-blond hair in a braid, went to Stel's message with the guard. The other two examined the ice, one to the north, the other to the south, walking in the typical loose-hipped gait of habitual runners, casting their eyes about, occasionally stooping.

The guardsman read the sign to Hagen, who smiled ironically at the thought of a man allowing himself to be so ruled by a family that he had to leave home because of them. "He will be happier out on the prairies, perhaps," he mused. "But let us look at the tracks, if they haven't been wholly trampled out by all you big-footed Pelbar." He picked up the tracks at the message, trotting easily out toward the channel, seeing Stel's footprints among the many similar ones as if they had been painted blue. About three-quarters of the way out, he stopped and bent down. The snow there was a light scurf blown onto the ice, next to clear ice.

"From here on out he backed up in his tracks," said Hagen. "A simple trick. Even foxes use it. Look. See the way the heel rolls? Why didn't you see that?" Hagen looked south at Assek. He cupped his hands and whistled. "Did he go that way?" he called.

Assek was several hundred spans away. He waved his arms. "Somebody did. A man of medium height," he called back. "Should I track him?"

Hagen looked at the guardsman with him. He shook his head. "No. But please check the tracks all the way out to the channel so we can give a clear report to the council. Ask him to follow the trace another half-ayas. And please come to Pelbarigan for some food and drink, and the pitched baskets we promised."

At the reassembled council, Leyye, the Southguard captain, reported Hagen's findings. The Protector nodded. "Well," she said, "then the matter is settled. Stel has left. If he does not return, then after the prescribed time, Ahroe will be free again. If he does, he will be subject to the discipline of his family—the Dahmens. However, I might point out that I have investigated the discipline that Stel was already under, and I regard him as a very sturdy person to have lasted this long. I suppose one might, with certain attitudes, demand that he kneel and press his forehead to the floor whenever a Dahmen woman entered the room, including his wife, or a five-year-old child—though some of us might consider that an odd procedure. But the withholding of food, wearing of weights, performance of extra duties, deprivation of sleep may eventually chafe at a person's sympathies. Were he to return, and more severe measures were applied, short of outright torture . . ." A murmur of protest from the Northcounsel caused the Jestana to raise her hand for silence. "If more severe measures were applied, short of outright torture, Stel would be in a position himself to apply for relief from the general council. I believe he could have applied as things stand, but he would not. Given his nature, it is my judgment that he will not return. He has been shown that there is nothing here for him, not even Ahroe, who has been taken from him. So, Sagan, you will have to endure without the sight of your son. I did that for quite a time, as you know, and my pity goes out to you." Smiling, she added, "I hope, however, that if Stel returns, for our sake, it will be somewhat less noticeably than Jestak. This council stands dismissed."

The entire Northcouncil rose to protest, with loud shouts of dissent and anger. The guard moved out in front of them and around the Protector, who simply smiled ruefully and raised her hands for silence again. "It seems we are not done, then. Well, Northcounsel, what is the will of your constituency?"

"Protector, we protest this decision in the most strong terms imaginable. We feel that it is perhaps time to call again for a general election. It is our unanimous view that guards, or perhaps Shumai, who are better at it, must be sent to bring Stel back. He has insulted the Dahmens, flouted his marriage vow, deserted his people, and deceived us into grief for his death and consternation at his lack of character. That the Southcouncil, and particularly the Arden, must bear, for it belongs to them and their loose methods. We demand this."

The Protector turned to the guard captain. "I do not see Aparet here. We will send for her. Now let us wait in silence. And have Hes bring the lamps."

Again the Protector sat with eyes closed and hands folded. A few of the council did likewise, but most were restive. It was a relief to watch Hes hobbling around slowly, deftly lighting the forty wax lamps in the hall from a long spill. The Northcouncil was especially grim. They looked at each other, nervous and angry, but the Protector's silence was one of the most basic orders of the council. It had often served to quell overflowing tempers. Finally Aparet came, her guardsman's tunic askew as she tried to smooth it down. The Protector motioned her to the dais.

"Aparet, it was reported to us yesterday that you had said to Stel, in ordering him out onto the thin ice through which he fell, that because of his reluctance to go, you were about to recommend for exclusion from Pelbarigan. Is that or is that not so?" Out of the corner of her eye, the Protector saw Ahroe wince.

"Protector, who reported that to you?"

"Witnesses. Is that or is that not so?"

Aparet dropped her head. "It is so, Protector."

"And was that the general decision of the Dahmens, or did you say that on your own?"

The Northcounsel rose to protest the question. The Protector looked at her but did not give her the floor. "Well," the Jestana said gently, "I see the Northcounsel protests my question. That is all right. I need not put it. I think it is clear that Stel had good reason to believe that it was the view of the Dahmens as a family, did he not?"

"No, he did not," the Northcounsel broke in. "It is evil to make that insinuation just because Aparet, driven to exasperation, let slip her tongue. You have—"

"Northcounsel," the Jestana interrupted. "You will recall, no doubt, other facts. Stel did in fact fall through the ice that Aparet ordered him onto, against his will. She ordered him to recross the ice he had just fallen through. The ropes were not in their usual places. Fourth, Stel had little reason to have felt welcome in the family of the Dahmens. The fact is that Stel had plenty of reason for thinking that he would be excluded from Pelbarigan, if not harmed, and so he excluded himself while he was still unharmed. Now you wish him brought back. Is it so you will have the pleasure of excluding him? However, I do not excuse him. He has wronged you. I, the Protector, say so. And if you wish the record to show that he has been excluded, I have no objection. Do you wish to say anything to that, Sagan?"

"What is there to say?" said Sagan. "You may do as you wish. We all know the facts, don't we. Stel has saved his life, but you want that collection of tyrants to look good to posterity."

"Well, then, though your expression of your opinion seems rather harsh, the Dahmens also may feel free to express theirs by excluding Stel. I might point out, however, that this is their ninth exclusion in the last thirty-two years. All other families together have excluded seven in total in the same period. But this is the right of the Dahmens. It is not the business of the council so long as physical abuse is not recorded or appeal made on such grounds by the one excluded.

"These situations are never easy. I would like to request that Sagan and Ahroe rejoin their families with the embrace of peace before we adjourn."

But Ahroe was no longer there. No one had seen her leave, but she must have slipped out during the North-counsel's protest. The Protector had to end the meeting without the ceremony. This troubled her, because it was more than a formality. It was a sacred pledge. Well, when Ahroe returned, she would reconvene the council, if necessary, for the embrace alone. It would be worth it. She left the hall frowning as she leaned slightly on Druk, her servant. The rest of the council followed, largely silent. The city was small enough to be deeply troubled by the vanishing of Stel. At this moment, they knew, he was out in the dark winter night, somewhere not too far off, but alone. While he did not have the tribesmen to worry about, it still was not a happy consideration to a close-dwelling Pelbar.

 III

AHROE had watched when the guardsmen and the three Shumai recrossed the ice spanner and walked briskly up the bank to Pelbarigan to report. Hagen and his two men did not enter the city, which plainly made them uneasy with its size and enclosure, but the group spoke in low tones at the gate. The guardsmen brought them drinks and a present of pitched baskets, which would hold water and yet travel well—much better than ceramics, which would not last long in the habitual rough journeys of the Shumai.

Ahroe's heart both rose and sank when she heard that

Stel was alive. Perhaps she might recover him. She still had her bride's ardor, though its fulfillment had lately been denied her. She longed to hear his wit, to see his whimsical smile and soft, gray eyes. And yet his flight meant that he had not only consciously rejected her but had deceived them all as well. A momentary fury rose in her, erasing her hopes. Stel had some other motive, some vision of life beyond their lives together, beyond Pelbarigan, some aspect of himself he had never hinted at.

All her Pelbar and Dahmen sense of female pride tightened at this. For a moment a whirl of anger almost made her stagger. She would pursue him and bring him back, perhaps even to reject him in front of them all. Had she not been at the fight at Northwall? Had she not run there herself and stood in the line of guardsmen blocking the flight of the beaten Tantal? Stel had done nothing like that. He was a builder, a worker in stone, a townsman.

But then what would she say to him when she had caught up with him? And what if she never did—out there on the vast snow-covered prairie and among the bare-branched woods. She really knew little of the wilderness that began at the west river bank. If Stel refused to come with her, what would she do? Would she take out her short-sword and make him come? If he still refused, how would she make him? Would she hurt him? And if he did come, what then? What of the family?

Clearly he hadn't gone to Northwall. That would have been easy. She began to surmise that he had gone westward. He had heard Jestak's story with eager intentness. He had listened to the Shumai with obvious fascination and had sat on the river bank with band after band of them, questioning them, mending their equipment with his deft hands as he drew out of them stories of their life. He had even reported much about them to Sease, for her records. A slight fear went through Ahroe. Perhaps he knew more of life to the west than she had realized. She remembered him telling her of rumors of a vast sea beyond endless mountains to the west, though none of the Shumai had ever been there. Who told him? She recalled how his gray eyes gained their hint of warm blue when he speculated on all this. He even suggested they might take a trip sometime.

Damn him. She had married a dreamer, unfit to be a practical and serviceable husband. But what if she really were pregnant? Did she dare appeal to him on those grounds? She knew he would instantly honor his responsibility. But that would be appealing to him, and a Dahmen never appealed. With men it was proper to control. And if they did return, how could they ever live at Pelbarigan? It would be impossible. Perhaps they could go to Northwall, or to the other Pelbar city, Threerivers, far to the south.

As she stood musing, the Shumai drank their steaming tea and ate honey-topped cakes, talking quietly. She caught a silence and looked up. They were watching her, and one was grinning. She detested his look, and, spinning on her heel, left, faintly hearing behind her a Shumai voice saying, "Now why would any man leave that?" It was followed by an ugly laugh, then a curt murmur from the old man, the one called Hagen.

About this time, Stel woke up. He had traveled south about seventeen ayas, searching the west bank for an entering stream large enough to be free of snow. He wanted to move westward. But he wanted no trackers—if he was followed. He knew he was tired, and in no condition to endure any sustained flight. A sullen fatigue had set in, and he moved dully, rehearsing his recent experience of cleaning Dahmen privies at night after drudging all day, of polishing equipment that didn't need it, washing, cooking, scrubbing, baking, sometimes nearly all night. He had been wronged, misused. He would not go back. Never.

But where was he going? He hadn't thought that through. Finally he had found a stream, entered it, by midmorning traveling up it some distance, only to have it narrow and grow snowy. Dizzy with fatigue, he had stopped, sat against one cut bank, and chewed dried meat and waybread from his mother's sack. Then he had dug into the snow of the bank and crawled into his feather-stuffed sleepsack. The day was dull gray, silent except for the piping of an occasional cardinal. Once, as the sun had passed its height, three tanwolves, trotting the crest of the bank, stopped. They watched the slight breath streaming up from the bank. The lead one growled in his throat, his back hair rising in a long ridge. Then the three turned and loped away. Stel never knew it.

When he did awake, he was startled at how much of the day had passed. He was hungry, dirty, unshaven, still aching with fatigue. But his mind was sharp. What had he done? Now he was wholly alone. Why had he done this? He felt blank, motiveless. It was as if he had grown sick and vomited, finally vomiting out his entire life. He felt like a skin full of emptiness. What would Ahroe do? Well, that would have to be her concern. But the shame of it. He heard of the occasional Pelbar outcasts, men who could not, for one reason or another, fit into Pelbar culture and society. He had always thought of them as misfits or disgusting freaks. Now he was one. Had they all gone through this? Had they found themselves standing outside their entire experience looking for another life?

Stel knew that he would have to do that. One doesn't find a wholly new self instantly. But there were other things to do. He would worry about the new life when he knew he had shed the old one. He would travel westward until he was sure that no one followed. He would go to the limit of his food, then try to survive until spring. He knew that was a vague plan. He would have to think about it, though, as he traveled. Binding on the crude snow sliders he had made from slats of the fishing shed, he started out.

He had curled the tips back by shaving them thin, heating them with boiling tea, and tying them with thongs. The bindings were even more crude, but sturdy. He broke some sticks for poles, to help propel himself, and started out. Almost immediately he fell. He had seen others excel at skill, but he himself was completely new at it. Well, he would have to learn. As afternoon darkened to evening, Stel moved westward into the vast whiteness, for all he knew empty of all human life between himself and Black Bull Island, which he knew to be a camp of Shumai old people on the Issou River, somewhere way out there on the frozen land. Where he didn't know. It was like striding purposefully into nothingness. But having nothing else to do, he did so.

Before the evening council meeting, Ahroe had decided to bring Stel back. She had prepared her equipment and supplies carefully and secretly, stowing it all in the room she had shared with Stel. She would have to wait until dark, and it was important to know the reaction of the Protector and the council. But her shame so rose that she could barely endure it, and then when the whole Northcouncil stood in a tumult of protest, she slipped out. It was dark. She could go.

As she entered her room, hurrying to be gone, a wave of strangeness went over her. How sweet their life had been, but for so short a time. Stel's clothing still lay on his shelves. The chest he had built and carved so intricately showed dully in the light of the fish-oil lamp. How much he had added to the room—bent wood hooks on the wall; a recurved bow he had made for her, bound and inlaid; mats of river rushes, woven in diamond patterns. No room had ever seemed so empty. Ahroe took Stel's razor. At least when she caught up to him, she could get him to shave. And as she left, she caught up his hand fishing line and a small wooden box he seemed never to finish inlaying. They would rest and talk, and that would give him something to do as they made their peace. He wouldn't have to look at her, nor she at him.

Ahroe didn't use the main entrance. She eased herself over the south wall with her guardsman's rope, slid down, shook it loose, and coiled it expertly as she ran down through the shadows, staying in the fringe of trees so the guardsmen on Gagen Tower wouldn't notice her. She was around the bend, over an ayas south, before she moved out onto the river for easier running.

It was only then that it occurred to her that she would have to cross the channel ice to reach the west bank. Ahroe was furious with her own stupidity. She would have to spend part of the night making her own ice spanner. But that would have to wait until she had traveled farther. The Dahmena might want to bring her back as well. Toward midnight she stopped at the head of an island near the east bank. Thick willows crowded at the north end, and using her short-sword she quickly cut a number of saplings, tying them into a large, loose mat with withes from smaller ones. It was a crude affair. Her bindings kept breaking. Finally she used Stel's fish line to fasten it together, ruefully cutting it into short lengths. She had watched him painstakingly braid it from thin strips of the inner bark of some tree she didn't know. It was too bad.

She held her breath as she slid the spanner out onto the dark ice. Cracks ran through it, with sharp, sudden noises, but she slid herself rapidly across, digging her smallknife into the ice for propulsion. It worked. But now that she was on the west side, what was she to do? She couldn't track at night. If Stel had turned west, she would miss his trail. No. There, in the light snow cover, were footprints. Then she lost them again on the clear ice. She moved slowly, beginning to feel her own strain and fatigue.

But she didn't know what else to do, so she persisted southward, finding no tracks. The night seemed to darken toward morning. Finally she stood, nonplussed, when a slight sound from behind caused her, with guardsman's instincts, to whirl and draw her short-sword in one quick movement. A figure stood there on the ice.

"Stand off," she said evenly. "Stel?"

"No, my love. I am Assek."

"The Shumai. What do you want?"

"To help you. Why do you follow him? I can be anything to you he ever was. And more."

Ahroe's short bow was strapped to her backsack. She surged with anger at her carelessness. But she still had the short-sword, and years of practice with it.

"Get away. I need no help. Least of all from you. Stand off. Come near and I will kill you."

"We have peace, remember? Is this a Pelbar welcome? You, the peaceful people?"

"I need nothing from you, want nothing, and insist that you leave," she said, surprised at the flatness and tension in her own voice.

"Well, you have already missed his trail. He turned into a stream over an ayas back. Doesn't that prove my help?"

"How do I know that? I would have learned it in the morning anyway. Now go."

"Do you think that twig in your hand could stop me if I wanted to take it away from you?"

"Then take it."

Assek laughed and made as if to shrug, but lunged for her wrist as he did. Ahroe's quick stroke with her short-sword caught him on the forearm and cut through his thick leather sleeve into flesh. "Ahhh," he muttered, trotting back out of reach, then kneeling on the ice holding his arm. "Damn you, Pelbar wench," he said, expecting a defensive posture from her, but, as he knelt, she had closed on him and stood behind him, catching his braid and holding the sword to his neck.

"Now," she said. "Will you go?"

Assek was enraged and bewildered, but he had no choice. "Yes, you fish-gutted, useless piece of river d—" He stopped and gasped as she twisted his head around, jammed his face into the ice, and put her knee against his back, slicing through his belt and removing his short-knife, tossing it aside.

"Now again," she said into the back of his neck, "will you go?"

Assek felt the sword point slowly bearing in. Fear mingled with his rage. "Yes," he finally said. Ahroe stepped up and back, holding her short-sword ahead of her.

"Stop at Pelbarigan and they will bandage your arm," she said.

"You barely scratched it, river dung," he said. But he held it with the other hand, and blood came from between his fingers.

"Nevertheless, stop there. Now, go."

"I am going, muck heap. Now keep on south and catch your manchild." Assek gave a bitter laugh and walked slowly north on the river surface. Ahroe didn't move, but stood facing him, sword out, until he was lost in the darkness. Then she sheathed the sword, sat on the ice, and cried, trembling with as much misery as she ever could remember experiencing.

If only Stel were here. Even his stupid male presence would have prevented the Shumai from making any move toward her. She could still feel Assek's quick male urgency, dumb as a beast, revoltingly opposite to Stel's gentle and playful nudgings toward love. Curse them all. Pell was right about the elaborate need to control the male. She knew, too, that she was not through with Assek. He would follow her, with his eyes that could track at night on ice. He would wait his opportunity, now not only with his desires but with his need to prove himself, his revenge. Had she not enough to worry about? Oh, Aven, what was she to do?

She stood, suddenly, absently dusted off the snow, and turned north to look for the stream Assek had mentioned. It was a chance. If Stel was close, she would find him before Assek could trouble her. As she walked, she unslung her backsack and took off her Pelbar short bow, hooking it on her shoulder strap with four arrows, each tipped with steel, each tip in a small wood-shaving sheath, a gift from Stel.

 IV

Before dawn a weary Druk awakened the Protector, knocking solicitously on the door. As she slowly came awake, she saw a light behind him, and the guard chief's shoulder.

"Yes, Druk, come in. What is it? Something about the Dahmens, no doubt. Come in. I can think from bed, surely. And surely I have enough on in this cold."

Oet shouldered by the startled Druk and said, "Protector, I regret disturbing you. Something has arisen. Someone was seen, a man, crossing the ice spanner a while ago. The guards didn't think to report it immediately, but I am surmising it is one of the Shumai, and Ahroe is out there. He turned and ran southward on the west side. What do you wish us to do?"

"It was not Ahroe?"

"No, Protector. Both towers agreed that even in the darkness they could see that he was too large."

The Protector sat up slowly, rubbing her face in her hands and sighing. "Send two guardsmen to the Shumai camp and find out. The old one, Hagen, has had tea with me. I believe we can trust him. Find out. At the same time, send two guardsmen across the spanner and south. Let them all be men. Let me know as soon as you learn anything. Wake me if you must. Ah, Ahroe, let us hope that you were shot from a large enough bow to fly far and quickly. But I fear not. And now, Oet, if I can, I will return to sleep." She turned down and away, settling herself, but Oet didn't see. She was already past the doorway, glancing at Druk curled on his reed bed in the small anteroom.

Hagen heard the guardsmen coming and was standing outside his log shelter waiting for them, a fur thrown around him, shifting from foot to foot. He held up his hand in the early dawn. "More tracking?" he asked.

The guardsmen panted hard, and one said, "We fear so, Hagen, but we don't know yet. A man was seen crossing the ice spanner a while ago and turning south. Was he one of your men?"

Hagen ducked his head inside the shelter, then disappeared, reappearing soon afterward. "Assek is not here," he said. "What concern is there? He will not track your Stel. There is no reason."

"Ahroe, Stel's wife, left last night. Will Assek harm her?"

Hagen didn't reply, but again disappeared into the shelter. The guardsmen heard murmurs, and with astonishing suddenness, Hagen and Ican reappeared, dressed and armed with spears and longbows, fur rolls slung over their shoulders.

"I fear he may do some harm," said Hagen. "He lost his wife last fall. He is a cross between an aspen leaf and a young bull. We will follow him." He and Ican were by the guardsmen and down the trail before the Pelbar could turn.

Stel had improved rapidly on the snow sliders, especially after he tired of falling and stopped to cut rough grooves down the bottoms. He continued all night and into the morning before becoming exhausted and finding a snowbank to rest in. But he had made nearly thirty ayas and was beginning to feel at ease.

Ahroe, meanwhile, had found the stream, entered it, and trotted up the ice until she saw the snow with Stel's tracks. There he had slept. That must have been last night. She shuddered from her fatigue and the knowledge that he was so far ahead of her. And she had no snow sliders. The snow lay scarcely more than a span deep, but nonetheless, he made better time. In spite of herself, she smiled when she saw where he had fallen and drawn a rough face, with downturned mouth, on the snow. Stel was always Stel. He surmised he would be followed, at least at first. Surely the face was for Ahroe. A complex wash of feeling went over her. How could he love her and run from them all? She kicked the face away and plunged ahead into the snow. The air had turned damp. What if it snowed? She would have to track him all day without stopping. She would have to catch up with him before the Shumai returned.

She continued walking as the day progressed, forcing herself increasingly, especially since the air grew dull and still, and in the third quadrant, slow snowflakes began to drift down, gently thickening as she followed the twin lines of sliding tracks across groves, brakes, and patches of prairie. She didn't stop to eat, but as she continued chewed on waybread and dried meat, just as Stel was doing.

Dusk came. She could scarcely see the trail. Stopping, she felt a silence fall that was worse than that of the caves beneath the city. A strange calm lay on her. It had warmed somewhat. Bone-weary, she decided she would sleep in a tree, using one of the traveling tricks of the Pelbar from the days before the peace. Selecting just the right one, a moderate-size maple with plenty of sturdy branches, she climbed carefully, working her short-sword into each branch at the base until she was about twenty spans up. Then she carefully cut into both the top and base of four adjacent limbs, leaving them hinged but nearly severed. Climbing farther up, she found a crotch and tied herself into her sleepsack. It was not comfortable, but in her present exhaustion, she didn't notice, and eventually she slept.

Suddenly, nearly at midnight, Assek was there. The tracks, now mere dents in the falling snow and dim-blue light, stopped at the tree. He smiled to himself, and taking out his second knife, a skinner, began slowly climbing. Yes, there was Ahroe's dim shape above him. He would cut her ropes and push her out before she could wake. Then, on the ground and injured, she would be his to do with what he willed. For a moment he hesitated. This was mad. It had gone too far. But she had cut him and he would have at least to even that score. He would see. Perhaps that would be enough. But Ahroe had a lovely face, straight-nosed, with thin and delicate nostrils. Her mouth was small and shapely. Her eyes, dark brown, were deep and penetrating. It was a face to be loved, certainly not to be sleeping in a tree in the snow.

Assek amused himself with his dreams as he moved up stealthily, but then, as he slowly shifted his weight, the branch beneath him cracked. He grabbed wildly, only to tear off another, dropping and snapping off four more, slamming into a final larger one and pitching into the snow.

He didn't move immediately. Snow fell on his face, which smarted from scraping against the tree trunk. He rolled over onto his knees as he heard Ahroe softly drop to the snow. Anger and pain shook him. He struggled to his feet and faced her.

"Are you hurt again?" she asked in a thin voice with an edge of mockery in it.

He couldn't even find his skinning knife. He must have dropped it in the snow. "Witch, river dung, Pelbar garbage, owl eyes, snake belly," he began, but he was staggering, and she hit him across the face, dropping him to his knees. Looking up, he saw dimly that she had an arrow nocked on her short bow. How could this be? He said nothing more.

"Do you want to die? I can't keep letting you go.

Sooner or later, you would get me. And I know you wouldn't let me go—at least until I was worth nothing to myself." Assek said nothing.

Ahroe drew the bow. "Now, do you want to die?"

Assek looked up at her with a bleeding face and a look of calm hatred Ahroe could feel even in the dark. He laughed silently, a bitter, aspirant laugh of pure frustration. "Please yourself. Kill me if you want to," he said quietly.

Ahroe let the bowstring go slack but kept the arrow nocked. The two confronted each other silently as the snow fell unseen in the night, hissing lightly in the branches and on the white surface of the woods floor. Assek laughed again. "Well?" he asked. "You make no sense. Your husband runs from you, and you follow him, armed to fight, to kill him or force him to return, and then, given two chances, you don't kill me. You Pelbar like to see people suffer. I saw it in your eyes at the gate back at Pelbarigan. I knew you would follow him. Right? Ahroe, the Dahmen, from the family of tyrants. I have heard of them this winter. The pitiless destroyers of men."

"And what are you doing here? Are you avenging my husband? No. You are a common rapist. Don't see yourself as anything else, anything worthy. Shumai scum and scruff. You are a disgrace. Why does Hagen stand you?"

"Hagen? You know Hagen? He doesn't stand me. We are fellows. I have always known him. We—"

"Then why isn't Hagen here with you? Him we know as a man of honor." Assek took a step toward her, but as he did, Ahroe kicked his legs from under him and whipped a rope end around his arms behind him. He thrashed at first, then cried out and lay still. It was plain she was practiced in what she was doing, and he discovered by the sharpness of the pain in his side that he must have broken a rib in the fall. She stood him up, he cursing her as she did. Pushing him against the tree, she tied him to it. Then she retrieved her bow, wiped it and the arrow carefully and deliberately, and stowed them away. Climbing the tree again, she brought down all her gear and packed it. Assek eyed her silently, head down.

Ahroe came up to him, took his head by the hair and lifted it up. She looked at him in the dim snow light. The blood was drying on the side of his face. She took snow and cleaned his face, gently and thoroughly. Then she found his hat and put it on him. He still said nothing. She searched the snow for some time in the gloom, finally finding his knife. This she put in her backsack. Then she came back to him and said, "I'm going to need that rope. I will have to let you go again. But I promise you that if you follow me again, I will have to kill you."

"I will. Why not do it now?"

She grabbed his head with both hands, shaking him by the hair, screaming at him, "Why, why, why are you doing this? Leave us alone. We haven't done anything to you." She dropped her hands, and Assek laughed silently again. Ahroe, enraged, hit him with one open palm, then the other. Then she dropped her hands again.

"I'm sorry," she said. "I shouldn't have done that. Don't you see I have enough trouble? My whole life has been shredded away, and now you track me like a tanwolf and try to destroy me."

"Then why not take me? I am not running from you. I am a man and will stand up to you. I will show you what men are all about. I will make a—"

"Oh, shut up. What do you know about what men are all about? Stel is five times the man you are. He—"

"Then why has he left you? Did you hold your knife to his neck too often? Wasn't he man enough to take it away?"

"You couldn't. No, I never did that to him. Never. Why do I have to tell you? Damn you. How do you reason with a common destroyer of women?"

"You don't. You give yourself to him, and he shows you how to live."

Ahroe hit him again, so hard she hurt her hand. The blood started to flow down his cheek again. She took snow and blotted it away again as Assek laughed. She didn't say any more to him, but untied him and shoved him away. He staggered but didn't fall, then stood, rubbing his wrists and laughing derisively. Wearily, she put on her backsack and started out through the dim woods.

Assek stood still for several minutes, then followed her, laughing again as he saw that she had lost Stel's faint trail in the new-fallen snow. He held his side. When the trail dipped through a brake, he had to move slowly. Going downhill was nearly impossible with his rib. He stopped at one straight sapling, took a third knife, a small one, out of his boot, and, kneeling in pain, slowly cut the winter-hardened wood through, then stood and trimmed the shaft, removing the side branches, feeling their bases with his hands, smoothing it all off carefully as he stood in the snow. The butt end he sharpened, then using it for a staff, he again took up Ahroe's trail. She was not walking quickly. Even in the dark he could see the fatigue in her dragging footsteps, which were not lifted above the snow anymore. She would not climb a tree again to sleep. If she did, he would spear her. After all, she was only a woman. He knew all her tricks. Like his own wife, Nimm, she had wronged him, and he would right all his problems here, once and for all. When he finally caught her, he would make her enjoy it; then he would make her suffer, not only for her own evils, but for Nimm's as well. Her husband would be a free man because of him.

By dawn the snow had stopped. Ahroe knew she had lost Stel's trail, but she hoped, by sweeping in arcs, to pick it up again. Now, though, she knew too that she had to rest, and had to find a place where the Shumai could not surprise her, or get to her, if he still followed. She had been walking out onto a prairie, and chose her camp with care there, at a curving bank of a stream, facing back along her trail. She prepared it meticulously, with Pelbar exactness, readying its defenses, slight as they were, according to her training. As before, she relied on the Shumai impulsiveness her pursuer had already shown. But here she would expect him to weigh and calculate. He would see the first traps, though she carefully concealed them. He might even see the second. He would not assume, she reasoned, that there would be a third set, so he would be safe. He would have armed himself, but not as she was. She would keep awake all day, then sleep only at night, when all her preparations were less visible.

Ahroe took out some dried meat and her last lump of waybread. She built a small fire and heated tea, sweetening it with dried honey. As the day progressed, the disk of the sun grew clearer, and as Ahroe looked back eastward across the open land, her head drooped repeatedly. By noon she was asleep

She was still asleep when, in the gray twilight, a dark figure moving along her trail stopped and looked ahead. Assek could smell her long-dead fire as a slight whiff. He moved slowly, and then, as the lay of things came clear to him, he smile at her naïveté, walked closer, and finally squatted down in the snow about fifty arms off, still and careful. His rib still hurt sharply, but he would let it hurt. When he surged in on her, he would be so fast that the pain would not reach him before he had her; it would have to be that way. He knew she would kill him this time if she could.

Assek cut the distance to her in half, then watched awhile. He would come around above. No, she had blocked that way with willow poles, and he would awaken her. Closer still, he could see the thin stakes along the trail by the stream. She would have put out small ropes or thread there to trip him. He could not cross the stream without making noise going down the steep bank, and she had broken the ice in the stream. Perhaps there were submerged stakes. He would go by way of the stakes on the bank, feeling at each step, moving like the steam of his breath.

Now he was close enough to hear her even breathing. He had made three spears and could throw one from here. Impaled, she would know who had won. But he wanted her whole. Any impaling could come later. Still Ahroe slept. He drew within eight arms of her now. Feeling ahead with a spear, he touched the last string, and, still and silent, focused until he could see how, in a final rush, kicking that string would lift the rack of pointed willows to catch him in the belly. Gingerly, he stepped over it. He could dimly see the short-sword in her mittened hand. Now it would be one leap on her, and, swallowing, Assek took it in a rush.

As he came down, though, Ahroe's four wires, taut and braced on a slant, caught him and threw him sideways into the stakes set in the bank. He felt a sharp, sudden pain. Ahroe had rolled away and stood up. She reeled a little, dizzy with sleep, but he couldn't get up.

She threw aside her sleepsack and stepped free, then came toward him.

"Ah, ah," he murmured, in spite of himself, trying to hold his mouth shut, gritting.

"Shumai. You again. And night," said Ahroe, vaguely. As she came to herself, she cleared away the light brush, uncovered tinder, and struck a fire. It blazed up, showing her face still puffed with sleep, and, as she looked at him, with horror. The stakes had gone through his side, and he lay, breathing roughly, his small knife still in his hand. Ahroe snapped it away with a stick, pulled him up, and bound his feet. He said nothing, his eyes swimming in pain.

Ahroe built up the fire, laid him out, shook out his fur roll and covered him with it. She looped a string from wrist to wrist behind him, leaving his arms loose but restrained. Then she knelt by him, lifted him up against her, and said in his ear, "This will hurt. I'm going to take out the stakes." His head fell limply against her.

He panted and coughed, whispering, "Damn you, fish belly," then screamed out as she drew back the first stake. The second, lower, was not in deeply, and he held his breath on that one, keeping silent.

Ahroe laid him back down. In the firelight she could see a slight trickle of red froth from his mouth. He panted, looking up at her as if she were some far thing in a mist. She finally began to come completely awake, and the sound of the wounded man's breathing, rough and gasping, made her put her hands to her ears a moment. Then, ashamed of herself, she set about to stanch the blood.

Assek, panting, said, "No matter. It is all over now. It is done."

"No," she said. "I will get you on a litter and back to Pelbarigan."

"No, it is done. I would not make it halfway."

"Why have you followed me this way? Why have you made me do this to you?"

"All women do this to all men, but not so, not so . . . obviously. Look at you and your husband. Is he not on a skewer?" Ahroe did not reply. Finally, Assek added, "It would have been simple if you would have loved me back on the river. I would have tracked your husband for you."

"You would have killed me, not only shamed me."

In spite of his wheezing, Assek laughed again, but this time lightly. "Yes," he said. "I suppose I might have. It is all so baffling. It is a great release, this dying."

Ahroe built up the fire again, gathered her things, and wearily began to put together a litter. Assek watched. "Don't do that," he muttered. "It will do no good. If you want to do anything, stay with me."

Ahroe returned to him, again wiped away the blood from his mouth, and knelt by him. He smiled up at her crookedly. "I'm sorry," he said. "I don't understand. . . ."

She stooped over him, put her cheek against his cheek, then wiped his mouth again. She smoothed his hair and held his shoulders lightly. Then she freed his hands. He didn't move.

"The Pelbar way. You are friendly now that I am helpless."

"No. I am now free to comfort you because I know you will not attack me. I see your hatred is all gone. That is the Pelbar way."

"And your husband? Let him go. Let him go and be free."

"What is he to you?"

"He," Assek gasped. "He is a man. It is a troublesome thing."

Ahroe could not think of a reply. For Assek, twisted as he was, it was a troublesome thing. But was it to Stel? She wondered. They were silent a long time, except for Assek's labored breathing. The fire hissed as the new wood, snow-dusted, dried out before burning. Ahroe saw there was little she could do but stay with the dying Shumai, so she sat with him, held his hand for a time, then prayed, holding the heels of her hands against her eyes in the Pelbar manner. Assek watched her with glazed eyes. His brow furrowed and grew calm repeatedly, like clouds passing the moon. It was as if he were finally perceiving the key to intimacy in gentleness and compassion. But that could not be right. No. The hunter's way had no place for . . . and yet . . .

Suddenly there was a sound, and Ahroe stood and whirled. A voice from the dark called, "Assek?"

"He is here. Who is it? Stand clear so I can see you. Don't come through my defenses. I am armed and will defend myself." Ahroe nocked an arrow.

"Is that Ahroe the Dahmen? Are you all right? I am Ican, sent by your Protector. Hagen will arrive when he catches up. Where is Assek?"

"He is here. Come where I can see you." Ahroe guided Ican through the defenses. The young Shumai was a tall, thin man, with freckles across his short nose. In spite of the cold he streamed with sweat from his running. He had a full mouth, now set tight as he saw Assek. His eyes, pale blue, were red from the cold and his exertion.

With only a glance at Ahroe, Ican went to Assek, kneeling down by him, taking him in his arms and putting his face by that of the dying man.

"Don't lean on his chest. He is having trouble breathing," said Ahroe. Ican whirled and glared at her, but said nothing. She had her short-sword out, holding the blade in her mittened hand. Ican glanced at it, then turned back to Assek, who nodded and smiled feebly up at him.

"It is . . . all right," he whispered. "She did . . . nothing wrong. She only . . . defended . . . herself. She is one . . . tough woman. . . . Take good care . . . of her. Do not . . . harm . . . her. Besides, she . . . would probably . . . kill you, too." Here Assek attempted a laugh, but ended in a fit of bloody coughing, then lay back still.

Ican sighed once, held Assek's hands a few moments, then turned to see Ahroe, her face set, tears gleaming in the firelight. Turning back to Assek, he crossed the young man's hands on his chest.

"He was my cousin," he said, his back to Ahroe. "I am glad you are all right. I will see if Hagen is coming." Ican plunged out of the firelight to have his grief alone in the winter night. Eventually, Ahroe heard him call from several hundred arms off. There was no answer. Then, in a while, he silently returned, his eyes more red.

"I am sorry for my cousin that he caused you this anguish and trouble," Ican said. "We were wintering near you to keep him away from our people. He has had trouble. His wife, Nimm, left him, with the child, for another man. She couldn't help it. Assek was strangely cruel to her, even when he loved her. Then when he tried to recover her, the whole band met him with spears, and he had to leave in shame. He has never been much good with women. With me he was as good a friend as I ever wanted. We read the tracks you left. You were lucky.

"After we saw what happened at the tree, Hagen had me run ahead. He is old. He was afraid for you. Assek could have easily killed you in the tree. His mistake there was in climbing for you. You took a big chance. Well, maybe not. He was destined for bad luck. He was always assuming that things would be some way, then going ahead as if his assumptions were realities. This was his worst. It has been a bitter life for him. I am glad you were kind to him here. He has had little enough of that. I could see that he had let the bitterness go, even at the moment of his death. When Hagen comes, we will find a place with rocks and give him a proper burial. You look tired. I am sorry for all this. Do you have any tea?"

As Ahroe dumbly made tea, Ican arranged Assek further, unnecessarily, then lay down beneath his fur roll, putting Assek's over him as well. When Ahroe gave him the tea, and some dried meat, he rolled over and sat up only slowly. Far off, they heard Hagen call. Ican answered in a long, quavering falsetto yell that made Ahroe's hair rise. Eventually, the old man came, tired and slumping, and took his tea without a word, staring at Assek, then Ahroe.

"Don't worry," he finally said. "We will not do anything but help. Do you remember when I first saw you? No? It was at Northwall, and you, limping from your running, bandaged my wrists. I was a captive on the Tantal ships. Now, Assek will keep. He has a long sleep ahead. I am tired as an old weed. Let's get some sleep ourselves."

Ahroe thought she could never sleep, there and then. But somehow the presence of Hagen brought a steadiness, a sense of mellowness and calm, that let her sink down into a level of peace comparable to that she felt in Pelbarigan, where she would watch the several stars that shone in through the tall, thin windows in the great walls of stone. The two men had moved Assek out to the rim of the firelight and arranged him carefully again; then they had settled down on either side of Ahroe. Hagen fell into a deep sleep almost immediately. As Ahroe finally relaxed she knew Ican still lay stiff and troubled. Once she heard him sob quietly. She didn't move. Finally, the cold night wind rustling in the snow and dry weeds lulled her into a slumber she did not awaken from until broad day.

 V

AHROE awakened slowly, feeling ill. The two Shumai had already nearly finished a litter for the body of Assek, and had built up the fire. Ahroe walked down the stream on the ice to a nearby bend, feeling dizzy, then nauseated. She threw up, repeatedly, though with little in her, and before she was through, Hagen stood beside her, supporting her, as she leaned against a bush. She stood up and looked at him through tearing eyes.

"Are you pregnant, then?"

"I don't know. It's none . . . I don't know. Don't say anything."

"I think you are. What does that mean to the Pelbar?"

"Without Stel? Oh, well. I would have a place, but not much of one. I would not get another husband. I don't want one. I want Stel."

"When we take care of Assek, we will pick up the trail again."

"We? I will do it. You—"

"No. We will. This is my world out here. I have nothing to do. My wife died on the Tantal ships. My daughter is married and now living down in the Arkon country. I was cutting wood for the Pelbar to try to help Assek, but he is beyond help. I don't think you would do well out here alone and in your condition. Do you know how immense this country is, and how empty? It is my world, and I am comfortable in it, but it is not yours."

"Well, let me think about it."

"There is nothing to think about. I am not going to let you go alone."

Ahroe drew herself up and looked at him. There was nothing in his face but pure frankness. He had achieved the freedom of the old. "Well, then," she said. "We will go together." Hagen gave her a brief embrace, patting her shoulder as one would a child. Ahroe felt a touch of anger at being so patronized, but she said nothing.

They took Assek back across the prairie to a small woods by a stream. A limestone outcrop rose on the inside of a bend of the stream. Near its summit a small open area lay flat and enclosed, a pleasant overlook, facing southward, toward the prairie, over which they could see their own winding tracks. Four sets had gone out, three come back. Using flat rocks from the outcrop, the two Shumai dug laboriously down through the snow and frozen ground, scooping and tearing a shallow grave. They laid Assek in it and built a large rock mound around it from stones. Ahroe gathered as they dug. More rocks crowned it, until the whole structure made a long, high mound.

As the afternoon sun, still a disk behind clouds, waned, the two Shumai prayed and went through a slow ceremony of burial. Ahroe stood silent and drained.

When they were nearly done, Ahroe saw two figures far to the east, coming along their track. "They are the guardsmen," said Hagen. "We ran ahead. They must have lost the trail in the snowstorm."

"I don't want to talk to them. They will want me to return," said Ahroe.

"I will go," Ican replied. "I will get our supplies for the woodcutting and wait for the spring run westward. Arch and Agona will wait with me, I am sure. Stel's trail must be north of us anyway. You go."

Ican embraced Hagen and looked at Ahroe. She went to him and gave him the formal Shumai parting, right hands, palms flat, touching three times. "Please don't tell them how well equipped Stel was. It would only make trouble for Sagan."

"Sagan?"

"Stel's mother. I am sure she will speak to you if you stay long near Pelbarigan. You will know her by her gray eyes. If anyone else says she is Sagan, she will likely not have them."

"Gray eyes?"

"Like Stel's. Here is Assek's knife. He dropped it climbing the tree after me."

Ican took the skinning knife and looked at it briefly, then put it in his coat. He looked again at Ahroe, standing straight-backed, a head shorter than he. A look of pain went across his face like a flight of birds. Then he embraced Ahroe, hard, and Hagen once more, and set off down the outcrop toward the guardsmen.

"We will need to arc out northwestward, Ahroe," said Hagen.

"You will lead, then?"

Ahroe gave one backward glance. The two guardsmen were standing, far off, in the snow, as Ican trotted lightly toward them.

The two walked and jogged northwest until well into twilight. Then Hagen stopped near a stream in a wooded cove. He looked worried. "I don't understand," he said. "Unless he turned straight north, we should have crossed his trail. Even after that snow, I know I would have seen it. And even with his snow sliders."

"Perhaps he didn't come this far."

"We will have to loop back. But that could have happened only if he stopped. Would he have stopped so soon? I hardly think it."

"He may have assumed that he was out of danger after the snow."

"Surely he would know we could track him."

"Stel is a builder, a carpenter, a stone worker. He sings well and plays the flute. He is not a hunter."

"We will have to camp now and loop back in the morning then. Now, do you have that small kettle?" Hagen took from a small bag the weed seeds he had stripped off stray plants as they walked. Ahroe unpacked the kettle and some dried meat. Both were very hungry, and unsatisfied by the small meal, even with sweetened tea. Hagen went away to set some snares, returning so quietly that Ahroe didn't hear him.

"I felt, almost at sunset, as if we had almost found him," she said.

"Near sunset? So did I. We call that the radiation of the quarry. I wish you had told me. It always means something. With us, if two feel it, we are much more careful. I am worried. I think we may get more snow."

In the morning, Ahroe again had difficulty getting going, but she was pushed by further anxiety now. Hagen's snares had caught one rabbit, a thin and stringy creature, but they took the time to roast it and eat it all with tea before starting out.

This time they arced back southward, swinging east. Within six ayas they picked up Stel's trail. Hagen swore quietly, kneeling and studying it. "This was made a full day ago," he said. "He must have stopped ahead. We were very near him."

They set out westward on the trail, trotting as fast as they could, Hagen looking back at Ahroe and occasionally waiting for her. Then as Hagen topped a small hill he stopped. Ahroe came up to him. Plainly Stel had camped below, among a grove of black oaks, and had made no effort to hide anything he did. As they came into the camp, they noticed an odd sign made of twigs bound with bark, in the shape of a fish with an arrow point for a tongue, and a notched, forked tail.

"That is Stel's symbol for me," said Ahroe. "Look, there is a message tied to it." She took down a large piece of bark from the twig construction and sat on her heels to read it. Hagen looked at her a long moment, then climbed the hill to look westward.

The message began with another arrow-tongued fish:

I heard voices a while ago, and from the hill I saw you and the Shumai walking north. How much I wish I could have talked to you, but you had your bow, and your companion, and I know that I can never return to Pelbarigan and slave for the Dahmens. They tried to kill me once and would try again. I mean to give them no more chances. If we could meet unarmed and talk, or even if I could talk knowing that you wouldn't force me to go back, I think we might reach some solution. But perhaps not. You seem to have accepted the Dahmen view of life and me, and perhaps even consented to my death in the river.

It will do you no good to follow me. I am fresh, rested, well fed, armed now, determined, resolved, fat, juicy, eager, and feeling the full vigor, as they say, of youth. If you follow, I will escape. If you catch up, which is not likely, that is to say, nearly impossible, someone will die—either the Shumai or me. I feel the snow coming. I have my sliders. By the time you double back, I will be far gone and going farther. Where I do not know.

Perhaps, if I live to be old, I will return to Northwall someday, and perhaps see you, and your next husband, should he survive, your children, and grandchildren (which, I hope, for their sake, are all women). I will never have anyone but you, for strange as it may seem, I love you, but I am giving all that up now. It is that or die, isn't it. There is your second cousin Spek, who will marry you, I am sure, once the desertion period has passed. I don't know how Spek is in your eyes, but a speck in the eyes is better than a Stel in the river. Perhaps my adventures will rival those of Jestak, though I doubt it, since I am more of a crow than a hero, slighter than a fighter, no substitute for a brute.

And so, Ahroe, this is good-bye. At some time, in some place, how much we could have loved each other. How many songs I would have sung you, how many chidren would have laughed with us. But it is all failed. My fault. I don't mind dying all that much, but not for nothing, not for your gang of Dahmen crones and witches. My price is more than a block of ice. May Aven bless you in all ways, give you peace and wholeness, grant you long life, friends, and a more adequate husband. Stel.

Ahroe looked up. Hagen had returned and stood looking at her. "He thinks my family meant to kill him. He thinks I knew it and agreed to it."

"It is beginning to snow."

"We had better hurry."

Hagen held up his hand. "No. He is gone now. Look at the signs. He can outrun us on the snow sliders. We are in for a good snow. Look. He has eaten well, even dug cat-tails for himself. He has made a bow and killed rabbits and even a tanwolf. That I find hard to believe. He has made himself a flute, even. Perhaps he was incautious to think that he would not be followed this far, but he is very resourceful. He has learned to use the snow sliders well, and already he is through with his first travel soreness. He left shortly after he saw us pass—so the tracks say."

Ahroe stood up. "I will follow him."

"You mustn't. There is the child."

"Who wants it now?"

"Atou—Aven, you call Him? Besides, it is in you. It will not go away. If you don't give it health, it will not give you health."

Ahroe kicked aside the fish symbol and started trotting along Stel's departing trail. Snow was falling now, and looking west as she gained the hill crest, she could see a gray wall of it, with Stel's tracks vanishing into it. Hagen came up to her. "We will go to Black Bull Island until spring," he said. "I will stay with you, and when the baby is born, and grown some, then we will go west and look for Stel."

"You said yourself that the country is immense."

"But it is nearly empty. Stel will look for people. I have talked with him and know how he loves people. If he is alive, we will find him with people. He is a skillful man and will be welcomed."

"That will be over a year."

"What?"

"Before we could go."

"Probably two years. Does he age quickly, this Stel?"

"I can't stand it."

"You could go back."

Ahroe shuddered. "No. I would feel their eyes on me always."

"If Stel can stand it, if Assek could stand it, if I can stand it, if Venn could stand it, then you can stand it."

"Who is Venn?"

"She was my wife."

"What did she stand?"

"She stood me. She stood the Tantal. What we all stand is what we have to stand. We can't step out of life as if it were a coat."

The snow now caught them in a whirl of flakes, the far world disappearing. Ahroe looked a long while, with Hagen standing by her. Finally, he touched her shoulder and said, "Come on. Stel left a lot of tanwolf hanging in a tree for us. It is stringy as wood and tough as leather, but I am hungry and I mean to eat some. Come on."

Ahroe didn't move, but finally, when the old Shumai had built a fire and had nearly roasted the remains of the tanwolf, she slowly came down the hill and joined him.

 VI

STEL was walking through flowers of a kind he didn't know. The breeze was dry and balmy, but a light dew held down the dust among the bunchy grasses. For the ten thousandth time, he scanned the horizon for some sign of human habitation or passage. Here there were no trails.

During the waning winter, he had run across ruins and spent three nights, ill and weak, beneath an enormous slab of artificial stone, canted down from a tall, single artificial stone pillar. Three others, still standing nearby, at different angles and heights, led Stel to surmise that this had been some sort of bridge. But there was nothing to bridge, and fragments of broken artificial stone lay beneath the structure. He couldn't understand, but at last he began to gain some sense of the strength and ability of the ancients, and of the colossal disaster of the time of fire. Jestak had told them of it after his return from the east, but no one fully accepted his stories, and even after his western journey, and his return to Northwall, most did not grasp their implications.

Here, in this place of desolation, this winter of wind, dry grass, white rabbits, and white owls, men had toiled to set up these towers. There must have been many workers. Stel had thought about it until he couldn't stand the sound of the wind curling in under the great slab, and so he had left, walking westward in a daze, turning south for a time, then west, then northerly again, without real purpose or much goal.

Should he have called to Ahroe? Should he have chanced that a meeting would have turned out favorably? Ahroe. The winter contained none of her softness, but only the coldness of the Dahmens. How many times, shivering in the wind, had the river risen up again around him in his imagination, the ice breaking again and again as he desperately tried to roll out onto it.

The muck of the thaw, too, which made his hunting harder, seemed more miserable, and when the high flocks of geese went over, snows, blues, the great dark ones, crying in their freedom and yearning for the north, Stel's heart wrung within him, thinking of Pelbarigan and the great passing lines of birds. What was there at home a strange lifting of the spirit was here so intense a loneliness that at times he covered his ears from the sound, squeezing eyes tight shut, eyelids smarting.

Perhaps it was his flute that made life endurable for him. In the evening, especially, Stel would finger his way through all the songs to Aven that he could recall, until the music itself populated the darkness, and the great meanings and human hopes lifted him from himself to ponder the sweeping themes of universal destiny. Still, he always awoke weary, and the hard sunlight brought with it the fact of his aloneness.

Now that he was walking through the strange yellow flowers, he went slowly, his belly full of fish snared in a slow-moving prairie stream. He played the flute lightly as he went, intermittently, having begun, with spring, to recover his vague purpose of seeking out the great sea of the west, if there were such a thing. It was something to do.

After playing the song called "Aven, My Wall, My Unreachable Tower," Stel thought he heard a phrase or two of it coming back to him, changed, in a different timbre. He stopped. No, there was nothing. He repeated the phrase, slowly and distinctly. Yes, there it was again. Stel stirred himself into a trot, moving northwest, up a hillside, toward the sound. He seemed to lose it. Stopping, he fingered out the phrase again. Very close came the quavering out of the return. Stel heard a scraping, and for a long moment, he saw the grinning face of a dark-skinned boy, his head shaved except for a long hank of hair braided out from the top of his crown. The boy's face turned solemn; then, like the fall of a tree, his whole expression turned to surprise and, shrieking, he disappeared down the other side of the rock and fled up the hill. Stel watched, then slowly followed. After half an ayas, he hit a path, obviously well used, passed between two large rocks, feeling watched, and heard, in the distance, a faint chant of numerous voices. Gradually it became audible. "Diu heer es nu may nezumi iro. Diu heer es nu may nezumi iro. Diu heer es nu may nezumi iro." The sound grew louder, and Stel, advancing in fear and anxiety, yet eager for humanity, saw a line of young men, all shaved bald, bare to the waist, dark-skinned and sleek, advancing single file down the trail, keeping time with their walking by chanting. They came toward him, seeming almost not to notice him, though they clearly did.

Finally the front man put on a high headdress of wood and colored feathers, raised his arms, and stopped, the column splitting, alternately, walking around Stel, passing him on both sides, close, he stopping bewildered, they then turning and stopping, though the chant continued, low and insistent, still in time, "Diu heer es nu may nezumi iro." The man with the headdress lowered his arms, and the men closest to Stel gently urged him forward by the elbows, still chanting. All the procession, then, moved down the path together, finally coming into the cleft of a small valley.

Many more people lined the path, perhaps eighty or ninety, Stel thought, the men all shaved, the women with very long hair. All were dark, and all looked at Stel with fascination. As they came near, all took up the chant. Stel and his procession were impelled toward a central square of flat laid stones, perhaps sixty arms around, in a circle. At one end of it was a raised dais, and on that a chair in which an extremely old man sat, bent, but leaning forward with eagerness toward Stel and his party as they came nearer.

The two lines of men brought Stel before the old man, then left him abruptly, moving to stand on either side of him. The man with the headdress shifted around behind. This close, Stel had a good look at the old man, who peered at him through bleared but dark eyes, his head thrust forward, the lines of his neck creasing the skin in deep folds, coming together below the throat like a leather necklace. Except for a cloth around his hips, the man was naked, and he was completely unadorned. As his mouth hung open, Stel could see only one tooth, in the bottom front, jutting up like a small rift of snow at the entrance of a cave.

Finally the old man rose, with surprising quickness, and came down to Stel, peering at him. Stel smiled. Then, catching a whiff of the old man's damp breath, like rotting fish, Stel drew his face tight in a noncommittal politeness. The old man walked all around him, growing more excited, finally thrusting his face close to Stel's, looking hard in his eyes. Then he took one of Stel's hands, which were hardened and dirty with the winter and his wandering. The old man peered at it, then thrust it down with a murmur of disgust.

He then returned to his chair and sat still for a very long moment, during which Stel was aware of silence and a quarreling of birds in the background. Finally, the old man stood up again, suddenly, and said, "Ik dik sa. Diu heer es nu may nezumi iro. Ik da sa."

A general roar of approval swelled up. Stel found himself impelled in a rush up a long rough rock stairs by and behind the old man, toward another paved area. In the center of it was one large, square stone, with a trough grooved into it, though a shallow one, as long as a man. Near one end stood a short-handled spear in a socket cut in the stone. It was upright, tipped with a large head made of glistening black stone, chipped neatly in the shape of a large narrow leaf. Beyond the pavement, two stone houses stood like overturned bowls, circular, each perhaps fifteen arms across. They were thatched with rushes. Glancing at them, Stel was startled to see that they stood at the edge of a rocky outcrop dropping off perhaps thirty arms to a dry wash behind. Then, in the distance, he could see in haze, trees and rising mountains to the west.

But he had no time to look. The chanting and chattering crowd brought him to the right of the square rock, and then a tall young woman came from the bowl-shaped house on that side. She was thin, dark-haired, lighter-skinned than the rest. She wore a long maroon robe and a heavy gold necklace, and walked in strangely high wooden sandals. The crowd suddenly fell completely silent, and Stel could hear the wood click as she slowly came toward him. He felt a series of chills chase themselves down his back.

She came all the way up to him, looking at him with eyes blue as chicory flowers. Like the old man, she walked all around him, slowly, with a look of growing contempt on her face. Stel said nothing. He felt like an object about to be bought at Pelbar trade week. Standing in front of him again, she took his face in her hands and opened his mouth, peering in at his teeth, then let go and took two sweeping steps back, glancing around at the crowd, then gesturing. She cried out, "Das corb furui? Das corb furui? Ah. Welve mo an das corb furui?"

The crowd sucked back, then stubbornly began again the chant, "Diu heer es nu may nezumi iro," but she suddenly let out a scream, flinging her arms in the air, pivoting to face them all. They fell silent.

"If you don't mind," Stel said quietly, "I'd really like to know what this is all about. I believe I've stumbled onto a stage during the winter festival. I will gladly turn around and . . ."

The woman whirled toward him, raised her arms, and shrieked out again. Stel gathered that she wanted him to be quiet. Then, startlingly, she took hold of a cord around the neck of her robe, pulling it with a dramatic gesture. The robe fell at her feet, leaving her completely naked.

Before she stepped out of her sandals, the crowd murmured in unison and knelt down, heads to the pavement. Stel didn't. He looked at the sky, then the far horizon, then at his feet, then at hers in front of his. He looked up. She stood glaring at him, proud and uncomfortably close. Stel had never seen that much of Ahroe, even, surely not in the sunlight. He was profoundly embarrassed. But she was intensely lovely, bizarre and different as she might be. Her beauty radiated from her like a fragrance. Every detail of her body struck his imagination as perfect. Stel felt slightly dizzy. She turned and walked slowly away toward the stone house, never looking back. Stel found himself looking at the dimples, one on each side, at the top of her buttocks. He had never seen anything like that before, and somehow they seemed at odds with her comic dignity. He laughed aloud. She wheeled around at the door of her house, her face contorted in anger, seeming not like a goddess of physical beauty, but simply a woman who had misplaced her clothing.

Stel laughed harder, but the crowd rose in obvious anger, and the woman vanished into her house. "Well, what now?" Stel asked. He was bewildered and weary, now more frightened. What had he blundered into?

Mutterings of "Nekko da," and "Slag da infed," came from the crowd, but quickly the same group of men who had ushered him so strangely into this society came up to him again. The man in the headdress stood in front of him.

"Nu Roti," he said. "Nu Roti. Vu ashi kisui da faimm. Bu nu klon vu maint." The men began their chant again, and nudged Stel forward into the other house. It was plain inside and dark. A bed lay on the floor, covered with a dark fur. Another hollowed stone stood on the right side. Immediately some of the men began to fill it with warm water, brought in leather buckets, and the leader gestured Stel to take off his clothing. They meant him to bathe, as he saw it. He didn't feel like being stripped of everything, but he saw no way out of it, so he decided to obey. None of the men left the house. When the bath was full, the water slightly steaming, Stel was lifted into it. Four of the men set about washing him, plunging him into the water, scrubbing him, especially his hands, with harsh brushes. From the tub Stel saw with dismay that his ragged Pelbar clothing was taken outside. Surely they didn't expect him to walk around in public like the woman. But he was very relieved when a short leather tunic was brought in, and his thick leather shoes came back cleaned and greased.

Finally they let him out of the bath, then let the water drain out of it through a plug in the bottom. While two men scrubbed the tub with red cloths, he was dressed and brought out of the house. By that time, Stel could see that there were even more people around the pavement, staring, especially coming close to look at his eyes, then running away chattering. He could catch the "may nezumi iro" from the chant. Here were a people, then, who spoke in a way unfamiliar to all the Heart River peoples, and even differently from the other groups that Jestak had met. Stel could make no sense of it at all.

A group gathered in front of the other house, chanting, "Ven maint, ven maint, vu das Diu." Clearly they wanted her to emerge and evaluate the new, cleaned-up Stel. But she didn't come. The crowd grew more angry, gesturing at the door. Finally she came to the door, again, to Stel's relief, in her maroon robe. She looked mildly at him, sniffed to herself, and went back in. The crowd fell silent. They turned to Stel. He simply extended his arms in the Pelbar gesture of puzzlement.

Then, amused with himself, he decided that if they wanted to be commanded, he would command them. "All right now," he announced, with mock sternness, "if you grass-eaters, you bald heads, don't mind, get out of here. Go on now, pack yourselves down those stairs. Time to go dig roots, time to count ants. Out with you." He took some of the nearest and shoved them gently toward the stairway. Somewhat meekly, they went. Stel kept cajoling them until the whole crowd left, except for the young men who had brought him there. They stood around the edges of the pavement. Clearly they had no intentions of going. He didn't urge them. He went instead to the man with the headdress and indicated with motions that he wanted something to eat. Instantly, two of the other men trotted down the stairs—for food, Stel assumed.

For a moment he glanced at the other house, but a curtain hung across the door, and the woman was nowhere to be seen. He decided to re-enter his own house. Food was brought in, and he sat on the floor, eating with as much dignity and decorum as he could muster, without utensils. Gesturing, he finally got one of the attendants to bring him his backsack, and took from it his small knife, cut the dry cake on his food board with it, ate only very small chunks, with the root vegetable, and some strange meat, taking as much time as possible so that he could look around, judging his situation carefully.

He had already decided he had to get out. Clearly they weren't accepting him as an ordinary human being. Clearly it had something to do with his eyes. They were all dark-eyed, except for old blue eyes in the next house.

As the day waned, Stel heard a stir outside, and the young men all came in to usher him out. Stepping out, he found the old man again, sitting in a portable chair. Again he went through his examination of Stel, and looking at his hands, murmured this time what was evidently approval. The old man then bowed deeply to Stel and, spreading his hands wide, said in a loud voice, "Nu heer lang ſo vu. Maint vu kaag atla. Nu paah, voor paah."

Then he bowed again, gave Stel a glance that seemed to have a leer in it, and went away, attended, slowly walking down the long stairs followed by his chair. Turning, Stel saw the woman in her doorway, smiling slightly, holding her door edges. Again she reached for the cord on her robe, but Stel turned on his heel and re-entered his house.

After nightfall, he heard in the distance some sort of celebration, with the dim chant, "Diu heer es nu may nezumi iro." He stepped out of his house. One of the young men sat on each side of the doorway. They didn't turn to look at him. Stel could see the glow of a fire from the pavement area below, and dancers moving around it, an alternation of shaved heads and dark-haired ones. Between him and the glow, the square central stone, with its trough, stood up, its short spear socketed, black against the firelight.

Returning inside, Stel took his short-sword from his backsack, lay on the bed, and began to test the mortar in the stones behind. It picked away easily. Working steadily, he loosened two adjacent stones, giving enough room so he could see he could worm through. Then he cut his bedclothes into strips for a rope. His old clothing had been returned, washed and dried, and he took off the tunic he had been given and put his old clothes on. Making all ready, he stepped briefly outside again. It seemed as if the dancers were coming closer. His guards didn't move. He returned inside, but hearing a sound behind him, he turned and saw the blue-eyed woman enter, carrying a small lamp. She smiled at him glitteringly, and again loosened her robe, standing in the dim light, bewitchingly beautiful, reaching out to him, and saying, "Vu kowabadda por nu, takai, takai."

From outside, Stel could hear, in low tones, the crowd mutter, "Vu kowabadda por nu, takai, takai," taking that up as a chant now. Stel felt his hands tremble. He moved toward her, took her in his arms, and, as she sighed in triumph, stuffed a fragment of bedding in her mouth, whipped her arms behind her, wound another strip around them, then fastened her kicking ankles and completed his gag. As she thrashed on the floor, he picked her up and set her down in the stone tub. From outside the chant, "Vu kowabadda por nu, takai, takai," continued, growing louder.

Leaning into the tub, Stel tweaked the girl's cheek, whispered, "Good-bye, old blue eyes," and kissed her forehead. Then he moved the stones and slipped out the hole, dragging his backsack after him. He slid down the rope of bedding, and, finding the rocky floor of the gully, paused a moment to hear the chant above him. All seemed undiscovered. There was no moon, but Stel recognized the stars of the bent kite sinking westward, and stumbled off in the darkness. When he had gone about a half-ayas, the dimming chant behind him broke up into shouts and cries. Stel began a trot, tripping and blundering in the darkness.

☐ VII

STEL ran, walked, and felt his way through the waning night into dawn, faintly hearing behind him a new chant, "Uhm, zym, nachtanali, nu ga hym," over and over. How the trackers followed him, he couldn't tell. Finally, coming to a north-flowing stream, Stel plunged in, allowing the current to spin him downstream, swimming and floating, sometimes through rapids, until the second quadrant of morning. He heard no more chanting, so pulled himself ashore among overhanging willows, moving back from the water to dry his gear. Everything was soaked. His remaining dried meat was swelled and foul-smelling. He buried it, dried his knife and short-sword on the grass, hung his tattered clothing up, and his now ripped sleepsack. Fortunately his flute was intact, though warped. His short bow seemed all right, though the string needed drying. The arrows all curved.

Eventually he heard the approaching chant, "Uhm, zym, nachtanali, nu ga hym," and stooping in the grass, saw the same young men, naked to the waist, paddling and poling a long log downstream, sweeping by him in the current, in rhythm, looking mindless or asleep, staring ahead. The leader had his headdress on, but it showed that he had been in the river. Each of the others had a red line painted on his shaved head from front to back across the crown. The paint was running. As they vanished around the next bend, Stel breathed his relief. He would wait until everything had dried. If they discovered their mistake, they would have a lot of river bank to search for him. He had time.

Or so he thought then. In the ensuing days, Stel eluded the trackers repeatedly, only to have them reappear, even as he worked westward up into the mountains. It was a mystery to him how they found him, always revealing their coming with their narcotic chant. Stel found himself internalizing it, even traveling as they did in time with it. When he realized this, he shook it out of his mind forcibly. But it returned, and so did the trackers.

Stel was growing sharply hungry, too, since he felt too harried to do much foraging. This was strange country with many scrubby pines, widely spaced. Few rabbits were present, so he shot small burrowing rodents with his short bow, trying to impale them before they could dive down into their clustered holes. He would clean them while walking, burying all he couldn't carry, finally building a fire and cooking several at once, when the wind was following him, then stuffing himself. He was tiring, and felt debilitated, but when he stopped to rest, eventually he could hear the chant in the distance, "Uhm, zym, nach-tanali, nu ga hym."

He thought of resistance. Surely he could shoot one or two from ambush and get away. But they had offered him no violence. All they carried was ropes. He didn't really know their intentions but felt only bewilderment.

Finally, as he rested high on an outcrop, thinking that he had at last shaken them, he saw them coming along an animal trail below. They missed seeing where he had left the trail, jumping on rocks as he turned up the steep hill. They ran on more than a hundred arms farther, then stopped, puzzled. They were right below him. On an impulse, Stel pried loose a large boulder, with much more difficulty than he had expected, heaved hard, at last balancing it, strained further, and sent it bouncing and rolling down at them, loosening others, soon a rock slide. The men looked up, stood strangely still, until the leader yelled out and they ran across the narrow canyon, rocks following, finally bounding among them.

Stel watched from a cleft in the rocks. One man had been felled. The others stood around him. He could see the leader gesticulating. Then two stayed with the prostrate man while the rest, resuming their chant, trotted slowly up the hill directly toward Stel. He could destroy them all with another rock slide, but his main emotion was revulsion at the man lying far below. He had done that. The trackers stopped chanting as the strain of their climb took their breath, but they continued, slowly but steadily, up the steep incline. Stel turned and ran.

More than an ayas later, Stel, turning, could see them still coming, far back, far below. He was nearing the rim of a sharp ridge, looking forward to gaining distance on the downward side, but as he topped the rise, he stopped, startled. All the landscape to the north was barren, eroded, treeless, plantless, gray. It was one of the great empty areas he had heard of, which the western Shumai said it was death to cross. Far below he could see what appeared to be more ruins of the ancients, straight lines, gutted with gullies, toppled walls among the gray and ditched land. Yet the trackers came behind him.

Turning, Stel ran on along the ridge, losing much of his lead as the trackers turned short. Stel now had two concerns, the men behind and the devastation to the north. Growing tired and short of breath, he was relieved when the rise ended and the land began to slope down. He could see water through the pines, and a strip of cottonwoods and aspens by its banks, far down, and turned toward it. The men behind him again began their chant, but only with hesitation. At least, Stel thought, they are winded, too.

Twisting to glance at them, Stel fell, tumbling down a wooded slope with protruding rocks, thudding and rolling, finally stopping himself. Scraped and shaken up, he had to try twice before he could stand. The chant grew closer. There seemed to be a small flat area ahead, and Stel stumbled toward it. He found a path, bordered with small stones. Not another village of these people, he thought. But there was no time to stop. The trackers drew very close now.

Flinging himself around a turn in the path, Stel almost ran into three thin figures. He stopped. They stood still, one raising hands to face, staring. All three seemed to radiate age, in their ragged gray robes, their complete hairlessness, their shocked faces. Two, Stel could see, were blind with cataracts. The other, with a shrewd and clownish expression, looked at Stel, then advanced, cackling, waving a long staff in arcs at him. Behind, the chanting grew very loud. Stel ducked under the staff and ran up the path, turning as the chanters came around the rock.

Seeing them, the old one screamed out, flung down the staff, and stripped off her robe, facing them with an ancient and wrinkled body, the skin hanging and flapping in loops like wilted leather pouches. The trackers stopped short.

"Agon, agon," the leader gasped. "Nu fleah fo yah nekko suur jambey."

Wheeling, the trackers ran back up the hill, never turning around. Stel advanced to the rock and watched them running and clambering. He felt the old one near him, but suddenly, with the retreat of the trackers, a wave of fatigue went over him so that he almost fell. Everything seemed dreamlike.

"Well, well, a traveler," the old one said. "Got caught up with the Roti, huh? You did very well to get this far. They will never come here. They think that this is the place of death and that you have entered it. You will have to stay with us. That is very good, good indeed. We have much work to do, and, as you see, we are much too old to do it."

"The Roti?"

"Them. The Roti. They sacrifice the blue-eyed, because they think they come from the sky." The old one laughed, then asked, "And who are you? We've never seen anyone who cut his hair like a round rock half in the earth."

"I am Stel, a Pelbar, of Pelbarigan on the Heart River."

"Never heard of it. Ah, well. You don't have to tell us. Not yet, anyway. Come along with us now. There are beans to hoe."

"Who are you?"

"I? Oh, yes. I am McCarty, and this is Gomez and Johnson. We are the children of Ozar. Or rather some of them. Come now. . . ."

"Ozar?"

"Yes, Ozar. Our mother. We came indeed from the sky, down with the great fire centuries ago. We have lived here ever since—up until now. We will soon all be gone. And especially if no one hoes the beans. Now, come."

McCarty turned and led the way up the path. She was a wreck of age and desiccation, but seemed sturdy enough. She had flung her robe over her shoulder, uncaring. The others followed, not noticing, tapping on the side rocks with their staves. Stel came behind, weary now almost to dropping, glad at least that they moved so slowly.

Ahead, the narrow flat opened out to a wide plateau on the slope above the tumbling stream. Stel could see a neat field, with many rows of beans. Other figures, all bald, all in the same tattered, nondescript robes, knelt in the field weeding, with infinite slowness. Some were blind and felt along the rows. Stel could see that some had pulled bean plants.

McCarty stopped. "There. You see? See why you must hoe for us? We cannot do it anymore. It was fine, for all those hundreds of seasons, until Kannaday convinced us that it was all right to cross the barren land when our stream dried up. Now look at us."

"Where are the young people? Where are the children?"

"None. No children. We have not seen a child in . . . in, well, many seasons. In fact, you are the first young man I remember for a long time." Here she laughed in a high thin quaver, and made as if to embrace him. Stel stepped back.

McCarty's face fell slack. "Ah. Once they were willing enough to take me in their arms. But nothing came of it. Nothing. Well, come now. We will take you to Fitzhugh. She still has hair. Like you. But it is all white."

Stel could see ahead a large building, made of stone and heavy timber, sagging, with a broad roof that sloped nearly to the ground, covered with neat tiles. Beyond it and against the slope was another building, very odd-shaped, like a crooked *T* with one arm canted back and down.

McCarty saw him looking. "You may not go there. That is Ozar, our mother, or rather, her house. She is only for us, the children of her children, all brought here in the great fire."

"We are all the same. Jestak says so, and he has been to the eastern coast and the islands beyond. Look. Can we not understand each other?"

"You do sound as if you were eating. What eastern coast?"

"Thousands of ayas to the east."

"Ayas? What is an aya?"

"An ayas? You don't know? It is two thousand arms. All the Heart River peoples know that."

"See? You are different. We use kiloms. A kilom is . . . well, we never travel."

"That is a minor matter. Look how easy it is for us to understand each other. You could talk to the Shumai, the Sentani, the Emeri, the—"

"You have met the Emeri?"

"No. I have heard of them. Jestak and the Shumai defeated them over two summers ago. But now they trade with the Shumai."

"They are a cruel bunch. They live way to the north of the empty land. Once they came this far. But that was before I was born."

"Who are the Roti? Why don't they talk like everyone else?"

"Who knows? They have always been there. We have never understood them. We have always hid our light-eyed children from them." Again she cackled. "But they will have nothing to do with us now, nor our cloudy-eyed people. We are to them death. They wish to taste the blood of the young."

Stel shivered. As they neared the building, seven more figures appeared in its doorway, looking much like McCarty and the others. Then another figure came to the entrance. Her robe was dark, and she had white hair, combed neatly and wound in a braid on top of her head. She appeared slightly younger. Her dark-brown skin contrasted starkly with the cloudy whiteness of the others. That must be Fitzhugh.

"Look. I have brought someone who can hoe. He says his name is Stel."

"That name is not on the list. I remember . . ." said one of the figures, vaguely.

"No matter. He is not of Ozar. He has escaped the Roti by coming here. Now he wants to work. Look, Fitzhugh. Hair. Look at his dark hair."

Fitzhugh came forward with a demure smile and took Stel's hands, looking penetratingly at his face. "Welcome, Stel. Will you stay with us? We aren't much, as you can see. We are near our end. You will stay, will you not? We are greatly in need. Now, are you hungry? Beans and fish is what we eat. Beans and fish. That is about all. There are melons, and sometimes nuts. But beans and fish is mostly it. Now, come inside."

Stel was startled at the contrast between Fitzhugh's warm humanity, the vacancy of the others, and McCarty's zaniness. His desire for sleep seemed to increase. Everything here seemed safe, mundane, quiet.

"Thank you," he said. "I am very grateful. Of course I will help if I can."

The beans and fish turned out to be gluey, but they were served with a boiled green that Stel found refreshing. He ate everything, his drowsiness growing. McCarty watched him eat, remarking, "Eats like ten people. Look at that. We shall never make it through the winter with that to feed. Let's hope he can work enough to make up for at least some of it."

Fitzhugh repeatedly tried to shut her up. She meanwhile continually questioned Stel, and his answers, guarded though they were, still lengthened the time it took to eat until he was unutterably weary, and feeling the bruises of his fall. He noticed less and less, finally dozing off staring at the small bit of metal Fitzhugh wore around her neck. It seemed to be another bit of flotsam from the ancients, and Stel had made out on it: 1992 RABIES VACCINATION COLO. DEPT. OF AGRIC. FREMONT CO. 2389. Well, that meant nothing.

Fitzhugh shook his arm gently, and when he opened his eyes, she led him to a small storage room with a stone shelf on which grass had been spread. He unrolled his sleepsack and spread it over himself, dropping almost immediately into slumber. Once, when the light from the small window showed it was near nightfall, he awakened. Fitzhugh was still there, sitting on an overturned basket. She was staring out the window. Her mouth was drawn in thoughtfulness and her eyes were still and narrowed. She didn't see Stel notice her. He soon drifted off again into a deep sleep that lasted until near dawn.

 VIII

JUST at dawn, McCarty burst into the storage room. Stel was still lying in a near-doze. She shook his shoulder and beat his back lightly with her staff. "Stel. Wake up now, hairy one. Come on, now. You've eaten our beans. Now it is time to grow some. Up now. We'll feed you now, but not forever. Up."

Stel rolled over and sat up. With one sweep of his arm he snatched McCarty's staff and flipped it out the open window. She stopped and looked stunned.

"My leg. My extra leg. Now see what you have done."

"Well, go get it. But don't ever hit me with it." Stel felt stiff, filthy, and again hungry.

McCarty left, calling back over her shoulder, "I hope you are that good with a hoe handle, big belly."

Stel bathed down at the stream, with several old robed people nearby. He didn't care. Most of them couldn't see anyhow. The others seemed shells of people, mumbling and saying inconsequential things. Again he ate beans and fish. Again it tasted gluey.

Then Fitzhugh brought him a hoe. "Well, Stel," she said. "There is no help for it. McCarty and the others will have you hoe if you are to stay. There will be time to talk. I am glad that you seem recovered. Anything you do will be a help. As you see, it is a bad time for us. When I was a child we were hundreds. Then the earth shook, and our stream stopped. Clouds of dust rolled over us and all our crops died.

"One person, Kannaday, convinced everyone that we would have to traverse the empty land to the north to seek help from the Emeri. I and Jaeger were left behind to care for Ozar. It was a hard time. The Emeri would not help—would not go near those who crossed the empty land and sent them back at swordspoint.

"While they were gone, Jaeger and I awoke one night to a great roar of water and found our stream nearly up to the level here. But it soon subsided and ran as it does now.

"We found later, when some of us went westward, that the earth had slid, forming a dam, and the water finally filled up enough to spill over it and then push it aside. It was a great catastrophe for us. We lost all our buildings down by the water, too, and our own dam.

"Nothing was the same when the people returned. Some sickened right away. Others lost their hair, and eventually all did. No children were born. People seemed to lose their purpose. Writing, art, music, even sports, slowed down and ceased as those who survived grew older.

"Jaeger and I had a child, but some of them stole her and killed her because they could have none. We had another. It was dark-eyed, so Jaeger took it to the Roti and gave it to them. Who knows. Maybe my own grandson chased you here yesterday. Life is a bitter thing. Now Jaeger has died, and I have to take care of this remnant until they die or I die. Why am I telling you this? I don't know. It would be good to have someone understand me before I die."

Stel said nothing. She had said that life is a bitter thing. He was beginning to agree. He put his arm around her, and her return embrace was almost fierce in its intensity.

McCarty came around the corner of the building, staff in hand, though, and Fitzhugh let Stel go. "There you go again, Fitz. Lover girl. What? Isn't he at work yet? Look, Stel the eater. I have my staff again. I think I need to use it on you. Wait. You owe me something. I saved you yesterday, when you ran. You have a beard, but no man's heart."

Stel hoed beans the rest of the day. He didn't mind, though his shoulder pained him dully. This was the first time since he left Pelbarigan that he was a functioning member of a society, and though this was a strange group, he felt much more at home than he had in all his winter of wandering.

Fitzhugh's brief commentary gave him much to think about. What terrible catastrophe had befallen the ancients that great areas of the land were so poisoned for so long that they could destroy a society that merely crossed the area? Would the land ever rebuild? From what he had seen of violence and misery, though, perhaps they would do it all over again. But then there were noble people. Stel knew them in Pelbarigan and among the Shumai. He had met Sentani during the last two years whose warmth and gentleness rivaled any he had known. And there were noble ideas and ideals, and the worship of Aven, with its whole code of ethics, that seemed so just and perceptive— would these not save the people this time? Could they not rebuild and rejoin? Stel finally began to grasp the vastness of the problem now being unfolded to the Pelbar.

He felt his own personal problem suddenly dwarfed. And yet wasn't that in miniature the same kind of thing that so deeply troubled whole societies, that may finally have erupted in the great time of fire that had destroyed nearly everything?

Suddenly the hoeing of beans seemed, though paltry and insignificant, the sort of social action that Stel admired. It was cooperation. He had missed it. He enjoyed the tinkle of his hoe on the stones, the bird song from the field edges, the rhythmic thud of the hoe. He felt a gust of peace pass over him. Yet there was Ahroe. What was she doing? Was she standing guard on Rive Tower? Did she ever look westward and think of him? Had she begun to think of other men? Stel hoped so. There would be a scar, perhaps a deep one, but the wound could heal. Worse ones did. If only she were here. They could care for the old together.

Stel's thought of Ahroe destroyed his slight sense of

peace. Again he felt himself an exile. Well, here was something he could do. His musings were interrupted by the arrival of a thin, robed figure with water, which he dipped out of a wooden bucket with a gourd. Stel drank and watched the person, who stared off at the sky. Was this a man or a woman? Stel couldn't tell.

"Thank you," he said, handing back the gourd. "What is your name?"

"Taglio. I am the last Taglio. Once there were four."

"A family?"

"A family? No. Taglio was on the list."

"The list?"

"Yes. The names Ozar left for her children."

"Are you a man or a woman?"

"A man? What do you mean? It has been so long. I went across the empty lands, you know. I don't remember."

"Yes. What was it like—the empty land?"

"I don't remember."

"What kinds of things did the ancients leave behind there?"

"Everything. All ruins."

"Do you remember nothing?"

"There was a wedge, a roof, all of metal. Or its ribs. But they had melted on one side, and run down. There was much glass. There were many streets, and foundations of something like stone. All in lines. I don't remember. There was a tower lying down, twisted. All metal."

"A tower?"

"Yes. We could see that it was very tall and had been held up by ropes of metal. But it was not for people to climb. It was too small. There was glass on top. We thought it was for a light. And there was an enormous lake, like a giant hole, to the north of the ruins. We had to go around the lake, so we all talked about it. But that was a long time ago. I was barely an adult. I was another person then. I was like you. Soon the Ozar will be no more."

"How wide is the empty land?"

"I don't know. It is a long distance. Many kiloms. Hundreds of seasons ago, some of the Ozar, it is said, went all around it. But none had crossed it. We were told that it used to glow at night. Many hundreds of seasons ago. Soon after Ozar brought us here. But I don't know. That may not be true."

"Where did Ozar bring you from?"

"From the sky. I don't know. That is what is said. It doesn't seem to make sense. Unless we came to destroy the ancients. But we are like them. Nothing makes sense of any of it. I can't hold a thought anymore. Ask McCarty."

Taglio shuffled off down the row with the water then, without another word. Stel watched the thin, robed figure, and a feeling of unutterable sadness came over him. He still didn't know if Taglio was a man or a woman. He turned to his hoeing with new vigor, counting as he stroked the weeds, driving thought out of his mind, piling the dirt around each stem with care, wondering if it would be possible to be true to anything. Didn't one have to know why he was motivated? Taglio, Stel thought, has ceased to care. He—or she—was operating like one of the wind machines that were used to draw water for the Pelbar since Jestak had learned of them in the east.

As spring turned into summer, Stel remained with the Ozar, hoeing their large field, cutting grass to go between the rows to hold the sparse rainfall, bringing water to them, renewing the fence of brush that kept out wild cattle, bringing withes for baskets, repairing the old dam, and working at a myriad of odd jobs that needed skilled attention.

The Ozar had a large series of ponds, upstream in a widened part of the steep valley, where it made a bend. Here they practiced fish culture, much as the Pelbar did in their own ponds near the Heart. Stel cared for the fish, caught them, helped clean and dry them. He also repaired the roof of the communal hall, the terminal, as the Ozar called it, though no one knew why.

Twice while working at the stream, Stel saw the Roti on the far hill, five of them, silent now, watching him from the height. He had made up his mind now that they were as McCarty and Fitz had described them. He wanted to make a longbow, if he could find the time. Whenever he had a moment of leisure, though, someone asked him to do something. McCarty, especially, seemed determined to work him every moment. He could have refused, but it wasn't worth it. The Ozar were to be pitied, not resisted. By the seventh moon cycle, or Pelbar Heatmonth, Harlow died, and Stel dug a grave on the hill among the rows of graves, all old, few marked anymore. When Stel inquired, he was told that they had lately been throwing the dead down into the great offal pit below the settlement. Stel knew it well. It had been a storage silo, a square-cut stone tower, beautifully made, and built against the hill downstream from the terminal. But at some time they had ceased to store beans or grain in it, and had begun dumping all sorts of refuse into it, as well as sewage. It was the foulest of collections, even oozing odorously from the cracks in the lowest stones.

They all referred to it as the "stew," and Stel soon surmised that this was McCarty's term for it. She herself had a horror of it and spent some time nearly every day digging at her own gravesite on the hill, so that when she died, they would not dump her into the stew. While she seemed sturdy, digging in the stony hill was far from easy for her, and she wasn't half done. Stel could see that she had been at it for some time. She tried to get him to dig for her, but he simply told her he was sure she would live forever.

But he soon regretted saying this. She would look at him knowingly, and remark, "I shall be the last to go. Even you, fat Stel, hairy one, will go before me, bearing a light for me to lead me into the country of darkness. The Roti will come behind us, pursuing you, and we will have to hurry. Then I shall frighten them back. But I shall be the last."

Stel bore McCarty as he had borne the Dahmens, with patience and determination. But she also made him feel vaguely uneasy. Fitzhugh, on the other hand, was his one delight—the only person he had met since leaving Pelbarigan whom he instinctively loved. It was Fitz who kept the whole society functioning. She had retained a human radiance despite all difficulties. She was also a consummate politician, smoothing away all domestic crises. In the evening Stel would seek her out and talk while she beat and spun the inner bark of a kind of tree they called the cordage into thread for cloth for the long gray robes they all wore.

It was tedious work. Stel saw he could fix a thread spinner for her, and a loom, if he were to spend the winter there. Clearly he would soon be their chief woodcutter, since the old ones had gleaned all the small wood for a considerable distance around Ozar.

Stel wondered about winter. Did he want to stay? Could he stand McCarty that long, in such close quarters? What would the old ones do without him? What would he himself do if he left? The winter might be severe in the mountains, and the Roti might still be waiting for him. Increasingly, Stel felt an odd sense of drift, perhaps, at base, because he had left Pelbarigan with no other motive but to live, and he had no clear purpose.

One evening he asked Fitzhugh if he would be welcome for the winter.

"Welcome?" She looked surprised. "We have grown to depend on you. To be frank, I was wondering how we would survive the winter. Five died last winter, and we grow rapidly more enfeebled. Look at them." She extended an arm toward the small group sitting by the large window opening overlooking the stream. "They don't play games anymore in the evening, or sing, or talk. They appear to be waiting. They don't pray to Ozar, either."

"Pray to Ozar? I didn't know Ozar was divine. I thought she was someone who brought you here."

Fitzhugh sighed. "That is just the trouble. Ozar was divine and wasn't divine. Now Ozar isn't for worship at all. We lack a real divine thing. I don't know, Stel, but I suspect that when Ozar arrived, almost everyone in her died. Only a few survived, and they must have been children. They didn't understand. They called Ozar a mother, as they grew, and they created a religion out of her. Perhaps the older ones taught it to the younger, either to fool them or to give them some explanation of things, inadequate as it might have been. And yet there must have been older ones because our language is well developed. It is hard to say. Ozar, as I see it, is nothing but some sort of conveyance, like a boat, but built to go in the sky, like a bird."

Stel felt a shiver down his back. "In the sky?"

"Ozar is supposed to be hidden forever in her building.

But when Jaeger and I cared for her, and all the others were gone, we grew so lonely and frightened, we dug into the house of Ozar, which has no door, as you may have noticed. We took lamps and went all through it. It is made of metal, and it is broken. On the side, now very faint, is written OZAR. Perhaps more. That is where it is broken.

"I don't know when or how Ozar became a religion. I don't think it was at first, because some things we still have were made out of it. I think, anyhow.

"Near the front of Ozar, inside, was a door. It had a sign on it that read NO ADMITTANCE. Jaeger and I pried it open and went in. It smelled horribly, but in it were two human skeletons in fragments of cloth. We couldn't understand the rest. They sat in chairs and faced a wall with disks on it, with glass fronts, and windows above it in a curve. Only one of the windows was broken, on the north side, where the hill had come over it. Don't tell the others anything about this, especially McCarty."

"Don't worry about that. McCarty and I are not the warmest of friends."

Fitzhugh grinned wryly. "I have noticed. You must watch her, you know. Just as she is watching us now."

Stel looked across the room to where McCarty sat with two of the more vacant old ones, looking at them.

"Don't notice," said Fitzhugh. "She is likely to come over here. I don't feel like a duel of words. I think, by the way, that McCarty has been in Ozar's house, too. I am not sure, but she has said things that seem to me to indicate it. She certainly has ceased to believe that Ozar is divine. I think everyone has. There seems little point in it. Ozar has never functioned in our lives that I can remember—except as a big building and a word. We thought, so our records say, that we were alone in the world, and that made Ozar special, but now other groups are appearing. The Emeri, the Roti, the Commuters, now you. You are, you say, a what?"

"A Pelbar. And there are the Shumai, the Sentani, the Eastern Cities, and many others."

"Yes. It would appear that many small groups survived the burning of the lands."

"Who are the Commuters?"

"We have met only one—a young man who left them

—not all that long ago. Several season cycles. He was journeying east. He never said why. They are herders of cattle. He said that the land to the west is very dry—across these mountains."

"Did he stay?"

"No. Only briefly. McCarty drove him off. He didn't have much patience. Not like you."

"Well, McCarty may still drive me off."

"Perhaps. She needs you and knows it, though. She herself has slipped in the past two or three season cycles. Watch her, though."

"Yet she certainly is better than the others."

"McCarty is my sister. Yes, it is true. She set out with the others, but she became frightened down in the ruins of the ancients, hid, and ran home away from the others. Whatever poison they all absorbed, she got much less of. She resents the fact I am free of it. She even returned to the empty land long after her hair fell out, and gathered dust there and put it in my bed. But Scribner found it and threw it away. Her journey there hurt McCarty, but she didn't care."

McCarty now came across the room, setting her staff hard on the stone floor with each step. "What is this, a conspiracy?" she said, less as a question than a statement. "You are going away with Stel, aren't you. And leave us. Leave me to take care of all these scarecrows. It won't work, Fitz. We will get you first. We will ask the Roti to help. We will put you both in the stew."

Stel and Fitzhugh simply stared at her. What was there to say? McCarty looked at them malevolently.

"McCarty," said Fitzhugh abruptly. "I want to show Stel the room of records."

"What? The room of records? Why? No stranger has ever seen it before."

"We have never regarded it as sacred. And Stel has worked now for us faithfully for several moon cycles. He has never asked for anything."

"He has certainly eaten. We will be fortunate to get through the winter with all he has eaten."

"Well, McCarty," Stel replied quietly, "I haven't eaten much of your food for several weeks now. I have hunted my own, or snared it, and eaten from the woods. I got

filled to the ears with beans and fish. Feans and bish. I
see fins growing from your ears. Your mouth works like
a carp. You flip your tail when you walk. Your eyes wave
like a crayfish. You are barbed like a catfish. Right now
your nose is as long as a gar's."

McCarty raised her staff. Then she lowered it. "Do
what you want about the record room," she muttered,
and walked away.

Fitzhugh looked at Stel. "Huh," she said. "Well, let's
go, then." She brushed her hands, rose, and led Stel
outside and across the field to a room set in the hill. Stel
had always assumed it was merely for storage.

Fitzhugh had a small lamp, which she had lit at the
kitchen fire. When they entered the dry darkness, she
turned up the flame. Baskets of dried beans stood along
the walls. At the rear of the room was another door,
which opened into a smaller room, also very dry, lined
with large cut stones. Along three walls was a stone shelf,
on which Stel could see a number of objects and some
stacks of paper, yellow and crumbling.

"Here is the list," said Fitzhugh. "Be careful. It breaks
if you touch it. This is where we have gotten our names.
See? Here is mine. Fitzhugh, G. Seat 19-F."

Stel looked at the ancient list, now browning, now faint.
Yes, there was Fitzhugh. There McCarty. It was a long
list, and, estimating quickly, he saw that it contained well
over two hundred names. The heading was obscured, but
he could make out: ". . . ger List: Flight 297."

Puzzled, Stel looked at Fitzhugh. She smiled quizzically back. "And here is something none of us can read.
It is not printed, but it is clearly writing. See?"

"It is script. Yes. I can read this. I think. Let me see."

The two very gingerly spread out the long sheet with
holes punched evenly along its two sides. There was a
printed heading, reading, "Schedule of Other Commercial
Flights Approaching KC/14:30 +− 30. 8/17." There
followed a list of numbers and letters. Below this in faint
blue was a handwritten paragraph:

As we came across Mo. whole landscape took fire.
Many spots, then several large bursts, prob. nuke. All
KC burning. Contn. w. to go beyond, but fire endless.

No radio contact. Air full of meteors. Went on. Over Colo. Still fire. Fuel nearly out. Denver all burning. Colo. Spr. nuked. Trying to ride over. Must land anywhere. Dear God, the world is ending.

Capt. Baron Jackson

Stel read it silently several times, slowly making it all out. Then he read it to Fitzhugh, who had been standing patiently, watching Stel's narrowed eyes flick across the lines.

"What does it mean?"

"Most I don't understand. What we thought. Ozar is a conveyance for flying. While it was flying everything caught fire. Finally it had to come down, and it came down here."

"It seems hard to believe."

The two fell silent for a time. Stel read the paragraph again, aloud.

"I have always wondered what it said," Fitzhugh mused.

"Are you glad to know?"

"One must always face the truth. Isn't that so?"

Stel paused. "Yes, I guess so," he eventually replied.

The two stood a long moment, then Fitzhugh said, "We can come back and see the other things some other time. Come. Let's go tell McCarty what the message said."

But when they got to the outside door, it was shut, and Fitzhugh found she could not move it. She sighed. "McCarty has locked us in."

Stel put his shoulder against the door, but it was solid, thick wood and didn't move. Taking the lamp from Fitzhugh, he scanned all around the door. It was set in a rock wall, with a rock lintel and a thick wood frame. Inside, the room was all stoned, not arched, as the Pelbar would have made it, but slanted inward and capped with wide, flat stones notched to fit the walls. Stel took out his knife and probed the frame on the hinge side. Dry rot had softened it. He knew that this, like all Ozar hinges, would be wood, resinous wood fitted with a round pin outside. But the frame was softer. Soon he had cut around the mortise for the hinges, and with a shove toppled the door outward.

Someone had pried one of the large rocks from the re-taining wall by the door over in front of the entrance, then wedged it with several sticks. Stel lifted the rock back into place and tossed the sticks aside. "That one is heavy," he said. "If it was McCarty, she must have had help."

"That could be. She could tell them anything. She is capable of it. She always was, but now that they are old, she sometimes makes fools of them just to be amused."

Stel mused as they walked. He would just as soon leave now, but they had come to need him. In fact, they had needed someone like him for a long time. It would be easy to stay there were it not for McCarty. And she had influence and a following among the old ones, too. Resentment of Fitzhugh's normality was not limited to McCarty. It just reached a peak there. Yet there was great appreciation of Fitzhugh, too, and this McCarty resented. A general mindlessness drifted through this small society, too, which shifted their thinking like light summer winds.

McCarty must have known that she couldn't keep them in the storeroom. She must have been harassing them. Her care for her own prosperity seemed to struggle against her desire for centrality and importance. She showed the quick reversals of small storms, like a succession of Crick-etmonth thundershowers.

As a result of the visit to the room of records, Stel quietly resolved to find a way into the house of Ozar. He would do it at night, repeatedly if necessary, to satisfy himself about what it all was. He would not even tell Fitzhugh, though he didn't really think she would care.

"Fitz, I think I would like to move my gear out of the terminal and sleep somewhere else," Stel said. "If there is hostility toward me, that might help lessen it. Besides, it is airless in there."

"I hope this isn't a step toward your leaving. I fear it. Sooner or later, you will have had enough."

Stel didn't reply. As they entered the terminal, they could hear a commotion at the far end of the main room.

"What is it, Foerster?" Fitzhugh asked.

"Cohen has died. He just came in, brushing dirt from his hands, began to breathe hard, and died."

"He will add to the stew," another remarked, imitating McCarty's voice.

"I will dig a grave in the morning," said Stel.

"No need. It will keep you from the beans," said another, laughing.

"The beans are fine. You can do the beans. I will tie a hoe blade to your foot. You are thin as a handle. Then you will work by merely shuffling about. Now if you will all move aside, Fitz and I will take care of Cohen."

Cohen was as light as a sack of dry leaves. Stel lifted the thin figure, which smelled like wet grass, and left the building, taking Cohen to the small shed where they left Harlow before burial. Fitzhugh followed with the lamp. As Cohen lay on a table, Stel remarked, "I guess rock-moving was too much for Cohen."

"We don't know that."

"No. There is the dirt on the hands."

"It is just dirt."

"Yes. Well, you are now down to twenty-five. Where was McCarty?"

"I don't know. She is given to disappearing. I will go and calm the people. Be sure and lock this shed. Here." Fitzhugh gave Stel the wooden rod, curved to the hole that would enable its user to push the latch rod aside. Then she turned and said, over her shoulder, "We will return to the room of records sometime. We will do it in daylight and take several others. Now I must get back to the people."

Stel watched her go, sure she was upset, but not sure why. He gathered his things from the small room he had been given in the terminal. Then he walked across the field in the dark toward a rock shelter he had seen from the field. As he walked, he was sure he saw a momentary light coming from next to the house of Ozar. Then there was nothing. Stel stood awhile, looking, but nothing more showed. Then he continued in the moonlight to his new outpost on the hill.

IX

THE next night Stel played his flute for the Ozar, while they all sat in the terminal hall. The first hint of late-summer chill had dropped on the plateau, and a small fire on the open hearth made him think of Pelbarigan. For the most part the Ozar sat, somewhat blankly, but some would absently shuffle out for a drink, or for no reason. Fitzhugh was spinning, as usual, until she needed to beat more fibers, and so stopped rather than intruding another sound. McCarty was not there.

Stel ended with a long hymn to Aven, Governor of all the earth and sky, whose beauty surpasses all earthly things, whose justice and perfection can be glimpsed slightly only in one's purest moments, when Her absolute flawlessness gleams like a hundred stars on a clear night. He was moved, himself, both by the thought of this transcendence and by his memory of the great chapel at Pelbarigan with its high ceiling, its balconies, its choir singing on winter evenings, their breaths steaming up in the light of the lamps. Ahroe would be one of them this winter, he thought. Her head would be bent to the music, perhaps sadder than she had been last year, when she could look across to him among the flutists, her smile flashing as she thought of their togetherness after the music.

Before he knew it, he had been silent for some time, and the hall was all but deserted. Only three of the old ones stayed by the fire, staring at it. Fitzhugh had begun beating fibers again, and had Taglio helping her, tapping automatically at the strands of tough fiber stretched over the soft-surfaced log.

On his way out, Stel said, "Fitz, somehow the wood I have been gathering for winter is diminishing. Not seriously, but noticeably."

"Yes, I know."

"You know? I thought that was a separate supply."

"It is. McCarty has taken it somewhere. A little at a time."

"What are you going to do?"

"I haven't time to watch her. It is her wood, too. We will find it."

"Well, good night."

"Good night, Stel. Your music has called up too many memories. It is different from what ours was. But the effect is the same. It hurts the heart. You must have experienced some great sadness. Why did you leave your people?"

"Someday I may tell you. Good night."

Stel left hurriedly and set out across the field between the rows of drying beans. He had found for himself five sleeping places, and chose a new one each night. Why was not clear to him. He had a vague presentiment. With the sense of secrecy typical of the Pelbar before the great peace, he had hidden his gear each day. Tonight he went for it to the hill behind the house of Ozar, and as he retrieved it, he again saw the tiny light from the odd building, vague and flickering, on the side away from the terminal.

Coming closer, he could see that a log, now largely rotten, had been rolled aside, and the light came from inside. Stooping in, Stel saw a dim figure beside the great bulk of Ozar, bent over, placing wood against the base of a large wooden pillar. He slipped in, moved around to the other side of the structure, there seeing other small piles around other pillars.

McCarty was leaving. Stel didn't move. She crawled through the small hole, then pushed back the log, plunging Stel into total darkness. Feeling his way around the great curved cool hull of Ozar, Stel groped along the wall, pushing the logs until he had the right one. He gently moved it aside and wriggled through the hole. McCarty, he could see, was walking back to the terminal in the moonlight, her thin figure high among the bean rows.

Stel watched until the moon passed over three pine tops, then took his own small lamp from his gear and re-entered the hole, pulling the log shut behind him. Lighting the lamp, he walked down the curved side of Ozar. Yes, there was the name, dimly maroon, flaked and fading. Torn from one side of Ozar's body, a thin, flat structure canted up against the hill. Stel sat on it. It was of a whitish metal, gigantic, made of plates fastened together with hundreds of small nails burnished flat to the surface. Windows in a high line receded into the shadow, and Stel slid over the flat structure and on back to the jagged end of Ozar, beyond the *R*. Twisted metal and wires protruded like vines. Climbing carefully up, he entered a long hall, with seats on either side, now just metal frames.

Ozar smelled of darkness and decay. A variety of tools and structures that Stel had never imagined lay strewn across the floor. Peeling from the wall was a cream substance that wasn't metal, nor was it wood. Stel broke a fragment of it off in his hand. It was brittle, but had a slight bend. It had not corroded. Scattered here and there were pearly-white drinking glasses, thin and fragile, and small bottles. Stel also saw wrinkled metal trays like those in the room of records. Ahead, where Ozar narrowed, stood the door Fitzhugh had mentioned, with the faded printing: NO ADMITTANCE. Stel's hand hesitated, but he took hold of the handle and pulled. The door grated open. Several small animals scurried by him in the dark, so jolting him that he almost dropped his lamp. He slipped inside and pulled the door shut behind him, then reopened it because of the close smell.

Stel shuddered as he saw the two skeletons, now quite scattered but still in their chairs. The one on the left leaned against the left wall, its head almost turned over. The dirt that had poured in the window half filled its skull. The one on the right leaned forward against straps. Its skull lay on the floor. In the silence, Stel peered at the disks Fitzhugh had mentioned. Each had labels, and arcs of numbers. Small knobs protruded in rows. In front of each skeleton a staff and a portion of a wheel slanted up from the floor.

As he stared, and grew dizzy with the strangeness of it all, Stel heard a slight sound. He covered his light, fearing to blow it out. A dim light from outside flared through the window of Ozar. Stel rose slowly and peered out. Several figures were entering the hole in the logs. At first Stel thought they were Ozar, but then he realized their naked heads were those of the Roti. He heard a voice say softly, "Yci, nu matte kudasy por das Diu nezumi iro. Ul coom a tha oka. Tyn nu ga hym. Uhm, zym, nachtanali, nu ga hym." The others started up the soft chant again, but the leader quickly put a finger across a couple of mouths, stopping them. Stel saw with some relief that one had an arm bound to his body. So he hadn't killed that man with the rocks.

But now what would he do? He shrank down between the two skeletons. Something pricked his palm. He jerked it up away, then, feeling, came up with a small object backed by a thin shaft like a needle. He felt it with his hands for a while, then put it in his pocket. He could hear the voices outside. Eventually they began to move around inside the building. Some were obviously agitated and fearful. Stel shrouded his lamp even more carefully. As he grew more and more used to the dim light, he saw a dark coat hung up on one wall. He touched it. The sleeve came off. But the cloth, though stiff, seemed quite sturdy.

Stel heard voices inside Ozar. Fortunately, he had pushed the door shut when he first heard them. But he knew it wouldn't hold if the Roti wanted to get in. At this point he wasn't even sure that they knew he was inside. The voices grew closer. Stel could hear the Roti shuffling through things inside Ozar. Was there dust? Did he leave tracks in the dust? He took out his short-sword. Then he put his hand on something made of wire. His fingers traced it out. It was like a Pelbar clothes hanger. Quickly he took the coat, took the needle thing from his pocket, and pinned the sleeve back on.

He could hear the Roti coming to the door. Hanging the coat on the back of one chair, he quickly propped the right-hand skull on top, and crouched down to the right, where the room bulked out. He held his lamp up inside the skull just as the Roti pulled the door open. In the dim light he saw three faces, then for an instant the reflection of the lit eyes and nose of the skull in six eyes. The compartment filled with a mutual shriek, and the door slammed.

The next moments combined a confusion of shouting, stumbling, and running. Stel heard, "Nekko, nekko, y da. Nu ga, nu ga vatay." Then the sounds scattered, and silence resumed inside Ozar. Stel slumped down on the floor, put the skull on his knee, sheathed his short-sword, and wiped the sweat from his hand. He felt limp. Then he began to laugh, at first silently, then quietly but fully. He sat and laughed off and on for some time.

Moving out through Ozar, carefully and silently, after placing the skull back in its corner and patting it a couple of times, Stel came to McCarty's log entrance. It was barricaded shut. No matter. Perhaps the Roti were watching it anyhow. He moved around to the other side of the log structure and made a new hole beneath a rotted log at the end of Ozar's other flat extension. Then he walked slowly back through the beans, climbed down to the stream, and in the chill bathed himself thoroughly. As dawn broke, he still sat by the stream, fingering the needle device that he had taken from the room of the skeletons. Now he could see clearly that it was a representation of two wings, all black, with a pin to fasten it on clothing.

Stel slowly climbed the hill and entered the terminal for breakfast, fish and beans as usual, dished out by Finkelstein, a small person with a perpetually solemn look.

"Back in time to eat, I see," McCarty yelled. "Ready to gather a little winter wood? The stack isn't building up very fast."

"It would build a lot faster if you didn't cart it off. You have half a moon cycle's worth in the house of Ozar already," said Stel.

The click of spoons and bowls stopped. "In the house of Ozar?" said Taglio. He was echoed by murmurs from a dozen others.

"That is a serious thing to say, Stel," said Fitzhugh, quietly.

"Nonetheless, it is so. I saw her last night. You can all go out there now and prove it if you would like to."

"You know we don't go to the house of Ozar."

"McCarty does. She has stacked wood all around the great log pillars inside."

"Then you have been inside the house of Ozar?"

"I was on the hill and saw a light. I thought I would check. I saw McCarty with some wood. She pulled aside a rotted log. I simply followed her in."

"But at least she is of the children of Ozar."

"Perhaps so. But even so, as you said, 'We don't go to the house of Ozar.' That is, none of us but McCarty does. And there were five Roti inside last night, too."

Above the general mutterings of consternation, McCarty shrieked out, "Now we know you lie. To the stew with him, the liar! Give him to the Roti!" She ended with a long, quavering laugh.

Stel simply said, "You need to grease your voice, McCarty. Go and look. Go inside and look at the tracks. I am sure you will see what I said you would."

"Go inside! Do you hear him? He would have us go inside the house of Ozar."

"It is time you went inside anyhow. The whole structure is in terrible condition. It will not last many more seasons. I am afraid I don't see why you refuse to go in. Clearly the children of Ozar built the structure. Your ancestors must have climbed all over Ozar to do it. Ozar must have stood there in the open some time before that was done. It has surely been repaired from time to time in the past. You don't worship Ozar. Besides, all it is, is a metal structure. I was in it last night, after McCarty shut the log behind her. She is always shutting me into something."

Taglio stood now, trembling, with much more resolve than Stel had yet seen in him—or her. Pointing at Stel, Taglio said firmly, "This person is lying to us. We have never gone to Ozar. Even McCarty would not. He has confessed he has been inside. We must be done with him. He has violated our most sacred trust. He has—"

"Your most sacred trust is not to go into a rotting old building?" Stel returned. "I find that a marvelous thing. That is birds flying upside down. The care you give each other is your most sacred trust. You have no real religion. You do have an ethics of a sort. What is an old building but an old building, even if it is Ozar's? What is it to

McCarty? Nothing. She has been there repeatedly. Go and see."

Taglio raised a pair of skeletal hands, crying out, "I will hear no more. This person must go."

Fitzhugh then stood. "No," she shouted, banging her wooden bowl on the table. "We will all go now to the house of Ozar. It is time we did. We should have done it long ago. No one has cared for Ozar, and if there is neglect, then it must be remedied. Of course, if we find the wood inside, we will have no way of knowing if McCarty put it there or if Stel did." She gave Stel a level and severe look. "We will all go but Stel. He is not of Ozar, so he will have to remain behind."

Taglio sat down with an audible plump. The others looked shocked and frightened.

"We will go," McCarty shrieked. "I will be the first. I have not been there ever. As Fitzhugh said, it is time we looked into Ozar's condition."

Almost mechanically, the rest rose, took torches, lit one, and walked slowly through the beans to the house of Ozar. Stel watched them go from the terminal, then he took down the stave he had found for a longbow and sat by the smoking hearth working it. The Ozar were gone a long time, but finally they came back. Stel could hear them stacking wood back on the great pile under the overhang.

Fitzhugh came in ahead of the others and stood regarding Stel. "McCarty is my sister, Stel. I will protect her lies against your truth if I must. This is the only place she has, and she must not lose it. You must see that."

Stel said nothing, but continued to shave the stave. Others began to come in. Fitzhugh continued, "It has been observed and decided that we have no proof that McCarty was ever in the house of Ozar. She entered first, through the opening you described, and so the tracks we saw were perhaps hers just made. We saw your tracks in Ozar, and we saw the bare tracks of the Roti. You were correct about that."

"You made one mistake, Fitz," said Stel, quietly.

"Mistake?"

"I never told you where McCarty entered the house of Ozar. It is no matter. I see it is time for me to leave.

It must be a matter of some wonder, too, that I would struggle to bring winter wood here, only to carry it off to the house of Ozar, giving myself more work. Never mind. I will be gone before the sun sets."

"Gone? We have only to thank you. You were right. We had neglected Ozar. If we do not take steps to preserve and repair the house, it will truly fall down. For that we will badly need your help, Stel."

The Pelbar stood frowning quizzically. Here Fitzhugh had shifted blame to him, only to praise him and ask his help. Well, maybe that shrill old catbird was worth it to her. On the other hand, she knew she needed his help. She would manage to put the matter of Ozar off while the more important business of survival took their attention. Perhaps it was just a game, a slow, ritualistic drama. The others, who had all been to the house of Ozar for the first time, seemed to be calm about the whole thing. Stel suddenly wondered if it were all a fiction and if they each had sneaked out there at one time or another to satisfy a curiosity about what was in the odd-shaped building.

Perhaps societies are bound together by such fictions. The Shumai certainly had trouble giving up the ridiculous notion of their natural superiority. What this collection of trembling bald heads had was Ozar. Fitzhugh had done what she had to. With them all staring at him, Stel had already begun to wander off mentally, wondering what fictions the Pelbar used to fuse their society together. The words of Pell?

But then he came to himself and said, "Well, then, I am very sorry that I entered Ozar's house when I should not have. I am glad that you will forgive me for it. I will stay here awhile yet if you permit it. See? I am making a longbow to kill a wild cow or two for you. If you dry its meat, it will help you in the winter. One cow is worth a lot of fish."

A general murmur showed that they had eaten beef in the past, but not for some time. Stel didn't tell them that his primary reason for making the longbow was the Roti. The Ozar now turned to their morning tasks. There seemed a gratification among them. They had been to the house of Ozar together for the first time in anyone's

memory. They had stood together and seen the tall letters on the side of Ozar, spelling out the name of the
great craft that had brought their ancestors all together
from the sky.

Stel caught McCarty looking strangely at him, but with
obvious triumph. "Well, old buzzard," he said, "you can
thank Aven for how that turned out."

"It has not turned out yet, hairy one," said McCarty,
adding one of her strange laughs.

 X

THE aspens by the stream were yellowing when Stel
finally killed a wild cow with his longbow—flicking one
long arrow into the back of the shoulder from behind a
tree. The black animal had bellowed, begun to run, as if
slow in discovering that it was dead, then collapsed after
a few steps, lying motionless.

Stel gutted the animal, skinned it, and cut off one hindquarter to take back immediately, wrapped in the skin.
The rest he cut up and put up in a tree.

When he arrived back at the terminal, the jubilation at
having meat was greater than he had anticipated, given
the passivity of the Ozar. They immediately set about cutting steaks off the quarter and roasting them in the fire.
Stel wondered if he ought not to kill a whole herd. But he
left them and went back for more. No one would come
with him, so eager were they for meat. It had been a long
season of harvest, with smoky fires drying fish, beans endlessly hand-shelled into baskets, all woven by the solemn
Finkelstein and a close companion, McPhee.

By midafternoon, Stel had brought in all the meat. He was alarmed at how the Ozar were eating it. "Fitz," he said, "after not having meat for so long, they ought not to be gulping it down like this. Will they be able to take it?"

Fitz herself looked greasy around the mouth. "They don't get much pleasure, you know," she replied, looking away. McCarty was urging further pieces of hindquarter on several of the old ones. Stel felt vaguely uneasy at her look. But he couldn't focus his feelings. So he went outside to begin work on the black hide. He had left his heavy winter coat out on the prairie when the weather warmed, and soon he would need a new one.

Before sunset there was no one working on the meat anymore. Stel had directed the old ones about setting up a drying rack and cutting the meat into long, thin strips for drying, lighting a smoky fire underneath. Going into the terminal, he found the place nearly deserted. Only Berry and Finkelstein sat at the bench near the unlit hearth. "Your meat has made everyone sick, Stel," said Finkelstein, staring at the wall.

"I was afraid of that. They all ate too much. A change of diet is not easy. Why are you not sick?"

"I didn't eat much. I was gathering withes for the baskets."

Stel felt uneasy. Nonetheless, he went outside and finished the drying of the meat, spending most of the night on it, cutting the strips, feeding the fire, turning the meat.

He was nearly done when McCarty appeared in the open doorway. "Poisoned them, did you? Never content to let us alone. Now you are fixing more poison." Then she turned and was gone.

Tired out, Stel slept in his room in the terminal. He had devised a locking system he was sure that none of the Ozar could master—not even McCarty. In the morning, a few drooping old ones appeared in the terminal hall. The place was a foul mess. Fitzhugh was nowhere to be seen. Stel set to cleaning up after the old ones, using a fiber mop and a wooden pail. His own stomach turned at the smell. Suddenly, Taglio appeared in the main doorway. "Stel, Fitzhugh has fallen in the stew," he quavered.

Stel dropped the mop and ran out by Taglio, heading

for the stone structure on the bank. Something was odd —was wrong—but he never realized what until he ran into the entrance and found himself entangled in a net. A group of the old ones surrounded him, and no matter how he struggled, grappling at them through the holes, they wound him up.

McCarty was there, as Stel now saw, directing everything. "Now," she shrilled, "into the stew with the poisoner. He has disrupted our life enough. Sink him." She flung up her arms, laughing, took a misstep, and herself disappeared over the edge of the pit with a yell. There was a general rush to the hole, and cries.

"Quick, get a rope," said Taglio. He turned. The only one around was holding Stel in the net. "We will have to let him go," he said. The old ones rushed to unbind Stel. He fought his way out of the net, tempted for a moment to throw them all in after McCarty. Taglio dropped the end of the rope to her as she flailed and struggled in the soup of filth. She took hold of it, but in her weakness could not hold hard enough to be lifted out.

"Loop it around you," said Stel. She was too frightened to hear, crying and moaning. The stench was almost unbearable. Stel turned to McPhee, shook her by the shoulders, and said, "Go get Finkelstein. He's in the hall. Bring the roof ladder. And get Fitzhugh." McPhee flung herself awkwardly out of the doorway. McCarty was sinking farther in. With revulsion, Stel took the far end of the rope, tied it to a small tree beyond the entrance, took off his clothes, and went down the rope to McCarty, slinging it around her armpits in the slop of filth, tying it in front of her, and calling for the old ones to draw them out. They couldn't.

"Let go, Stel," said Taglio. "We will pull McCarty out and then throw the rope down for you."

"I will when you jump in, Taglio," said Stel.

The ladder was finally brought, and Stel directed how it was to be tied fast at the top. Then he took the whimpering McCarty on his back and climbed slowly, with slippery hands, back up out of the stew and dumped her on the stone slabs. Fitzhugh came in, rubbing her wrists. "I was tied up by someone last night," was all she offered. "Finkelstein just freed me."

"Well, that's nice," Stel replied, dripping with the stinking muck of the stew. "Taglio, bring my things—all of them—down to the stream. I am going to wash."

Taglio started to resist. Stel hit him open-handed, with a filthy palm, across the cheek. The old one fell. "Finkelstein, you do it," said Stel. The short figure looked, opened his mouth, shut it, then went to Stel's clothing and picked it up.

Stel said nothing more but went down to the stream and sat in the cool water, scrubbing himself with sand, clumps of grass from the bank, and finally with some wood lye soap he had directed Finkelstein to fetch for him. Several times he retched into the water. So that was it with the Ozar.

Finally he felt fairly clean. He climbed out and dressed. High above, in a line, a number of the old ones watched him. He slowly climbed back to the terminal to assemble his gear. As he came up, McCarty, still dripping with the stew, went down to the stream, though she had found water to rinse herself. She had stripped off her robe and was the same human ruin Stel had first seen in the spring.

"May the vultures of the mountains drink from your eyes," she said to him as they passed on the hill. Stel said nothing.

He took his time preparing to go, taking an ample supply of dry meat from the racks. No one said anything until he was ready. Then Fitzhugh, by the door with a small crowd of the old ones, said, "Of course you will feel you have to go now. I wish you well. Don't stay in the mountains long. Winter will come early there. We regret what has happened. We are grateful for all your help. You have gotten us through this winter anyway. We—"

"It was McCarty who killed your child, wasn't it," said Stel.

Fitzhugh stopped, stunned. "That was never proved," she said, quietly.

"It was proved to me this morning. You may keep what you have harbored."

"Did McCarty burn the ancients? Did McCarty bring down Ozar? Did McCarty create the Roti, the Emeri? Did McCarty thrust you out from your own people to wander friendless across these wastes?" Fitzhugh spoke in a monotone, unsmiling. "Or are you here because of the McCarty in you?"

"What of Jaeger? Did he end up in the stew? Was he already d—"

Stel was interrupted by a shriek from Fitzhugh, who covered her face and turned to go into the terminal. Stel quickly went to her and turned her again. "I am sorry. There is no use in our parting like this. There is that which is not McCarty. Good-bye, Fitzhugh. I fear for you now with her loose, but I have no say in the matter. Now—"

"No, you have no say."

"Thank you for helping me with my things, Finkelstein." Stel took both their hands, then the hands of each of the others, for they all held them out mechanically.

Taglio said, "I am sorry. I have remembered now. I am a woman."

"Oh. I should have known. Well, Tag the wag, keep yourself far from the stew, lest McCarty's next conquest be you."

"Me? What have I done? I never—"

"No, you never. I am sorry. Forget it."

Fitzhugh came forward and embraced Stel, saying, "May your Aven go with you and lead you to a better place than this."

"May Aven stay with you and lift you above the skies of Ozar," he returned. Then he walked westward without looking back until he was high above, and the house of Ozar looked like the print of a gigantic, broken-winged bird, plowed into the hillside. Only one figure, like a speck, still stood by the terminal. Then another came. That must be McCarty, Stel thought, then looked ahead again, through the yellow-leaved aspens and the dark-green pine.

XI

As Stel left the cluster of old ones, Ahroe, far to the north and east, lay in a log house of the western Shumai. She was in pain. Bending over her, a heavy blond woman, with a downturned mouth and crow's feet by her eyes, said, "All right now, everything is fine. Now, push. When the tightening comes, push against it."

"Ahhh, ahhh. I will try. I thought I pushed the last fifty times."

"You did. You did well. This is your first, and it is sometimes not so easy."

A voice came in the door. "Is everything all right in there? What is it?"

"Go away, Hagen. You are as bad as a father. We will call you. Keep the water boiling."

"Ahhhhhhhh. Oh, Aven, let this stop."

"What are you doing to her?"

"Shut up out there. Haven't we enough to contend with? How many babies have you had? Now, Ahroe, push again. All right. Now we are doing fine."

Not long after, Hagen, stirring the fire, with six hands, as the Shumai put it, heard the cries. For the first time in a long while, he prayed, not for the child, but for Ahroe. It had been a long birth, after a long walk west. For the child he cared little as yet, but Ahroe he had come to love.

They had spent the winter at Black Bull Island. Getting there was not as easy as he had hoped, chiefly because of a new storm, with bitter cold. They had had to sleep nestled together in snow caves, and Hagen had teased her a good deal about it. One night, with his arms around her from behind, both cold and shivering, he had told her about Venn, his wife, and how they would sleep that way. "But of course," he added, "I didn't leave my hands *there*," shifting them slightly.

Ahroe had stiffened beneath her coat, and he with his heavy mittens on had laughed. A great white owl hooted outside the snow cave when Hagen's laugh rang out, and, glancing out, Hagen saw it, ghostly in the dark, gliding off toward a farther tree. Ahroe had stiffened even more at that, and Hagen had laughed again.

Then she had said, "Don't laugh so loud in my ear," and he had taken that to mean that she trusted him, accepted him as family, knew he meant nothing but a joke, and in a rush he had seen her humanity fully, her youth, toughness, and vulnerability. They had gone to sleep then, quickly, and after that he had trouble seeing her as anything but his daughter.

With spring they had walked westward, Ahroe growing heavier. They went slowly so Hagen could be sure she was steadily well fed, and as summer progressed they walked more slowly yet, finally arriving at Ayase, in the southwest part of Shumai territory. Hagen had one cousin there, Ral, a man who had been northwest to Emeri territory, had been enslaved, and had been freed by Jestak's expedition.

His face lighted up at the sight of another Pelbar. "That Jestak," he told her, "knew what he was doing. And he did it well. Now, you stay with us and we will take care of you. Bara will help you have the child. And I have learned to milk cattle from the Emeri, so you will have plenty of milk."

He had embraced her odorously and warmly, and they had moved into his hexagonal log structure. Ahroe had worked as hard as her condition had allowed, doing what the Shumai thought of as "woman's work," though she had also done some blacksmithing for them, light work, since the Shumai were at best poor metalworkers still.

"Well, are you going to squat out there all afternoon dreaming?" Bara was smiling, jerking Hagen out of his reverie. "Come in now. Now where is that water? You can stay only a pigeon's flight. She still has to be washed some. And so does he."

"He?"

"He."

"Ah, well, with someone like Ahroe, one always hopes for a copy."

Hagen dusted himself off and entered the dim house, blinking away the dazzle. Ahroe lay nested in cattle-skin robes like a child with a doll next to her. She smiled weakly.

Hagen's old hunter's hands smoothed back her hair, which didn't need it. "Well," he said.

"See him? I have called him Garet."

"Garet?"

"Stel's grandfather. Look there. It is Stel's chin."

Hagen looked, but it looked just like any other baby to him, slightly purplish pink and grotesque, with wispy hair, engaged in its own contemplations, eyes shut like tight mouths, lips working. "Well, Garet," he said, "you . . . you are a real baby, all right."

Garet sniffed and wriggled, then settled back to his deep concentrations.

"Being born is a lot of work, eh, Garet?"

"Work! What did he do? I have done it all—with Bara's help. What do you know about it?"

"Well now," said Hagen, with mock severity, "I've had my own babies before you were even born."

"Venn did."

"Well, yes, but . . ."

"Anyway, give me a kiss, Hagen, and then I think I will have to rest some."

Hagen did, then stepped outside, where Bara was stirring cloths in the hot water. They looked at each other. Hagen shrugged and said, "I think I will go up the hill."

"Bring back some wood when you come."

Hagen turned. "Bring some wood? Bring some wood!"

"Yes, bring some wood."

"All right," he said, starting off without looking back. "I will bring some wood." Bara watched the old man walk stiffly away and laughed to herself, shaking her head.

Back inside, Ahroe, looking at Garet, did indeed see Stel's chin, as well as his forehead and cheekbones. For a few moments she resented this. What had he done to deserve that recognition? Right now he seemed so far away their life together drifted like a dream, an alien passage, and yet so was this hexagonal house so far away from all she had been accustomed to. Why had she come this far? If Stel was still alive, where in this vastness was he? Maybe his bones had been bleaching somewhere back on the prairie since he had died in the winter cold. She would return to Pelbarigan with the child. No, she would not. It was possible to live out here. She would continue westward, but not now, not with Garet so small. They would live here for the winter and then go on, again slowly.

Hagen wouldn't mind the slow pace. He seemed the most free person she had ever met, completely footloose, but she knew he would stick with her as long as she wanted it. He seemed to accept this. It was as if it were a boy's adventure in a world of boys. She had never really seen the verve of boys among the Pelbar, where they were disciplined early, and gentled. Among the Shumai they were rogues. They needed discipline. Well, she would see that Garet got it, even though she knew little of such things. As much as possible, Pelbar children were cared for by men. The thought of having to tend Garet, wash him, cleanse his clothes, irked Ahroe a little. But the Shumai women did it as a matter of course.

Where did she fit into all this? Of course a guardsman's life was often endlessly routine, with endless watches, though the rigor of the training and intensity of the skill gave it a piquancy she enjoyed. But now she would have to put guard training behind her. She was a mother with a very tiny child and only Shumai women to turn to. She would have to be a mother, impatient as this made her.

Winter on the plains went slowly and monotonously. Ahroe helped Bara do all the work Shumai women were accustomed to, and found it intolerable drudgery. There seemed always something to scour, soak, cook, mend, arrange, warm, serve, or fetch. Her hands were always dirty or greasy. If she only knew how the Pelbar made soap. Stel would know. Occasionally Pelbar soap made its way this far west in trade, but they had guarded the secret of

its manufacture during hostile times because they had to
have things to trade that the outside tribes would need.

The Emeri made a soap from some weed. But Bara,
who was not used to it, scoured with sand and rushes. She
had lived with grime all her life, and with cold and deprivation, and she seldom noticed them.

Garet also took time. Ahroe had to learn child care,
too, largely from Bara, adding refinements of her own for
his comfort and cleanliness. She nursed him in the house,
and the Shumai came and went without noticing, as was
their way, though she always reddened a little with embarrassment, especially when Quen, who was her age, a
cousin of Bara's, arrived. He was tall and lank, freckled,
a hunter, unmarried. He was also soft-spoken and gentle,
but Ahroe sensed soon that he had developed an active
interest in her.

But he traveled a great deal on winter hunts, and so his
appearances, though too frequent for her comfort, because
of his attentive eyes, blue and searching, would be followed by days or even longer periods of family quiet.

Hagen went with Quen on shorter hunts, but the old
man's stiffness seemed to grow on him. He seemed repeatedly startled by his own age, as if it had ambushed him,
been defeated, but lay in wait again outside the firelight
after a long run or a cold hunt.

As Garet grew and fattened, Hagen became more interested in him, delighting in making the baby laugh tooth-
lessly and fling his body into repeated stretchings. Hagen
did this generally by imitating all the birds and animals he
could call. Occasionally, as when he did a wild black bull,
Garet's face jerked into surprise, then wrinkled into a
wail. Bara would say, "If you're going to do that one, do
it from the top of the hill."

Hagen would rock the child back into contentment, taking his time, and clearly enjoying it. As the nights
warmed, he made Ahroe a back frame for Garet. They
would set out again, he assumed, before the grass stems
headed.

In the first flush of spring, when the great crane flocks
swept slowly overhead, and the geese, and smaller birds,
returned to the plains, Quen seemed to settle into Ral's
camp, helping him with his small herd of milk cattle, and

being close to Ahroe as much as he could. Everyone noticed it. Bara called him aside one afternoon, as she stirred a large pot of fragrant stew, in which large meat chunks seethed and rolled.

"She's married, you know."

"Who?"

"Ahroe the Pelbar."

"So?"

"So you ought to be at Maden's or with your Uncle Ekhel. There you will find Shumai women good for you. Ahroe is a person of honor. She—"

"Where is her husband, this Stel? Is he alive?"

"No one knows."

"What good is he? How will he help her? She has a child. How is he a father?"

"She has Hagen for help right now."

"An old man?"

"Nonetheless, your anxieties will do you no good. Why not let them fade and dry, like rain in the sand? You will only make a mess."

Quen stood silent for a while. "I can only try. It wouldn't be a settled thing for me if I didn't."

Bara lifted her large wooden ladle and let stew slop back into the pot. "Can you see her doing this the rest of her life? I cannot. She combs herself like a mantis. She scrubs, wipes, and fusses endlessly."

Quen grinned, as if lighting his freckles like candles. "Yes, she is clean, isn't she."

Bara laughed. "One more thing. Remember, she was trained as a Pelbar guardsman. She is no wilting flower. She will take your proposals amiss."

"I mean nothing but to ask, cousin. But I must do that."

Yet he didn't—for quite a while. And when he did, it was meekly and quietly. Still, Ahroe whirled and glared. "I am married," she said flatly, turning back to the wild sheepskin she was softening for the baby.

Quen said nothing for a time. Then he said, "I have thought about that. What kind of marriage is it? Didn't he leave you? Don't you have a child? I will honor the child as my son. I will care—"

Ahroe stood and faced him. "Get out. Leave me alone."

Quen's eyes narrowed. "I believe I have just as much

right here as you. I am of the family. You are not. I have
made an honorable proposal, and I think a good one. I
am thought—"

"Stop." Ahroe put her hand to her short-sword, and on
an impulse flicked it out.

Quen looked at her in amazement. "I'm sorry you did
that," he said. "You can refuse me if you want, but I have
offered you no hostility, and I'm afraid I will not tolerate
anyone's drawing a weapon on me like that."

"Then what will you do? It is here. I have had to defend myself before with it, and will do my best again."

"Defend yourself?" Quen made a move toward her,
with almost dreamlike slowness. She backed, feinted, and
as he came on, with his hand out, slashed to nick his forearm. But it wasn't there. He had her wrist, and moving in
a blur, threw her down. She spun her leg to trip him, but
his leg was rooted like a tree.

"Now," he said slowly, "drop that before I break your
arm." She didn't let go. Quen moved as if to twist her arm
back, but suddenly jammed her face into the floor. She
seemed to see a flash, raised her head with blood streaming from her nose, and saw him, through tears, standing in
front of her with her short-sword. Without hesitation, she
rushed at him, feinting, reaching for an armlock. But he
spun the weapon away, caught her, swung her, jabbed his
elbow in her eye, and dropped her on the floor. She rolled
away, stood again, panting, dazed with pain, facing him.

Quen stood still. "Now, sit down," he said. Ahroe stood
her ground. "Sit down or I will knock you down." Ahroe
continued to stand, her eye already puffing closed. "All
right," said Quen, lunging toward her. She stepped back,
turned, and tripped him. Quen spun, saying quietly, "Very
nice," as he kicked her feet from under her. Ahroe fell
hard, and almost as she hit, Quen was sitting on her back.

"Now," he said. "I can see that my proposal has been
rejected. That hurts, of course. It hurts me more to hurt
you. But I will not have anyone, even a woman, hold a
weapon on me and simply walk away. If you play a man's
game, you'll have to play it by men's rules."

Ahroe's eye hurt fiercely. With her one free hand she
felt her nose to see if it had been broken. She said nothing.

"I'm sorry, Ahroe, that you reacted as you did. I'm sorry to have been that repulsive to you. You may keep your precious coward, this Stel, and welcome to him. Hagen told me about that wretch, Assek. I am not an Assek and decline to be regarded as one. I did not start a fight, but I have never yet shrunk from one. Now don't you agree that it was a fair fight? After all, you did start it with that long knife."

"Get off me, you fish-gutted rat snake."

Quen took her wrist and twisted it. "What did you say?"

"Get off me."

"Now, in polite company, what was the rest?"

"Please, Quen, you are going to break it."

Quen stood up. In the dim light, he watched her roll slowly over on her back. "Well, Ahroe, when you start a fight with somebody who hasn't offered one, have a good reason. And let there be a reasonable chance you can win it. I myself don't stand in front of black bulls."

Ahroe felt her eye. "Look what you have done to me," she said, but when she could clear her good eye, she saw she was alone. She dragged herself to her feet, and, groping, found her short-sword on the other side of the house, then sheathed it. Ahroe ached. Her eye felt as if it were dragging the whole side of her face down.

Bara appeared in the doorway, saying, "What is wrong with Quen? He is leaving without even staying for . . ." She came over to Ahroe and held up her face, scrutinizing it. "Did he force you? Did he—"

Ahroe shook her head.

"I didn't think he would."

"He wanted to marry me. He wouldn't stop asking."

"And you. Did you attack him?"

"I took out my short-sword and told him to stop."

Bara whistled softly. "Oh. Well, sit down, and I will get some water and clean you up."

When Bara returned, Ahroe had scarcely moved. Bara did her best to clean and ease her, but the whole side of her face had swollen.

"Pell was right. Men uncontrolled are not fit to live with."

"Just be calm. Lie down. I will bring Garet to you when he awakens."

"You don't agree. Look what he did."

"But you said that you took out your sword."

"He didn't have to prove his big male superiority. He just had to leave."

"You really asked him to prove himself, didn't you?"

"I only wanted to be let alone. I am married. It is indecent to propose that I marry again. Besides, I—I love my husband."

"Do you? Is he alive? I don't mean to trouble you, Ahroe, but I think you should listen. You see we live a wild life. Fighting helps us survive. You have seen Quen come in from hunting. That is a kind of fighting—for the sake of others. He can't just stop being that way, like pouring water on a fire. He has trained for it since he was a small boy. He—"

"But I didn't—"

"You took out your sword, Ahroe. That is a threat. Quen's whole life involves handling threats with his physical skill. Do you hold up a house with twigs? No. You use logs, and the strongest your horses can pull."

"Look what he did to me, and you—"

"Accept your responsibility. Ahroe, don't be angry with me, but I am glad this happened. No, no, don't get up. I wish he had been easier. Hagen told us what happened with Assek. You handled him well. But I am glad now that you see that doesn't always work. Because the sapling has resisted the badger, will it stand up when a bull leans on it? Look. Men tend generally to be stronger than us. You may not like it, but that is the way it is. If you know the rock is hot from the fire, don't pick it up. Get a tongs. And in this case the tongs is being a little diplomatic."

"He was just proving he was a male, and so, superior."

"If you'd have been a man, he'd have been harder on you. Look. What did your family do to your husband? Did he run away of his own accord? Wasn't it because he didn't accept his place as a man? Isn't this the same in a way? Besides, you are wrong about most men. Look. I know you met Assek, but for every Assek there are a thousand others. Even here, when Ral says to me, 'Do this,' or 'Do that,' and expects me to, he wants me to be happy. If I am not happy, he is not, and he knows it right away. Most men are that way. Quen is angry because you have a baby and no father here for him. He—"

"It is none of his business. How would I—"

"He has fallen for you, Ahroe. Or did. Does the sun tell the opening leaves to shut because light is none of their business?"

"It is not the same."

"With men it is—most men. Some are evil and violent. Quen treated you awfully roughly, but only when you stepped into his ground."

"His ground?"

"Fighting. He does it very well. Many men do. Apparently, Stel never did."

Ahroe tried to laugh, but it made her face hurt. "Stel? No. I never saw him fight. He took little guard training— only what all had. He—"

"Was he strong?"

"Yes. He is. He does stonecutting sometimes. He could always lift a great deal. But I could have beaten him in a fight if he—"

"Did he know enough not to try it out?"

Ahroe said nothing, partly out of pain, partly in thought of Stel. He certainly was not helpless. She never thought of fighting him. They had been instinctive friends from childhood, from the time he had given her a practice boat he had made in his woodworking class. He had come up to her and said, "Are you Ahroe Dahmen? Here." And he had walked away embarrassed.

Bara had brought Garet, who was waking. "Did he try it out? Would he, if he were here, have felt pity for a strange young woman with a baby and no husband anywhere?"

"Yes, of course. But he wouldn't have beaten her into the ground."

"At least his pity is like Quen's. His pity turned to love. I tried to tell him to leave you alone, but he thought he could see a way to help you—by giving of himself."

"All this doesn't sound like what happened."

"No. But you had a hand in that. And we fear the windy storm that makes the grass green. Now, I must go and cook. You are going to have some black eye there. But it will heal. I am sorry, Ahroe. But things will calm. After the worst wind, the river water becomes smooth and clear." Bara put her arms around the younger woman and patted her a long moment, then got up to go out. At the door she turned and said, "I am sorry, Ahroe, but I have been thinking about what I have told you a long time. You are not among the Pelbar. Walk gently when you cross a quaking bog. Talking is a method. You don't always have to fight.

"Another thing. I know you think we here, we women, have a bad time, with all the dirt and work, but remember that it is not amusing for the men to stand in a freezing rain on a hunting station for most of a day and have the cattle turn aside an ayas back and never come. They have to do it, and the tough survive it. Your Stel had other skills, and other needs, and you could treat him differently."

"I never—" Ahroe began, but Bara had gone outside again. Then she lay back and nursed Garet, who drank greedily and long. Ahroe watched him dreamily through her one open eye. Hagen came in and then came over to her, kneeling down. When he saw her face, his showed shock and anger.

Ahroe put her hand on his arm. "No. Don't do anything. I had a hand in bringing it on."

"He had no right—"

"Please let it go. I would not have you hurt. I have things to learn, too. I have been thinking of Stel. If I knew then what Quen has just taught me, maybe I would be home with him now, or at Northwall."

"Just the same, he—"

"No, Hagen. Please. Look what Ral and Bara have done for me. And you. I have eaten Quen's meat. I have never done anything for him. He is rough, isn't he. I am glad Assek wasn't so fast and strong. Now please let me think this all over and be quiet."

But Hagen still sat there, angry and upset. Ral came in, knelt at her other side, looked at her face, and whistled long and low. "Well, Ahroe, it looks as if you stood in the way of an axe."

"I think I did."

"A dull one, too."

"Too sharp for me."

"Are your teeth all right?"

"Yes. All there."

"And that nose. Is that a bruise? Or is it broken?"

"A bruise only."

"He is a rough boy, isn't he. But he went too far this time. Only a touch will trigger a deadfall, but then all that weight comes whunking down." He sat a moment, then leaned quickly and kissed her forehead. "I still have three cows to milk. Hear them out there? They are saying I have neglected them. When are you going to help me milk, Ahroe? Ah, you yourself are being milked still, aren't you." But he was on his way out and didn't wait for any answer.

A half-month later Ahroe and Hagen set out again. Her eye was better, but for a small arc of red in the white, and her nose had resumed its narrow shapeliness. The whole camp said good-bye, and watched them up the hill. Bara called, "I hope you know what you are doing. Come back anytime. Bring Stel when you find him."

They waved back, then didn't turn again. Ahroe couldn't. Again she felt cast adrift, by her own hand, but Hagen was there, and old as he was, remained wholly devoted to her. Ahead of her, he walked stiffly but steadily westward, and she had a sudden inkling that it was all a grand adventure to him, for the first time going west of Shumai territory into a new land, the eastern face of which shone this morning with the sun over their shoulders.

The first two weeks passed without remarkable event. They went slowly because of Garet, resting and foraging. Ahroe could see that Hagen still enjoyed himself. Then, topping a rise, they looked at a new scene. In the distance, the landscape looked brown and lifeless, eroded into deep gullies, steaming with dust.

"What is it?"

"It is an empty place. It is death to cross it."

"Do you think Stel did?"

"No. I think he would know. If he came this far west, he is probably to our south—if we have not overrun him again. But I know of no people to our south, and I surmise he may have continued west."

"Then we should go south around the empty place?"

"I think so. From here. We would have to anyway. Ral knew of no one there. We should skirt the empty area and continue westward. Let's back off it a little to be safe. I saw another empty place once, far to the northeast, west of the Bitter Sea. They always come where there was an ancient city. The broken roads run into them. Sometimes you can see ruins out in them."

The two turned south around the great burn of ancient times. That same morning, Quen returned to Ral's. He had been troubled ever since his encounter with Ahroe. He had gotten no peace. He had finally decided that whatever Shumai rules or attitudes are, he had been wrong. After avoiding the place as long as he could, he finally came back so that, if nothing else, he might rid himself of the massive emotional upthrust that troubled him days and nights. Omar and Wald were with him.

Ral greeted them outside the animal pens, hands on hips, his blond braid over one shoulder, his leather smock dark with dirt. "They have gone," he said. "I was expecting you. You were too violent with her, Quen."

"Where?"

"Westward."

"Does Hagen know about the empty places?"

"Yes. I am sure."

"Then what?"

"I think he thinks Stel is to the south and west."

Quen frowned. Wald muttered slowly, "Well, if they go to the empty place, then turn south, they will come to Roti country. I hope the woman has dark eyes."

"What of the baby? Have his eyes turned dark?"

"Gray. Like his father."

"If his father went that way, then that was an end to him. Gray, you say. Well, boys, what do you think?" Quen stared into two sets of eyes as blue as his own.

"I say we'll have to go and get them."

"What is all this?" Ral asked.

"The Roti. Haven't you heard of them?"

"No. The Roti?"

"No wonder. Few know of them. They speak some unknown language. They capture blue-eyed people and sacrifice them."

"Garet?"

"Him they would let grow up. Then they would kill him. It all has something to do with—well, with sex. The whole bunch is sex-crazy. They think blue-eyed people come from the sky and are gods."

Ral whistled. "I will come, too."

"No. You have too much to care for here." Quen called this over his shoulder as they already began a loose Shumai trot up the grassy hill, Ral somewhat bewilderedly watching them go.

 XII

IT took Hagen and Ahroe three days to arc around the empty land southward, reaching a country of higher hills, dotted with broadly spaced pines and rough clumps of grass and brush. Hunting was poor, but Ahroe shot several burrowing animals with her short bow. They were smaller than the woodchucks of the Heart River, larger than the ground squirrels that squeaked and hid as the humans approached. Hagen called them prairie chucks.

The night of the third day they slept by their small fire. Hagen felt uneasy. He was sure he had heard something. Yes. He sat up. Suddenly, he was lashed by a noose around his neck, then quick coils around his body. As he shouted, Ahroe jumped up and a noose whisked around her. She cut it off with a sweep of her short-sword, but another, then another, wrapped her, and she too was en-

snared. Five figures with shaved heads slid into the firelight. One picked up Garet, who screamed and cried.

One with a strange headdress cried out, "Puus da oun
das tan. Coom. Fro das coeden."

Another added twigs, and the fire flared up. All of
them ignored Hagen and Ahroe, clustering around the
fire with Garet, forcing open his tightly shut eyes.

"Aaahhhiiieee," the leader cried out. "Diu heer es nu
may nezumi iro!" They all took up the chant, dancing
around the fire with Garet, who shrieked in total fear,
swung above all their heads. They turned to the two
bound adults, who twisted and fought against the leather
ropes. The leader put his foot on Ahroe's neck, looking
at her eyes.

"Naaah. Heo nyet das may nezumi iro." Then he
turned, handed Garet to another man, and as he went to
stoop by Hagen, suddenly his chest sprouted the point
and shaft of a Shumai spear. He grunted and slumped.
The man with Garet whirled as another spear went
through his hip. A third snatched up the child and ran
from the firelight, while the other two seemed to vanish
into the shadows.

Hagen had rolled over and was sawing his wrist ropes
against the spear tip. "Quen," he said. "It is Quen. And
some others." And as he said it, Quen came into the firelight with Garet.

"That was a long run," he said. "Wald and Omar are
with me. They are after the others. Here." He laid the
baby by Ahroe, sawed through her bonds, then what was
left of Hagen's.

Ahroe, still bewildered, took Garet, and said. "Dear
Aven, we are so glad. . . ." But Quen had put his knee
on the Roti's back, yanked back his spear, and run off
into the dark, pausing to give a long, quavering yell. An
answer came from the south, but none northward.

"Here comes Wald," said Hagen, rubbing his wrists, as
a thickset but slender man plunged through the firelight
running northward. They heard his receding footsteps,
and a long silence. Ahroe strung her short bow and laid
out her five arrows, letting Garet cry. Hagen stood at the
edge of the firelight, his spear held close to him. Another
rope swished out over Ahroe's neck, and Hagen followed

it as it pulled taut to the Roti who threw it, running his spear into the man's midsection. Two others jumped on him. One had a knife, but as he raised it, Ahroe's short-sword raked into his ribs and through them. The other turned as Hagen tripped him, but scrambled up and ran into the dark.

Ahroe rushed back to Garet as two Roti appeared on the other side of the firelight. She snatched up her short bow, nocked, and shot without aiming. The front Roti buckled and pitched into the fire. The other stopped, turned, and dragged him out, as Hagen returned with his spear and, swinging it by the butt, cut the man's knee. The Roti yelled and dropped, seizing his leg with both hands and writhing. Hagen took one of the fallen ropes and snagged his ankles, then turning him over, wrapped his neck from behind. Then he took the end and bound the man's arms behind him.

Quen and the others returned. "One got away," said Quen.

"Two," Hagen replied. "One from here, too. Mean stuff."

"You will have to kill that one. And the others, too."

"Kill them?" said Ahroe.

"They want the child, for his gray eyes. Or any of us for our blue ones. They sacrifice the blue-eyed, with . . . while . . . Anyway, they sacrifice them. They think blue-eyed people are gods from the sky."

Ahroe felt a wave of fear and revulsion. Taking up Garet, she held him to her and sobbed, fighting back her emotion with all her guardsman's resolve, but without effect. The men looked at her, silent and embarrassed. The three younger ones sat down, winded and tired. Hagen built up the fire, bound the Roti Ahroe had wounded, and dragged him into the firelight. Hagen was limping, having wrenched his back. The Roti breathed with diffi-culty. Ahroe continued fighting her emotion, her head against Garet's. The infant continued to wail.

Quen came over and squatted down in front of her. He put his hand on her hair. "You are thinking of Stel. You mustn't worry. He may not have encountered them. There are not—"

She looked up. "Stel?"

"I have heard that he has gray eyes."

Ahroe grew still, but her breast heaved as she sat thinking. "No, I was thinking of Garet. Stel? You think they might have sacrificed Stel?"

Quen paused, then said, "If he got this far, all the way from the Heart, by himself, he was a man of resource. Maybe they didn't get him." He paused again, a long while, then added, "Ahroe, this isn't the time, I know, but I have felt so bad about what I did. There are rules, and there are feelings. And I went by the way things have always been done. I was wrong. What can I do? It was not right. It is something I can never make up. It—"

"You and the others have just saved our lives, Quen."

"Well, but that is not the same. That is only . . . well, it has nothing to do with the other."

Ahroe stood up and took Garet over to Omar, then came back and put her arms around Quen's neck. "I am tired, and you did really hurt me, but I am not so stupid that I don't know who my friends are. I am sorry, too. It was my Dahmen blood, forcing things my way. I had no right. The irony of the whole thing is that if you weren't the kind of man you are, you could neither have made such a mess of me nor come here so fast to save us."

"You had a better right than I did. I know you were anxious. I was wrong. And I know these things are never made up, no matter what. They are always there."

"It didn't happen, Quen," she said into his shoulder.

"But, well, all right. Now we had better be busy. There is much to do. We have to get out of here, for one thing. Tonight we had better move on a little. Then we need a rest. I am like an old rabbit skin."

Ahroe, turning, saw Omar almost asleep with Garet, held like a sack of seeds. Hagen was binding the wounds of the Roti, moving stiffly with his hurt back. Wald was watching the darkness.

They did move on, lining up the dead Roti. Ahroe had prevailed on the Shumai not to kill the hurt ones, so they left them tied lightly. They went southward through the darkness, then turned west. Before morning they found a hill with a high escarpment, and there spent until afternoon sleeping and resting. They saw no more Roti.

"We will take you west beyond them," said Quen.

"Then we will go back, or else go around the empty place. North is Emeri country, but we are at peace with them, and I would rather risk their whims than these ghostly people. At least you can talk to them."

Setting out again, they began to see signs of habitation, in a lack of dead lower limbs on trees, or on the ground, and then on a hillside below was a path edged with stones.

Hagen had been limping, with his twisted back, but when he tried to go down the steep hill to the path, he fell behind. His face was contorted with pain. As they turned around and looked at him, he said, "Go on. I did this once before a long time ago. I will catch up with you." But they decided to go together, painfully slow as this was.

Reaching the path, they found it well constructed, but little used lately. Hagen walked more easily on level ground, and the group pressed ahead.

"This is not Roti work, I think," Quen remarked. "These are other people. The Roti all live nearly together to the east. Look." He pointed ahead to the Ozar bean fields, now largely gone wild. Advancing farther, they saw three figures, all dressed in loose gray robes, standing near a low, rambling building. Two were bald. They drew quite close before being noticed. Quen held up his two hands, and the one figure with hair, a dark old woman, advanced slowly.

"You are welcome here," she said. "I am Fitzhugh, of the children of Ozar. This is Taglio and Finkelstein. We are all that is left of the Ozar." Then as her eyes swept the small group, she caught her breath as she saw Ahroe. "A Pelbar? Another Pelbar?"

"Another? Stel is here?" Ahroe's hopes rushed together like water and rock. Was it possible?

"Stel was here. He left us last autumn going west. He was with us for nearly a half-cycle of seasons. So you must be Ahroe. He told me about you. You look worn." Advancing, she took the younger woman's hands, smiling shyly up at her. "And who are these?"

"Quen, Wald, Omar, Hagen. And this is Garet," she added, turning around. The baby regarded Fitzhugh solemnly, then reached out a hand. Fitzhugh gave him a finger.

"Stel never said he had a child," she said. "He looks like him. Look. Both chin and eyes."

"Stel never knew about him."

"Well, come inside. I can feed you fish and beans, but not much else. That is what we eat."

Quen made a face sideways to Wald. But they all were hungry. "Can you defend yourselves against the Roti here?" Hagen asked.

"They are not interested in us. I haven't seen them since Stel left. A group of them followed him here, but they think of us as death, so they stayed away. This spring, way up that pass in the west, I found five of them, dead. They had evidently lain there all winter. I found three of Stel's arrows with them. They must have followed him. Peaceful as he was, he seems to have defended himself at last. There is one on the shelf," she added, pointing at the slender arrow, now warped.

Ahroe picked it up. Even weathered, it showed Stel's deft exactitude. "He must have made a longbow."

"Yes. Yes, he did. He killed a wild cow with it with one shot for us. That was just before he left. I suppose if he had not, he would have been here still, but for my sister, McCarty. The meat made all of us sick. We ate too much of it, not being used to it. McCarty encouraged it, then blamed Stel. She hated him."

"What did he do to her?"

"Nothing. She hated what she couldn't control or understand, and that was anybody without guile. She hated me, too, but we were sisters, and there was some regard for that in her, I suppose."

"Where is she now?"

"Dead." Fitzhugh sat down from her stirring of the pot of fish and beans, motioning Finkelstein over to take it up. He took the ladle without a word.

"After Stel left, the rest of the people, especially the blind ones, began to realize what they had lost. They began to blame her, avoid her. She convinced them that Stel was waiting for them to greet him in the house of Ozar—up there. She got them all to go there, blind and senile as they were, and managed even with the seeing ones to trap them inside, then burned the whole building down on them all, herself included."

No one said anything for a time. "Now we three are left," Fitzhugh said. "And now I think it is time to eat." Quen went outside and looked in the direction Fitzhugh had pointed. Against the hill slope lay a blackened mass, in the middle of which a rounded bulk sagged and protruded. Then he turned and went in. He would try some beans and fish after all—until he could hunt.

☐ XIII

STEL had killed the five Roti. As he climbed up through the trees and scrub grass, he heard the familiar chant. He was still angry and bewildered by what had happened to him, still smelling the stew faintly in his nostrils. He was weary. Yes, there they came, rattling and sliding down the slope, mindlessly chanting, now unfurling the coiled ropes they carried at their waists. Very deliberately, anger boiling up in him, Stel strung his longbow and nocked an arrow. He strained the bow back, aiming with care. The arrow flashed out, piercing the first two men completely through and penetrating the third. The fourth and fifth simply stopped and looked, unbelieving. Stel drew again and killed another. The fifth looked, screamed, and came for Stel, swinging his rope. Stel waited until he was sure, then released his third arrow at that man's chest. The Roti pitched forward with only a grunt and lay on the ground twitching.

Stel sank down on the grass. Putting out a foot, he unstrung the bow. Then he rolled over and put his face to the stony ground. What was he to experience next? He lay in utter misery of spirit for some time. Sitting up, he tried to remember where he was, what he was doing there. He took care not to look at the dead men, nor retrieve his arrows, for all the labor they took to make. He could make more. In the mountains. Alone. Far up in the cold wind, then the snow, he would camp and methodically make new arrows. Why would he? He didn't know. Men needed arrows.

He was conscious of putting one foot in front of the other, drearily, as he went slowly up the hillside. Eventually he would camp, but only after nightfall, only after he could not look back and see the Roti. But what had they been? Nothing. Even now they were returning to the grass, leaching down like dry grass itself. He too was the same. He had no solidity, no direction, no future. Why was he climbing the hill? He didn't really know. He was wind, moving like the wind in his face. It was not wind. It was simple movement. As he reached the saddle of the westward hill, the sun was setting in red streamers, long flags of blood-red light, stretched and flowing. Stel kept his eyes down, but saw the rose glow on his legs and boots.

He camped that night under a hulking, reddish misshapen rock, building a large fire that threw its moving shadows off the rock and the shrubby pines beyond it. Were there Roti to see and come? He didn't care. What was wrong? Somehow he seemed subtly unfit for human company. Was that it? He had gotten along well enough at Pelbarigan before his marriage. What had it aroused in him then that twisted all awry? Or was it not him? He tried to review it all, but everything seemed to spiral in his mind like the rising flames.

No Roti came. Stel was half disappointed. He didn't sleep, but let the fire die down toward morning anyhow. As the sun rose, there were only upward wisps of smoke. He stood and stretched, somehow felt better, with each pine needle, each grain of rock now distinct and in its place in the clear sunlight. He was thirsty but found no water in his pitched bottle. He would let it all go and move on, still westward, toward the higher country, which seemed to expand in its dimensions, with the clarity of the air, and the jutting mountains, which could be seen so long before they could be reached.

Stel found a stream tumbling through the red rocks,

drank, and carefully bathed himself. He boiled a grain mush and ate it sweetened with honey Fitzhugh had given him. He still felt empty, but he wasn't sure whether in body or in spirit. If he had had a motive for his travel, or a desire to see what no Pelbar had seen, even Jestak, that was gone. If only Ahroe were here. Then what? He didn't know. Well, he would go on.

Stel continued west for some days, through a high country of short pines, some aspen and cottonwood in gullies, and open meadows of bunched grass, now drying with the fall season. High peaks with snow on them appeared to his north, then far ahead. He finally descended into a great basin of dry land, with a herd of black cattle apparently undisturbed by anyone. On the valley's west side he could see a long range of snow-topped mountains, with pines thick on their sides. It seemed a barrier. He would try to make it beyond them before winter set in, though he could see that on the rims and crests it was already winter. No matter. He would try to traverse them anyhow. Stel crossed the basin slowly, killing a heifer on the way, smoking dried beef from it, and working the hide for a winter coat. He wished he knew more about tanning, for the black hair came off in bunches as he worked on the skin. Was there no way to keep it on? He finally decided to make the coat in two layers, stuffing it in between with grass, working in the evenings. He was startled, one morning, to see that snow had moved down from the peaks at least five hundred arms. It was time to be going.

As Stel began his climb, he found fragments of ancient roadway, interspersed with great sections in which the falling rock had torn it all away. Here, perhaps, was a way, winding through the mountains. He could see by the occasional notches in the mountainsides that the road followed the shoulder of the steep grades with a steady rise, not too steep, sometimes doubling back. The ancients, with their characteristic massive energy, had somehow gouged away great slices of rock, cutting deep gashes into the mountain faces, and plowing away boulders as high as the wall of Pelbarigan. And the mountain, with its timeless passivity, had also characteristically shrugged aside all that work in its great rockfalls. But here, perhaps, was a direction.

Picking his way into the increasingly cold mountain maze by day, Stel worked on a new pair of snow sliders in evenings. He shot and ate a new kind of rodent, not the woodchucks of home, nor the smaller ones of the plains, but a shorter and fatter rock dweller, a friendly animal that whistled and hid when he came near. It took two for a dinner, and Stel would rather have laughed at their peerings and twitchings but for his hunger.

Finally, after nine days, the road disappeared upward into the snow, and Stel strapped on his snow sliders and continued his ascent. For a moment as he bent down to fasten them, he seemed across the river at Pelbarigan again, and then, when he stood, slightly dizzy, blood rushing, he almost expected to look back across the river at the looming city, knowing Ahroe was there. What he saw almost startled him—an empty, cold, and beautiful land, a home of giant crows, rushing water, gigantic rocks, and the tall, thin, spiring evergreens. He was momentarily bewildered at his own presence. Then, as if the strange, passive hostility of the country had suddenly taken shape, an animal, dark, shaggy, enormous, terrifying, rose ahead of him on its hind legs, far taller than Stel, its massive front legs hanging, tipped with long, curved claws, eyes nearly buried in its heavy furred head. Stel held perfectly still. What was it? The beast was testing the wind, which blew crosswise between them. Stel made no sound. The beast seemed puzzled, not quite aware of the nature of the vague, strange stimulus that had brought it upright. Finally it lowered itself and moved down through the trees.

Stel held himself still until he saw the beast emerge far below on an outcrop. He found he had been sweating. He knew then he wanted to get out of the mountains, but it still was a long way, a climb ahead, then a descent. He set to it.

Late that afternoon he came to the crest of a pass. It seemed he was on the rim of the world. Far to the east he could see the descending crags, the winding valleys, the dim outline of the west edge of the basin far away, with its brown hills. To the west, against the haze of the waning sun, the wild grandeur continued. Stel felt a strange, savage elation. He was standing alone at the world's summit. He had come by himself. This was beyond anything Jestak had found. And yet why was he here? He still was not sure. He began his careful descent. There were still remnants of the winding road of the ancients, notching the rocky mountainsides.

For two days Stel trended downward, below the snow, again below the tall, thin evergreens, but still in the wild mountains, still on or near the ancient road. Emerging into a flat meadow, he came suddenly to a cairn. This was strange. Surely it was a Pelbar waymarker. Yes. How could that be? It pointed farther, clearly down the road. Yes, here were the distance marks. Fourteen of them. Fourteen ayas westward, clearly marked—and then the mark of Pell. Stel sat down. He reached out and passed his hands across the cuts in the rock. There was no mistake. These were not only human marks, but Pelbar ones. Was he insane? Jestak had not been here. Who, then? He would continue. If this was a waymark, then there should be another in four ayas, then one more two ayas farther along.

Stel hurried on, scrambling down the rocky sides of hills, trotting across the meadows, forcing the undergrowth. Estimating the first interval, he found the next waymark on an open shoulder of the ancient road, clearly marked. Again Stel stopped and studied the cairn. According to Pelbar custom, this one contained no marks at all. Now Stel was sure. Somewhere ahead there were Pelbar—or at least one. Or there had been recently. There would be time before night to get to the third cairn. That one should be unmarked as well.

As the sun was setting, Stel found the cairn, not only in an open grassy area, but one clearly kept visible by the pruning back of the encroaching brush. Somewhere, eight ayas ahead, then, was some sort of Pelbar structure. Stel could hardly force himself to stop, but he did. There would be time in the morning. He might easily miss his way at night. And knowing Pelbar habits, both of secrecy and self-defense, he wanted to come visibly. But it took all of his stolid self-containment to sit by his fire, working on his coat, pushing the twisted sinew through the rows of holes he had made in the hide, pounding grass for lining, shredding it into the doubled pouch of a sleeve, blowing on his fingers in the cold, sipping occasionally from his lightly boiling stew. He would be ready to continue in the early light.

He was half afraid of another human contact. His recent ones had gone so badly that his self-confidence wavered like the last unfallen aspen leaves. As he lay in his sleepsack that night, watching the slow overhead passage of the stars from twig to twig, he thought of the strangeness of his whole experience, the emptiness of the wide land, his intense aloneness, the indifference of the land and its cold, the remoteness of the stars themselves. What pattern had Aven in Her great thought? Ahroe, where was she? Was she still in their small room at Pelbarigan? Was she directing the weaving of river rushes for winter mats? Surely with all the evidences of pattern, of order, of the array of species, of human accomplishments, there must be a niche in the system for someone like himself. He caught himself wondering if he existed only to represent exile and anguish.

He knew without doubt that there were Pelbar ahead of him—or had been recently. How would they receive him? What would he tell them? Would he read their defenses correctly? He had never heard of western Pelbar, but perhaps they had been lost, separated in some dim period of the past, and had wandered this far away. He had. Perhaps this was to be his function—to reunite the Pelbar colonies.

Light came long before the sun was to push above the rims of the high eastern mountains, and Stel had picked his way through nearly all the final eight ayas before it struck down to the now nearly bare aspens among the pines, bathing their light-tan trunks in its clarity. Stel was strangely elated.

Rounding a curve in the shoulder of the hill, he looked ahead toward a thin column of smoke that rose, then spread like a gauzy sheet, vague and continuous, across the valley. Following it down, Stel saw, with a sinking disappointment, the familiar Pelbar structure, a square of rock, tucked in against the hill. It was small. Here was no city. Unless it was an outpost, it was the home of only a few—perhaps even of one person. But it was Pelbar.

Stel advanced into the open and studied the situation. Yes, there would be the pit trap, and beyond the next

curve the rolling snares. There might also be a ditch
trap, but that would be close in. In front of the structure,
a short-bow shot away, was the familiar message stone,
small but prominent. Stel would work his way across the
perimeter of defenses to it, announce himself, and wait
for a reply from the structure.

As he mounted the message stone, Stel took out his
flute, and when in formal position, he played, slowly and
loudly, a hymn of Aven, praise for the beauty of autumn,
the cleansing white of winter, the rebirth of spring. The
square stone structure remained impassive. He played
through the hymn again, then became aware of a face,
dimly seen, at one of the two high windows. It looked
old and gaunt.

Finally, the door opened, a pivot door beautifully concealed in the front face of the structure. A small old man
emerged, dressed in a formal Pelbar tunic, but made of
small furs sewn together with no great skill. He stood just
beyond the entrance, leaning on a staff.

"Greetings from Stel Dahmen of Pelbarigan," said Stel.

"Dahmen?" the old man repeated in a high quaver.

"Dahmen, by marriage, son of Sagan, a stonebuilder,
Arden by birth, a carpenter and workman of Pelbarigan,
here through self-exile."

"Exile?" The old man laughed a strange laugh, then
came forward slowly and mounted the stone.

Each man put a hand on the shoulder of the other
and repeated together, "May Aven protect, guide, govern, and direct you. May She enrich your ways with
kindness and temper our meeting with Her love and
decorum. May we be the better for this meeting."

The old man silently looked at Stel for a long time, his
eyes slightly sunken with age, but dark and penetrating
in the thin face, which showed a strange, contradictory
combination of fragility and sturdiness, Pelbar reserve
and toughness. "Come inside," he said abruptly, and
turned, then added over his shoulder, "I am Scule, also
Dahmen by marriage, sent to be our western outpost.
Come."

Stel sighed slightly and followed Scule in through the
pivot door, which the old man shut and bolted after
them, as was proper. Then he opened an arched wooden

door to their right and motioned Stel to precede him into the room. Stel could see another arched wooden door ahead of him, and a high window, through which a thin ray of light streamed. He bowed to Scule, then entered the room. Scule stopped to fool with something in his belt, saying, "Continue through the next door. I am coming."

Stel moved ahead, took hold of the ring in the far door, and swung it toward him. For a slight moment he was puzzled. Behind it stood a blank wall. But as his first thoughts flashed through his mind, he heard the familiar grate of a wall trap, and, spinning, saw the door he had just entered disappear as a rock wall thundered down into place. The old man had trapped him. How could he have been so stupid, so incautious? Why would an old Pelbar want to trap him? Stel sank down against the wall and looked around.

He was in a tall, arched room. The window was too high to reach and too small to squeeze through anyway. At the top of the arch was another small square hole, where the final keystone might have been placed. It was dark, but Stel knew that the old man would soon be looking down at him through that gap. He studied the surrounding stonework. The keystones on either side reached across the adjacent stones in the arch, thus effectively keying that row. It was well done. For the present, he would have to wait and talk to the old man.

Before long, his thin voice called down from above. "I have been waiting for you for thirty-five hard winters here. I knew the Dahmens would want me back. I knew they would send. I have made ready for you." He laughed nervously.

"What? The Dahmens send me? What for?"

"No use pretending. Have waited too long. Knew they would not consider exile enough when they discovered how I had fooled them."

Stel shook his head. "Nobody fools the Dahmens. What are you talking about? The Dahmens fool everyone else. They are canker in the stomach of Pelbarigan."

The old man laughed. "No use talking. I know."

Stel thought rapidly. What was he talking about? He had fooled the Dahmens? And over thirty-five years ago?

What was he talking about? A thought began to dawn on Stel. He stood up suddenly, looking up. "You. You are not Scule. You are Soole, exiled for the unspeakable, who went willingly, leaving a trap for Visib, your bride, which killed her as she re-entered your room. I have heard your story. How they searched for you and never found you. You are here? I can't believe this. And I have come here through all this trackless wildness and have also been trapped. I thought you were from the dim lost past."

After a silence, the old man chuckled again. "For Visib? It killed her, then? I was not guilty of the unspeakable. Visib herself was. I found out. When she learned that, she found ways of accusing me, of exiling me not long after truceweek, sure I would be killed. I turned it on her, and now I am turning it on you. I knew they would never give up."

Stel felt dizzy. "On me? What have I done?"

"You are a Dahmen searcher. I knew they would come. Anyone traveling westward comes to the two great burns, the empty places, which overlap. If he goes south, around the edge, he comes to the great basin, continuing west. From there he can go south around the mountains, or the ancient road will suck him up here, through the pass. You have been clever, but not enough to fool Scule."

Stel sank down again. "I am not fooling anyone—except myself. I am also an exile. Just let me go and I will never return. I am going westward. I saw your signs only yesterday. I want to get out of these mountains before winter. Now, raise the door. I will not bother you. You ought to know by your own troubles how deep mine are —deep as a mine, higher than these peaks. More than pique. I am weak as a reed. I reek like a weed with my own agonies. Let me be gone. Without gain. Never to return again."

Scule laughed again. "Good to hear a Pelbar pun again. But you don't fool me. There is no friendliness in it. See your longbow. Now will let you think. Will lower you some food and water and return tomorrow. You may think in silence until then. Don't worry. Have plenty of food. As I say, have been expecting you, Dahmen, and have prepared extra food for you every winter. Expect you to tell me of Pelbarigan, then finally to confess."

"Confess what?" But there was no answer. Eventually, a thin seed broth and a bottle of water came down a thin rope from the hole. Stel untied it. Again he said, "Confess what? What am I supposed to confess? That I came here for you, to bring you back? That is not true. How can I confess that? It would only be a lie. Am I here to lie here until I lie here? May you confester with your nonsense. And what if I do confess? Will you then kill me? Will Scule make a skull of me? Probably. You encourage me not to confess in every way—not knowing, too, what to confess. You confuse."

From above the old man's voice whispered, "There will be time," and then was silent.

There was time. Stel talked upward at the roof hole occasionally, but since no answer came, he finally stopped. He felt the old man was never far, perhaps watching him from the upper darkness. What a fool he had been. It had been his trust of a Pelbar welcome, and the appearance of the far door, perhaps, that had entrapped him. Scule was clearly mad. Stel had heard of him as a child, as a whispered legend, again a warning against the dangers of freeing men from the governance of women. So Scule said that it was Visib who had committed the unspeakable. Stel half believed him. But there was no time for that. Clearly he had to find a way out.

He fell to examining the stone room. Scule must have been a master stoneworker. The work was beautifully and carefully done, with each stone cube keyed in without mortar, so carefully joined that not even a knife blade could be slipped into the cracks. Stel knew the keying would prevent any slippage. Eventually he found the swingrock in the floor that would enable him to void himself into a space below, but even there the surrounding joining was so solid and careful that Stel felt he could not work it loose.

He was further alarmed when he realized that the wall trap was so notched in place that Scule probably could not dislodge it if he wanted to. It would have to be dismantled stone by stone from outside, if Scule were still strong enough to do that. It was a one-way trap, a dead end. Stel turned his attention again to the window. There seemed little hope there. It was the top of the arch that seemed most promising. As he studied it, Stel felt that the two keys adjacent to Scule's viewing hole were simply slipped into place. If they could be dislodged by a very hard shove from below, a portion of the arch would come down.

Probably some weight lay on top to prevent that. Yet Scule wanted to look down, so there was likely not much weight. But the arch was too high anyway. Stel would have to shove the stones loose with a pole, and he had none. What of the false door? Examining it, Stel found that it was only thin veneer over wood that Scule had cut into, across the grain, deeply. So he had thought of that possibility, too.

Stel examined what he had with him, mentally. He didn't take anything out of his backsack, because the less Scule knew, the better. He had his flute, thrust into a side pocket, a short selection from the words of Aven, his clothing, a considerable supply of dried meat, some ground seeds, his small iron pot, his shortknife, his short bow and seven arrows, his sleepsack strapped on top, a coil of rawhide string, five rodent furs, a small bag of various furs, his fire kit, his needles, and soap. Outside, he also carried his longbow and nine arrows, his short-sword, the half-made coat, his snow sliders, his water bottle, and a tinder pouch. All those outside things Scule could see.

When, after what seemed an age, the sun set, and the dim light from the high window faded out, Stel became frightened. Darkness pooled and gathered here the way it did in the caves under Pelbarigan where the ice was stored. Not even a star showed out the window hole. Cold seemed to flow in on him. No light survived anywhere.

For a long time, Stel sat in silence. Then he felt the walls in the darkness, stone by stone, to see if Scule had left a key anywhere, a single stone that could be pushed, sliding back a hinged stone structure. When he was sure he had tested them all, he went over all again, tapping with the butt of his short-sword. Everything was solid. He could tell that the room was backed by rock on three sides, only the one with the high window being an outside wall.

Finally he sat down again, thoroughly alert and awake. He would have to await Scule's decisions, his pleasure. He took out his flute and reassured himself with a long session of playing, almost all hymns to Aven, running through at least three dozen, slowly and with dignity, playing the melody through as many times as there were verses, thinking the verses. The music filled him with relief, but when he stopped, the silence seemed that much more oppressive. After a long time, he grew drowsy, finally crawling into his sleepsack and dozing off.

It was full daylight when he awoke. A new water supply lay on the floor, and a stew containing both meat and vegetables. Stel stared at it a long time before eating and drinking. Then he used the remainder of the water to wash himself, and grinding his short-sword on the floor stones, shaved as well as he could, without mirror or water surface. Finished, he sat back against the wall again. The silence continued.

At last the voice from above asked, "Ready to confess?"

"I have nothing to confess. I am an exile, like you. I married a Dahmen girl, but I was unable to be as fully servile as they wanted. For my wife it was one thing. For the whole family it was another. I had to escape when they tried to do away with me. I have been wandering now since just past last midwinter. For nearly a whole year now. You are mistaken. Now let me out so I can go beyond these mountains before full winter sets in."

"What lies then beyond the mountains?"

"I don't know. I have heard that there is a great sea to the west, beyond much. I was told the Commuters live beyond the mountains. They are herdsmen."

"Beyond the mountains is dryness, rivers contained in canyons, then more dryness a man cannot traverse. There is no great sea."

"You have been there?"

"Far out in the dryness. Then returned to the mountains where I could be alone and await the Dahmens. You."

"To be alone? Who was there? The Commuters?"

"Yes. The herdsmen. They drove me off."

"Why?"

From above there was only silence. At last Scule said, "I will ask the questions. You will answer them."

"No. I will answer some, and you will answer some."

"You forget. You are the prisoner."

"Only my body. Not my spirit or my will. I still can choose to answer or not to answer."

"And I can withhold your food and your water. I can watch you die. You can do nothing."

"You would do that to a Pelbar who has done you no harm? Then you did murder Visib just as they say at Pelbarigan. And for no reason. I think she did you no harm, as I have not. I think you are mad. You have always been mad. And I think you may well have committed the unspeakable."

From above again came only silence. It lasted all day. Stel paced, examined, and thought almost to distraction. Again at night he played his flute, then slept. In the morning no food was lowered, no water. By noon, Stel's thirst had become extreme. By sunset he simply lay, dull-eyed, his tongue swelling in his mouth, as the evening cold again poured in through the window.

Finally, in the full darkness, a voice from above said, "Play your flute."

"Too dry," Stel croaked.

From above he saw a light. A bottle of water swung down on its string, hanging just above his reach. "Will you play?"

Stel managed to say, "Yes, if there is enough water." The bottle lowered, and Stel drank it all. The bottle raised.

"Now play."

"Not enough water. I need more."

After another silence, the bottle swung down again, full, and Stel drank deeply, managing, as he did, to pour some into his own pitched bottle under his coat.

"Now play."

Stel sat against the wall and played the long hymn to Aven, source of the river, bringer of rain, sweller of flowers, stretcher of cattails, blesser of mankind.

From above the voice said, "Aven did not give you the water. I did."

Stel played again, a psalm for kindness, placed in the hearts of women by Aven, given them to govern justly as She Herself did.

Again the voice said, "Am kind because of myself, not because of Aven."

Stel did not reply. He played again, here the ancient hymn to gentleness, care for the children, forgiveness of the folly of men, firmness in adherence to the laws of Aven.

"Play something that is not a hymn. You are worse than the winter festival."

Stel played a love song, the song of Iri, whose eyes seemed deep as the ancient quarry pools. Then he played the song of defenses, the guardsmen's anthem, the prayer "for arms as strong as river-bluff stone/Defending the city though fighting alone."

Scule cackled lightly again. "The Pelbar think those river bluffs are high. They have never seen mountains. Now it is time for you to apologize."

"Apologize?"

"For what you said."

"When? Oh. Well, perhaps you didn't commit the unspeakable. I really don't know. I don't care, either."

"Perhaps is not enough."

"I don't know, do I. I have heard from childhood that you did. You are a legend, a warning against men. But enough of us were glad that you put one over on the Dahmens."

"Perhaps is not enough."

"Do you want me to say that you never did?"

"That is the truth."

"How do I know it?"

"Do you enjoy thirst?"

"No. It is awful. Thirst is the worst. I will say it because it pleases you. No, Scule, imprisoner of the innocent. You did not commit the unspeakable. Now. Does that make you feel better? How much weight has that? A forced admission of something no one can know."

From above there was another long silence. Finally,

Scule said, "So they say that of me at Pelbarigan. And what do you suppose they say of you?"

Stel mused. "I have often wondered. I have my family. My own. I know they have borne shame for me. I know, though, that they feel I did what I had to do. Sagan advised me to go Northwall. It is my wife I think of." Stel himself fell silent, thinking of Ahroe.

"Do not think," said Scule. "Your wife will not remember you. By now she is either married, or, in the manner of the Dahmens, committing the unspeakable. She—"

"Stop, you crazy old pervert!" Stel had jumped up and shouted at the gap in the roof. "What do you know? You are mad. You wouldn't know decency if you trapped it. Curse you. You know nothing of my wife." Stel stopped for breath, as his shouting seemed to echo and re-echo in the tall dark room.

Scule laughed. "You know I am right. You would not get angry otherwise. However, you have called me that which I will not allow. You will now know thirst." Silence followed, then another distant laugh from Scule. So now there would be more thirst. Damn him. At least Stel had a little water to hold out with.

Slowly his anger subsided into despair. He crawled into his sleepsack, taking a small gulp from his pitched bottle. He could vaguely hear wind outside and feel a greater cold. What if Scule were right? What if Ahroe had married again—no. Not yet. The time prescribed for waiting had not passed yet. But what if she had forgotten him? What if they spoke of him in Pelbarigan as they had spoken of Scule, who had become a legend of evil? Stel didn't sleep for a long time. Finally he took out his flute and played a few hymns, lying in the sleepsack on the stone floor. He grew more calm. Finally he stopped in the middle of a hymn, heavy with drowse, and pulled in his arms for warmth. Above, though he didn't see it, Scule looked down, troubled because the hymn was not finished. The old man frowned down through the dark hole a long time. He could hear Stel's heavy breathing.

Stel dreamed of the great beast in the mountains. It rose again and again before him, its head dimly searching, nose testing the air. It seemed to enlarge and expand, hanging over him. Slowly it became Ahroe, then the beast again. Then the dream blackened into sleeep.

In the morning the gray light brought a swirl of snow-flakes into the window gap, and added cold. Scule didn't come. Stel got up, went through a Pelbar exercise routine, then returned to his sleepsack, stiff with the hardness of the stone floor. Pulling his head inside the sack, he sipped at his pitched bottle, but sparingly. If he was to suffer thirst, at least he would last as long as he could.

Scule didn't appear all day. Stel remained most of the time in the sleepsack, but when he felt warm enough, he worked further on his winter coat. Night fell, with the blue cast of snowlight. Again Stel sipped at the pitched bottle, alarmed that he now neared the last of his water. Hunger cut his stomach. Night brought further despair. Ahroe. He had, after all, deserted her. He had violated the promises of his marriage. Did he show resemblances to Scule? What if Scule were telling the truth? What if Ahroe—no. What if, though, she saw him as a weakling, unworthy of being remembered? Well, what difference? He could not go back. But Ahroe was not like the other Dahmens. She had the steel of a guardsman's sword. She would have de-fended him. But he left. And she hadn't defended him. But she had followed.

Stel slept. Again the dream came, the vast, shaggy shape, merging into Ahroe's. That night Stel drank the last of the water.

Again the next day, Scule did not appear. Stel again went through the Pelbar exercises, but listlessly. Again his thirst was acute. Doggedly he worked on the coat, and stuffed his thick, soft-soled boots with four of his small furs. Finally he returned to the sleepsack. He had not touched the dried beef. Better to suffer acute hunger than to add to his thirst.

That night the dream came again. But it seemed to gain dimension. The great beast rose and hovered in the room itself. Then it shrank down and became Ahroe. She took out her short-sword, and, holding it up, blew on it, chang-ing it into a torch, which lit the whole room. She seemed not to see him. Stel got to his knees and reached for her. "Ahroe," he croaked in his thirst. "Ahroe. Here. Here. Help me."

"I had a husband," said the vision of Ahroe, in slow, measured tones, her voice, but flat. "His name was Stel. I thought him strong. He was weak. He left me. He would not accept discipline. Some say he was unspeakable. I don't know. I thought he loved me. He left. I followed, but he eluded me. Now, with my sword of flame, I am going to kill his memory." The face of the vision suddenly twisted with hatred, advanced on the kneeling Stel, and swept the flame through him again and again, in wide arcs. The pain seemed to cut through him. Stel shouted out in agony again and again. The vision laughed in the voice of Scule, blew out the sword, sheathed it, and said softly, "Now. It is finished. There is no Stel. There is no . . . what was his name? He had no name. He never was. I had a nameless misfortune, but now it is over."

Slowly the vision vanished. Stel groveled on the floor. Slowly the darkness and cold returned. No. It had not happened. He was in Scule's prison, in the mountains, in winter, without food or water, a prisoner of a bitter old madman. Well, it did not matter. Perhaps the vision was right.

What was he to do? He was confused. Perhaps he would return to the book of Aven. Nothing mattered, the book said, but to be just and merciful, to love. What about truth? Was he beaten? And did it not matter that this miserable old man had tortured him? Would he bear it as long as he could, as he had at Pelbarigan, then contrive in the dark to put an arrow into Scule as he talked down the hole, knowing that it would mean his own death?

No. He would not do that. The old man might kill him, but Stel would not kill him. In the first place, he would remove his own hope. In the second, some unknown thing had given this old man his cycles of misery. He had objectified all that in Stel, with his myth about the Dahmen searchers. If he killed Stel, then at least he might be mollified. At least there would be one human life, however twisted, where there otherwise would be none in all these mountains. Stel again slept.

In the morning, water was on the floor in a stone jar, and a rich stew. Stel crawled to it, and ate and drank very slowly. It was good. He returned to the sleepsack and crawled in, wearing his winter coat. That day Scule said nothing, and Stel slept most of the day. The night resolved itself into dullness.

In the morning, the voice from above said, "You must apologize."

"I apologize," said Stel, still in the sleepsack.

"You must also confess."

"I confess. What am I confessing to?"

"You must confess that you have come for me, sent by the Dahmens, by the unreconciled relatives of Visib."

"That is not true. But I confess."

"If it is not true, why do you confess."

"You seem intent on it. It does not matter to me."

"Who is Ahroe?"

"Ahroe?"

"In the night you cried out for Ahroe. She is your wife, then, this Ahroe?"

"What does it matter?"

"She is named for a relative?"

"What does it matter?"

"If I tell you why, will you tell me about her?"

Stel didn't answer. Scule repeated the question. Stel still didn't answer.

"More thirst, then?"

"Old man, you may kill me with thirst if you want to, though I don't wish it. But there are some things I will not discuss with you."

Scule pondered this. Somehow he knew Stel meant it. Something switched in him. Somehow he didn't want to kill Stel. It was himself on the floor below, being tortured by himself. Well, didn't he deserve torture?

"Then tell me of Pelbarigan. How is it there? Do they withstand the outside tribes as well as they did?"

Stel sat up. He told Scule of the fight at Northwall, the Pelbar united with both Shumai and Sentani to free the slaves of the Tantal. With the old man's questions, he talked for much of the day about the city. Scule was a blood relation of his cousin, Ruudi, as he found out, though none of Stel's.

Finally, toward evening, Stel said, "Old man, I saw, in the mountains, a giant beast, dark and shaggy. It stood up in front of me like a man, though taller, with long claws.

Then it dropped down again on all four feet and walked down the mountain."

Scule said nothing for a time. Eventually he said, "You are lying. There is no such beast."

"I saw it. I thought you might know it. It makes no great difference, though I have dreamed of it. It could crush a man like an egg."

"There is no such beast. It is the devil beast flag of the Commuters. You say you came from the east. How did you get around to the west?"

"It was just as I told you."

"You must be taught not to lie."

"As you wish, but please, no more thirst. Try some other way. You will see. I have not lied."

Scule hesitated. "I will cut your food ration."

"It is already slender enough."

"I will withdraw myself from you."

"As you wish. You are touchy company. Touchy unlucky. I wish you would touch the latch key."

From above there was more silence. Stel sighed to himself. How long, now, in how many situations, had people tried to dominate him? This was the worst. This made the Dahmens seem kind. It made McCarty seem reasonable.

In the morning the half-rations began. Stel had carefully counted his strips of dried beef the night before. There were forty-seven. He would chew a half-strip each night, in the dark. That would help his hunger.

The silence from above persisted for twenty-two days. Stel grew more listless and withdrawn. The routine of blankness and cold made him simply await the change in mood he felt eventually would come. Meanwhile winter set in more deeply. Stel was never really warm. The numbing chill seemed to make him shrink further into himself.

For a time he seemed the only man in the world, a speck of heat in a whirl of cold—single, remote, unique. So this was what aloneness was. Real aloneness. Cut from past, future, warmth, relation. He would shrink like a dying fire, to one ember, then go out. A drift of smoke would rise to nowhere and disappear. Was this, then, the consequence of leaving Pelbarigan? To step into chaos, then into nothing? No. There was always Aven. And there are the consequences of Aven in human behavior. Somewhere. Could they be here? If he were to burn out like the ember, then he would burn out giving light, giving heat to the uncaring darkness, even to the mad Scule.

Finally, Scule spoke again. "I am going to cut your rations further," he said abruptly one morning. There followed for Stel a period of deeper hunger and cold. He finally lost track of the days, forgetting to cut the notches into the wall with the tip of his short-sword. He dreamed again of the great beast, but it did not change into Ahroe. It seemed to loom and loom, growing and fading. Finally Stel began chewing a whole strip of beef at night, but still the darkness brought with it racing fantasies. Stel had even stopped playing the flute. He tried to think the songs to himself.

At last, when his beef, even so rationed, was running short, he saw in the pitch darkness, as he huddled and shivered with cold, that he was in error. He must give out himself. If the old man withheld what he needed, that was none of his affair. So he was to die alone here. He would die being himself, not only himself, but the best of Stel he knew. He tried to play, sitting up, curled in the sack. His fingers refused to work right, even on slow songs. The results were clumsy beyond belief. Stel laughed to himself, then aloud. He tried again, but it was no better. He played the hymn to the spring river rise, that brought the Pelbar so much wood in the time of hostilities that it seemed like a blessing from Aven. Then he played it again.

The third time through, Scule's voice came from above. "Stop. If you are going to play it, play it right or not at all."

"My hands are too cold."

"Then stop."

"What if I don't? Will you cut off my rations altogether?"

"I may."

"I will stop."

"You need not stop. Play it right."

"You seem not to understand. I would if I could. I am too cold and hungry. You are, you know, slowly killing me. But since it offends you, I will stop. I will listen to the sounds inside me, where they don't depend on my fingers."

From above, after a silence, Scule said, "I saw them."

"What?"

"How can you be hungry? Why do you return? I saw the tracks."

"What tracks?"

"The devil beast. You are the devil beast. You make the tracks, then return to mock me."

"No, old man. You are the devil beast. He is within you. He will never let you alone because you nurture him." Stel suddenly felt recklessly playful. "At night, when the moon grows, you become the beast. You breathe down at me, slathering, and saying to yourself, 'What now can I do to Stel to torture him? I am a Dahmen. I must torture people. I know no other way. Touch is torture. My hands are claws. I must slash and lash. I was silly enough to put Stel behind these stone walls, so I must use the claws of hunger, of cold, of silence, of any cruelty, to reach him with those.' You are the beast. But I have now gone beyond you. I am in the mist. Your claws rake through it and cannot wound it. Only the body bleeds. Not the soul. I know now what you fear and have always feared. You don't fear the Dahmens. You don't fear me. You don't even fear the great beast. You fear yourself. You have come here to the mountains hoping never to be found, yet preparing elaborately for it, because you fear what you might do. That is what Visib did for you—or to you. You may have thought you killed her. But you must kill her over and over every day in your thought, in your horror at it all. I see now that you never did the unspeakable. You fear only its possibility and what you did do, in your desperation. And I thank you for it."

"You lie again," Scule shouted down through the hole. Then, "Why do you thank me?"

"It is guilt, Scule. I see it now. I saw the beast as Ahroe. My wife, Ahroe. I saw it as myself. But it is not. It is really circumstance, and perhaps weakness in us, so it is what we do, what rises up within us when bad times come. But when spring comes, we shed our shaggy coats. When it is time to eat again, we do so because we have used up the last meal and are done with it. I am free of you now, though you have still imprisoned me." Stel laughed, shivering with cold.

"You are crazy."

Stel laughed again with the irony of this. "No, old man. There was a beast. I saw him. You saw his tracks. I mean a real beast. But he is just a beast. The one we fear is the one we fear we are. It is the one our mothers redeem when they forgive us as children, dropping their tears on us. And as men we must forgive ourselves. Forgive yourself, Scule. And give me something to eat."

"It is the middle of the night."

"Nonetheless, I am hungry. Feed me."

"You are crazy."

"And you are not guilty. Now, feed me."

Above there was a slight rustle, but after a while a small light appeared, and a stew was lowered through the hole, with hot tea. Stel took it, thanking Scule, and ate it slowly and with relish.

"That was good. Delicious. Now how about an old blanket. Surely you have one to spare. I am freezing down here. When my blanket comes, that much more of the devil beast will leave you."

"You are crazy," Scule said again. But he forced a robe made of small, sewn animal furs down the hole.

"Thank you again," Stel said. "And now good night. May you sleep in safety and the comfort of Aven."

Stel lay down. He had, at last, some direction. He would do what he could to entertain, amuse, educate, and cure this old man. Perhaps he would save himself as well. But inadvertently he had released himself from his own sense of guilt. At least, most of it. He was in, after all, a Pelbar society, small and queer as it might be. He would see if he could free the old man from the long memory of Dahmen cruelty and his own weakness.

In the ensuing days, and weeks, Stel not only amused himself by cutting splints from his snow sliders to make drumsticks, with which he drummed out patterns of sound on the stone floor, but even got Scule to lower him material for another flute. Since no drill and no pithy wood were available, Stel got Scule to burn a hole in the flute shaft with hot metal, then shaped the instrument, put the finger holes in it, trimmed it, and tested it, finally giving the old man lessons.

Occasionally, when Scule wanted him to confess his mission from the Dahmens, the relationship grew tense again. But Stel knew that there was a finality to that, and that if Scule ever became convinced that his delusion was fulfilled by Stel, the old man would probably abandon him to starve. So Stel tossed off his confession agreeably enough so that Scule knew he was just saying it. Eventually, Stel could see that the old hermit had ceased to believe his long-held myth that the Dahmens would get him.

Winter continued, but Stel was warmer now. He agreed to sew up a pair of fur mittens for the old man if Scule would give him materials for a pair of his own. Eventually Stel made socks as well, for both, with fur inside.

But he was not free. One night he strapped the thin remains of his snow sliders near the ends and tried to reach the keystones by the roof hole of his room. They barely reached. He could exert no force. He carefully dismantled the makeshift probe. Nothing else came to mind, though he pondered his problem endlessly.

Winter deepened. Stel got Scule to stuff the high window with a sack of leaves, but this so dimmed the interior of the room that it seemed to plunge him into a continuous night. Scule told him that the snow had drifted nearly to the height of the window, as it generally did. The old man was used to such winters, and spent much of the warm season preparing for them, but the endless cold, wind, and snow appalled Stel, intensifying his isolation.

One day toward evening, as he was idly decorating his drumsticks with fine carving in the dim light, almost working by feel, he heard a sound at the window. The sack pushed in, followed by a great, furry arm, claw-tipped. It was the mountain beast. The animal held, and tugged, as the drift outside sagged under him. Finally the paw slipped back outside.

Stel shouted for Scule, repeating his shouts until finally the old Pelbar came to the roof hole.

"What is it now?"

"He was here. The mountain beast. He was at the window."

Scule disappeared and was gone a long time. Then he

returned. "I saw him going down through the trees. So you did tell the truth."

"Yes. For once I am glad the walls are strong."

"He wanted you. What have you done that the devil beast should want you?"

"It is only an animal, big and hungry. It must have smelled your cooking."

"I think it wanted you."

"Are you secure up there? Have you any windows large enough for it?"

"They are too high, even in the drifts."

"Can you bar them?"

"Why should you worry about that?"

"If you die, so do I."

"Remember that."

"I don't ever forget it. You are my jailer and jeerer, cook and lock, watcher and witherer, mother and smotherer."

"Enough. Your rattling on gets too much after my years of silence."

Though that ended the incident, Stel continued to worry. The great arm of the beast was the most visible living thing Stel had seen now in almost four months. Scule remained dimly above his hole. He took care to exercise every day, especially after he discovered he could not pull his longbow.

Winter and monotony continued. Scule continued to feed Stel well enough. He took his daily flute lesson down through the roof hole, though he showed little talent for it. His old fingers would never be very nimble. But Stel could hear him practicing above at times, working through slow, measured songs. The two seemed to be becoming an odd sort of domestic couple, jailer and jailed, like many marriages, Stel wryly thought.

The crisis came suddenly. A storm of even greater fury than usual blew snow outside. Stel had exercised, cleaned his cell, prayed, played his hymns, and eaten. Somehow he felt uneasy. Something was wrong. He didn't know quite why, but he strung his longbow, which he could draw again. From above he heard a sudden rending of the hide windows of Scule's room. The old man shrieked. The wooden frames cracked and splintered. Sudden smoke

and snow blew down the roof hole. Stel nocked an arrow.
A heavy growl told him the beast was forcing his way
into the room overhead. He must have the old man
trapped, judging from the cries of terror. A rending of
frames told Stel the animal must have muscled his way
into the room and rushed across it. Stel saw a great foot
fall through the roof hole. Instantly he drew and shot,
piercing the foot before the beast could wrench it up
again. He heard a roar and shriek, as the beast tugged
against the stout arrow. His foot filled the hole, giving
him no purchase against the shaft to snap it.

Stel saw that the beast would do what he himself had
sought for so long. He was tearing out the keystones. In
the dimness Stel put another arrow through the foot,
drew his short-sword, and stood back against the wall
as the beast's foot came free, tearing out the stones. As
the whole end of the room thundered down, the beast
came with it, roaring into the dark hole.

In an instant Stel was climbing over beast and stones,
slashing the animal once in the face, then throwing the
sword up into the room above, leaping to grab the edge
of the floor, scrambling up, turning, and heaving loose
edge stones down on the beast scrabbling up the stones
below him. It was no use. The beast was too big. Stel
turned, grabbed his short-sword, and, as the animal put
one forepaw on the rim of the hole, Stel hacked at it
repeatedly. The beast sank back, then tried the other foot.
Stel chopped mercilessly across it, and the wounded animal fell back into Stel's prison with a rumble. He could
see it in the dim light, rising and falling, a great shape
writhing in pain, its front paws now useless.

Stel turned to Scule. The old man was lying in a corner
where the beast had swept him. He turned the wounded
man over. Blood welled in lines from his side, and a little
frothed on his lips. He groaned. Stel ignored the beast,
stuffing the window hole with bedding as well as he could
while snow and cold poured into the room. Then he built
up the fire, laid the old man down on his straw-filled mat-
tress, covered him with a coat, and heated water on
the fire. He found some old cloth, which he put in the
hot water, then found a short bow, old and slack, with
seven arrows.

With these he shot the wounded beast slowly and deliberately, until it sank down in a corner. Then, shuddering, Stel again went down into his prison and brought his own gear up, returning to skin the great beast. He placed the giant pelt, hair side down, over the hurt man.

Scule had said nothing. He lay moving his arm vaguely, breathing with difficulty. Stel bathed the wounds in his side as gently as possible, but Scule winced and writhed weakly. Stel could do nothing but try to make him comfortable, bathing and binding. Returning to the beast, Stel cut meat from the carcass and boiled it, feeding Scule the broth. He himself ate the first free and unportioned meal he had had in the whole winter. The meat was gamy and tough, but nourishing.

Finally, late that night, Scule stirred and opened his eyes. He seemed to recognize Stel. "The beast," he murmured.

"I killed it. It is in the pit. You are lying under his skin. You have eaten broth from him. He was only a beast, and now he is dead."

"You have me now."

"What? Oh. What do I want you for? I am not from the Dahmens. You know that by now, don't you?"

"Had believed it for so long. Suppose I knew. Then it is not true?"

"No. Things are as I said they were. Now lie still. You will be fine. But it will take time."

"No. Am all broken. Can feel it. It is just as well." He sighed faintly. "Bequeath all this to you."

"What?"

"All my things. My house. Stores."

"Wait now. You are . . ."

"No. Now we will both tell nothing but truth. There is no need to shroud . . . my dying from me. Not a grave matter. Am glad to have met you. Would not have liked simply to die, after all that waiting." He fell silent for a time. "There is a shining sea," he added. "Could not make it across the dry country. But there is one. Some have made it. The Commuters know of it. You must go there for me. Should have gone. Feared the Dahmens. All was open in the dry country. Felt safe in the mountains."

"Quiet now. I will go, eventually, when you are all right. Perhaps you will come, too. But not now."

Scule smiled oddly. "Stel, you know the old woman, Ahroe, for whom your wife, Ahroe, was named?"

Stel was puzzled. "Yes, a bitter old woman who died five or six winters ago."

"She . . . she was . . . I used to know her."

"She must have been young."

"But just as bitter. Stel . . ."

"Yes."

"It was she I meant to kill, not Visib. Knew I would get someone. You have made these days hard for me telling me it was Visib. Loved her, Stel. Even though she . . ." He stopped. Tears welled in Stel's eyes. So this was the end of a story of bad human workmanship. Scule had participated, been murderous. But he was also the victim. How weary and sad it all was.

"You said, Stel, that a mother's tears can redeem the beast. It is a father's for a Pelbar man. It is yours for me. I see them. Never thought a Pelbar would ever cry over me."

"For any man, Scule, it is a mother or a wife, a woman. That is something no man, even a Pelbar, can do. It is the special province of woman, hard as they try to deny it. But don't worry. Your mother cried for you often enough."

"Do you know that?"

"The family is at Northwall. They raised a poem stone there. There was much argument about it, but Northwall would not agree to take it down."

"What did it say?"

"I don't know. I have never been there. But it must have been good because it made the Dahmens so angry."

Scule started to laugh, lightly, in his old man's cackle, but ended coughing blood.

"I will return to Pelbarigan, Scule, and I will tell them the story as you have told it. I promise."

"No. The Dahmens will make enough trouble for you."

"Nonetheless, if I live, I will go."

"But go to the shining sea first."

"The shining sea? I will go westward, and I will try to

go to the shining sea. Now you must rest. I have to plug up your window better. It is cold in here. Look, the snow is still getting in."

Stel worked much of the night, both on the window, which he eventually shut with stone from the prison room, and the beast, which he butchered, drying long strips of the dark, heavy meat over Scule's fire. Toward morning he looked at the old man again but saw he was not sleeping this time. He was dead.

Stel was suddenly very weary. He carried the body to the cold storage pantry, wrapped it, and left it there, returning to curl up by the fire in his own sleepsack, with the beast's pelt over him, sleeping undisturbed until midday.

It was no weather to travel. Stel took his time, examining all of Scule's house and possessions, taking the old man down into the prison room and entombing him in a structure of the rocks he himself had so carefully cut. The storm had ceased, but it was bitter cold. Stel ventured out through the window. It was a joy to be free. He would find wood suitable for snow sliders, then return and set up housekeeping in Scule's house until the weather broke. How different was the silence of outdoors from the silence of his prison room. It was singing with wind and branches, with cruel cold and the silent music of free air and icy mountains. Scule, Stel decided, surely must have felt some of this. He must have.

☐ XIV

THE snow was still deep at Scule's house when Stel left it. He had carefully dismantled all the traps outside, digging down through snow and ice to do it. He had arranged the house as an open one for whatever traveler might happen to come. And by the prison room, the roof of which he removed, making a stairway of rocks down to it, Stel chiseled an inscription, working with an old maul and the nub of a steel chisel he found in Scule's tools.

Scule of Pelbarigan, who set out for the shining sea and stopped in these mountains. Lived by himself, without speaking to anyone for many years. Killed by a great unknown beast, Scule leaves this house for all who pass. Soundly made, it will serve the travelers of ages. As you rest by his fire, think of the skill of Scule, the stone-cutter, and his faithfulness to his work.

STEL DAHMEN OF PELBARIGAN

Shortly after his departure, Stel was surprised at how few ayas he was from an ancient town—this one fairly free of snow, being down beyond the narrow gorge in the high, steep mountains in which Scule lived. It was not a poisonous empty place, yet was a ruin, the first Stel had ever been in from ancient times.

Overrun with brush and forest, the ruin still revealed the layout of its streets. Tumbled in, and burned in some wild fire, the buildings were still largely visible—at least the stone ones, and those of the small bricks that even the Pelbar still made at Threerivers. It was all decayed. Stel examined the ruin for some time. Gaps in the few standing walls and fragments of glass on the ground showed there had been large, glazed windows. The surfaces had a wonderful flatness. Still standing were several stanchions of the light, white metal of the ancients, perhaps for outdoor lighting, but they were so high that Stel could not see how they could be ignited at night. It seemed very impractical. Perhaps they had another function. On north slopes west of the town, Stel found, in the tangled mountain growth, the rusted remains of lines of towers, leading uphill. But too much time and weather had passed by here, and he could make nothing of it.

Back in the city he found a fallen statue buried in leaves and brush near a brick ruin. It was gray. He thought it had been of a man, but the face had washed away. He seemed to be holding a long stick or club in front of himself. Stel cleaned it off and stood it up, heaving hard against it, then leaning it back against a shrubby pine. Did it have an odd hat on? He thought so.

They could do so many things, the ancients, but something had destroyed it all. It was like his own experiences. Men were much better with their building, their weapons, their entrapments, than they were with each other.

He turned westward, very soon running into a small empty place, not half an ayas wide. In its center he could see a ruin of buildings on a flat site tucked in under the north slope of the lower hills. From there the land trended downward toward the west. The hills were high, but rounded, reddish, and covered with tufts of brush and short pines. Stel followed a rushing stream that carried snowmelt, frost cold, out of the mountains. Here too were fragments of ancient road and occasionally a small ruin. But the whole district was now empty of people.

Stel had been traveling slowly, fishing and hunting, for nearly two weeks when he came upon a small rough shelter of brush, clearly made by humans. As he looked around, he saw brush enclosures, and strange animal droppings, all old. So herdsmen of some kind lived here.

The dwellings were simple and crude. But no one was there now, or had been for a while. Stel had continued west for two more days when he heard a child's crying.

Plainly it was a cry of distress, piercing and quavering. Trotting ahead, Stel found a child, a small dark girl, sitting by a mound of fur that Stel soon saw was a woman. She had fallen and lay still at the bottom of a slope of loose rock.

Stel's sudden arrival raised the child's cry in pitch, but he simply hugged and patted her briefly, saying, "Don't worry, little one. Your Uncle Stel will take care of everything." Then he turned to the woman. Her skin was dark and smooth, a little like that of the Roti. She had a rounded face, now scratched from the fall, and long, straight coal-black hair, thick and rich, held in a single braid behind.

Stel rolled her over slowly and bathed her face with water from his pitched bottle. She opened her eyes and looked at him vaguely, then focused with surprise. "Commuter?" she asked, in a strange dialect.

"No. Pelbar. Lie still. I will take care of you."

"Pelbar? What is Pelbar?"

"A people from the east. Where do you hurt? Have you broken something?"

"Leg, I think. You talk like Commuter. Where is Blomi?"

"Who? This little girl?" Blomi had quieted down and sat on her heels watching, her face tear-streaked, her small hands clasped in front of her. For the first time, Stel saw they were surrounded by medium-size horned animals, with slotted eyes, quiet and quizzical. He started.

"What?"

"They will not hurt. They are quiet and tame."

"What are they?"

The woman stared in disbelief. "They? Goat, of course. Are you stupid? You not Commuter. What you say you are?"

"Pelbar. From the east. There are none of these there. Now let me look at your leg."

Feeling carefully, he determined that one bone in the lower leg was broken. Stel bound it up and splinted it. He washed the woman's scraped legs and arms and covered them, using his small collection of rodent furs. The woman, whose name was Catal, had come early to the summer pastures. She was not expecting her family for some time. She wanted to return to them now, with the goats, of course, Stel carrying her on a litter, dragging the rear ends, driving the goats, and herding the little girl, Blomi. Not only that. She wanted to go south, across the line of rounded mountains.

Stel hesitated a few minutes. Plainly it would have to be done. He could not leave her, and he didn't want to stay with her. But it was not easy. Scrabbling up the slopes, watching the goats, carrying his own gear as well, hunting, milking the goats as Catal taught him, with Blomi laughing at his clumsiness, and caring for the two soon had Stel nearly exhausted. They had to go farther than he had surmised, or Catal had said, and after three days, he found out they were only halfway. Tired of the bumping, Catal wanted to walk, but even though they tried crutches, it would not work on the rough ground.

The one compensation was Blomi. Stel had forgotten the delight of children. She talked to him endlessly, sometimes lapsing into the tongue he couldn't understand, sometimes in "Commuter," as she called the common tongue Stel knew. She was better at it than her mother. The goat people had come from the south only eighteen summers ago, and they traded with the Commuters to the west.

Blomi snuggled up to Stel at night, putting her small arm around his neck. She was not heavily dressed, and slept by the fire without cover, and Stel knew she was by him for warmth, but he still felt the charm of her small softness, and her presence was a compliment. To have one's own child—what a delight that must be.

Blomi got Stel to tell stories and play his flute, and especially delighted in the frog game, the finger people of the house, or the rime for toes:

> These little fish swim in the current.
> These five fish swim near the shore.
> Along comes the great big catfish—
> No little fish anymore.

This was accompanied by hands approaching her toes like gaping mouths, or even Stel's mouth, opening and clicking his teeth. Blomi always squealed and held her feet in her hands. Then she would put them out for him to do it again.

"Do it to Mother," Blomi shrilled.

Stel looked over at the silent, watching Catal. "She wouldn't pull her toes away. Her leg is tied down."

"Then you would pinch them," Blomi said, laughing.

Stel fell silent. Catal smiled at him. Stel felt uneasy after that. What was the woman thinking? Well, he would be rid of them both soon enough, though he thought of leaving Blomi with some regret.

The third day after involved a climb that the goats managed with ease, but for Stel, dragging his heavy load, it was a great trial. He had to stop repeatedly, sitting and panting. Catal was somehow impatient. When they finally reached the rim rock, he saw the hill slope southward gently, and a trail winding down. Far below, in a canyon, smoke rose.

It was late in the afternoon that the strange procession straggled into the open canyon floor with its rough shelters. About twenty people, as rudely dressed as Catal, almost all dark-skinned, came out to look. No one rushed forward. A strange atmosphere of tension hung like the smoke in the air.

"Where do you want to be put down?" Stel asked.

"There," said Catal, pointing.

Stel saw a brush shelter. In front of it a thin young man stood, this one not dark, but light-brown-haired, blue-eyed, with a sparse beard and long hair tied behind with a thong.

Stel dragged the litter to him. The man didn't move. He put it down. "She broke her leg. Now, do you have water?"

The brown-haired man paid no attention to Stel. He said a short sentence to Catal in a strange language. She replied in a long, impassioned speech, full of contempt, ending by spitting.

Stel was uneasy. He strung his short bow and took out several arrows. Let them settle their own problems. He untied his backsack from the litter. Stooping to Blomi, he kissed her and said good-bye. But she was crying.

"You can't go now, Stel," she said.

"Why not?"

"You were with Mother."

"Yes. Depending on what 'with' means. Then what."

"You must fight Father."

"You knew this? Why didn't you tell me?"

"Mother said—Mother said it was the only way to save her and get her home."

The brown-haired man brought a long, braided whip out of the brush hut, and began whistling it around his head. "Come on, now, you green-livered woman stealer. I'm going to peel your hide."

"Not again," said Stel, stepping back.

"What mean, not again. Not first time? Well, it will be last."

"Another gang of crazy people."

"I'll show you crazy. You die for that." The brown-haired man lashed out at Stel, who jumped back in time. "Stand still."

"You stand still. You see that log?" Stel pointed to a curved juniper log near Blomi's father.

"What about it, green liver? Of course I—" He stopped when Stel's arrow thunked into it.

"Now, take that out carefully. Feel the point. Do it." The brown-haired man did. "The next one goes through your belly. Do you want that?"

"Through my belly? No. How'd you do that? Fight fair, green-livered lizard."

"Lizard now, is it? Or is it green-izard lizit?"

"What?"

"Now, back off, or I will kill you, purely and simply. I am going to retrieve that arrow, then I am going to wash myself in that stream, and then I will leave. Any questions?"

Blomi's father backed off. "You can't do that," said a greasy-faced man, squat and dark.

"Why not?"

"You must fight."

"We just did. Didn't we, brown hair. You won, didn't you."

"You do nothing rightly."

Stel laughed. "All right, snake belly. Maybe not. But that is the way it is going to be."

"No one calls me snake belly. For that you will die," said the greasy-faced man, advancing with tightened muscles.

"Wait," Stel said, holding up his hand. "All right, grease face, you are not a snake belly. Now I live, right?"

"Grease face?"

"An apt description."

"You die for that." He too carried a long, braided whip, and he curled it out, catching Stel around the wrist. But Stel's razor-sharp short-sword cut it off as the man pulled. He sat down in the sand, got up, looked at his whip, and screamed.

"Look what you did! A new whip."

"For that I die, right?" Stel turned slowly, watching them all. They stood still. An old woman spat at him, and began cursing him in her unknown tongue. Stel took from his backsack a small piece of glass he had picked up at the ruin and held it in front of his face, pointing at the woman.

She stopped. "What you doing?" she asked.

"Have you never heard of a mirror man?"

"Mirror man?"

"This has the power, with my magic, to turn your curses back on you, doubling them. Do you feel them yet? I see your chin beginning to grow more hair. Are your teeth loose yet? Your eyes already sag." Involuntarily the woman put a hand to her face. Then she turned abruptly and walked over to her hut, entering it. Stel looked at the rest, his arrow nocked.

The brown-haired man shouted from the entrance to his hut, "I don't have to take care of the child. I don't have to keep Catal. They are yours now, you snake."

Blomi screamed and cried, sitting in the sand.

"Then I will take Blomi and care for her," said Stel, stooping to the child. "Do as you please with Catal, you lice-ridden toad wart. Or should I say, toad-ridden lice wart? No, that would be louse wart."

Blomi reached out for Stel, who picked her up and walked briskly out of the camp the way he had come. The girl said nothing, but her chin trembled as she looked back. "Don't worry," Stel whispered to her. "It will be all right."

"Where are you taking me?"

"We will go to the Commuters until they all calm down. Don't worry. You will be with your mother and father soon enough."

"Why did you do those things?"

"I think they would have killed me for helping you. Would they?"

"I think they might. It is really because Mother and Father fight all the time. How long before they will come and get me?"

"I don't know. They will have to calm down. What's the matter? Don't you like me?"

"But they are my mother and father."

"Yes, my little love. But we will have to give them time to realize that. Sometimes children have to help educate their parents, you know."

"Educate?"

"Teach them."

It was not as long as Stel supposed. Before they reached the first hilltop, the brown-haired man ran after them, panting hard as he came near. Stel turned.

"We—we have decided. We will keep the girl."

"What will happen to her?"

"Nothing. We cannot let her go with a murderous crazy man."

Stel put Blomi down. "Good-bye, now," he said. "See that murderous crazy person over there? Run to him. He will take you home."

"But that is my father."

"Yes. I am teasing. I am the murderous crazy person. Now go." He kissed her forehead. She took his bent head, with deliberation and dignity, and returned a wet but formal kiss. "Teach him the finger games, and the little fish poem. You may civilize him."

"Civilize?"

"Make him as lovely as you are. Now go, little flower."

She ran to her father, who picked her up. "What is your name?" Stel called.

"Why should I tell you, goatsucker?"

"Well, at least you didn't say, 'For asking that, you die.' "

"His name is Coffi," Blomi called. Her father squeezed her in irritation.

"Good-bye, Blomi. Good-bye, Coffi," Stel said. "May the blessings of Aven be on you both."

Coffi turned without a word and strode down the hill with Blomi. She called, "Good-bye, Stel. Come back sometime. When they have all calmed down," but her father twisted her arm, and she put her face into his neck. Stel could see him comforting her and scolding her at the same time as they grew small in the distance. He stared after them a long time.

Then, despite his weariness, he walked long into the night before stopping near a small stream he could bathe in. He wanted no more of the goatherders. But that night he missed Blomi. It would have been nice to have a child, a small one to educate him.

 XV

AHROE had a problem. Hagen's back did not ease. It grew worse until he couldn't get off his bed. His pain was extreme, even in rolling over. Omar and Wald were restless to return home, but they didn't dare go without Quen. They would make it through Roti country in a single run. They didn't want to leave Ahroe and Garet, either, lest the Roti take the child. Quen wanted her to return to Shumai country with him, but his motives were mixed. Hagen, Fitzhugh assured them, was too old to be of interest to the Roti, despite his blue eyes.

Fitzhugh suggested a solution as they all ate supper in Hagen's room. It was cramped, but it made company for him. "Quen," she began, "you must allow Ahroe to continue alone. She knows that Stel is ahead now. Hagen can stay with me until he is well."

She smiled over at him. Plainly they were already fond of each other, the two older ones. "I have taken care of people all my life now, and all I have left are Finkelstein and Taglio. I have scarcely anything to do. His hurt will rest out. I have seen it before. But he cannot be moved at all. It may take all summer." Hagen winced. "But he will be well. Then he can return by himself. I am sure that Ahroe will find him once she has located Stel."

"If she ever does," said Quen.

"You must not try to stop her, Quen. You see that, don't you?"

Quen did not reply. But Hagen said, "How can I let Ahroe go on alone? We have come well over a thousand ayas together. I was there when Garet was born. I have carried the child for days together. He—"

"What is the purpose of her journey, Hagen?" Fitzhugh asked.

"To find Stel. I know."

"And Stel deserves to be found. Remember that I know Stel. But for my sister, he would be here now with you. Stel is the father."

"Hagen is the grandfather," said Ahroe. "But Fitzhugh is right. I have to go. Garet is not safe here without all of you, and it is right that you three go home."

"I see nothing right about it," Quen growled.

"I am Stel's wife, Quen, and I am going to find him."

Quen left the room. "Wald," said Hagen. "You and Omar will have to see that he doesn't follow her."

They nodded.

"Then it is settled. Garet and I will leave in the morning. You two and Quen might come a few ayas with me, to see there are no Roti, then return, if you will do that."

"Good. We will."

"Hagen, we will return for you. We will—"

"Don't worry about me. I will be all right. If it is easier, don't even come this way. You may be a long time. I really feel that you will find him. I pray that someday

I may see you again. I am sorry that I will not be with you. But I have seen enough of you to know that you are tough and strong. And I want you far away from these Roti crazy people. Just come in and see me tonight, please, so I can say good-bye."

Ahroe did come in, alone. Hagen was silent a long time. He finally said, "Ahroe, put your arms around me. Be careful, please. Don't move the bed much."

She did, easing herself down next to him, and saying, "A Dahmen doesn't get to have a father like you, Hagen. I see it is not a matter of blood. It is something else—what the society allows and what the two people feel."

"We did have a good time out there on the plains, didn't we."

"Yes. Especially you. It got a little heavy there for a while." She got up, tugged his beard a couple of times, and stood still holding his hand. Then she went to the door, and the old man covered his face with his hands.

In the morning they said good-bye again, but quickly and in company. Hagen saw her in his mind's eye, setting out, with Garet nodding on her back, and the three Shumai, ascending the westward hill.

Fitzhugh came in. "They are gone," she said. "Now, would you like to help me twist fibers, or would you like to rest?"

"I think I maybe will rest, Fitz." He smiled up sheepishly, unused to helplessness.

"You can help me later." She brushed his hair out of his face and left the room.

Above, the four travelers were standing by the scattered bones of the Roti. Quen whistled softly. "So the innocent Stel has a sting after all," he said.

"Come. I want to go on." Ahroe moved ahead, as the three looked at each other.

After ten ayas, Ahroe said, "All right. This is far enough. Thank you for coming. I will go on alone now. Come, let me thank you." She embraced them all warmly, Quen last.

"It is not right. I will not let you go."

Omar and Wald took his arms.

"May Aven bless you," Ahroe said. "This is a hard good-bye for me, too." Turning, she walked rapidly down a hill and disappeared around an outcrop of red rock. The three watched awhile.

"We will go now, Quen," Wald said. Quen shook them off. Then he turned with them and trotted back to Ozar.

Ahroe felt strangely free now she was alone, walking rapidly over the rough terrain, trying to put as much distance between herself and the Roti—as well as Quen—as she could. Hunting as she moved, feeding Garet, bathing and caring for him, enjoying the freedom of her aloneness, she felt a strange exhilaration. The country was so big, and so empty.

At last, she came down into the same basin Stel had traversed the previous fall. It took most of a day to walk across the floor of the valley. Ahead stood a wall of mountains, north and south, still snowcapped. As she looked at them, she doubted that Stel had simply gone straight up them. The west end of the basin also stretched north and south, with remains of an ancient road going in either direction. The north seemed to climb into the steep mountains. Stel was a river person, she reasoned, and so probably went south, seeking water he could follow through the mountains. In fall, with winter in the heights, he would not have gone north.

So Ahroe turned southward, away from the steep road to the empty house of Scule and across the divide. But after twenty ayas or so, she was not sure. The mountains continued to her west, and all water still flowed east, toward the faraway Heart River. She was sure Stel meant to go west. Fragments of another ancient road split west and led her up into high country. Eventually she too reached the snowfield of the high mountains, soggy now with spring, but still deep and cold. She too shot the small, whistling rodents with her short bow, making mittens and a hat for Garet from the pelts. She too came to what seemed the rim of the world, with the pure joy of the climb and the height, and, looking far to west through the cool, clear air, saw a ribbon of water. It was obviously flowing west. A long look showed a big, rough country ahead, and Garet was crying. Ahroe sighed, picked him up, and began her long descent.

She was a week in the mountains, eventually reaching the river, which had cut a deep, narrow gorge through a scrubby plateau. Ahroe followed it, descending for water now and again, to bathe, and to wash the baby.

Then one day as she reached the rim of the canyon, she was aware suddenly of three young women standing in an arc, with spears, watching her.

"Greetings, sister," the tallest called. "You have entered the country of Jahv. Have you come to join us?"

"Join you? No. I am Ahroe Dahmen of Pelbarigan. My child and I are passing through. I am sorry if I intruded. Most of this is merely empty country. Would you prefer that I withdraw?"

"No. Come with us. Your child—what is her name?"

"Garet. He is a boy."

The Jahv started. "A male child, then. We will relieve you of him and put him with the males. You will be free of him."

Ahroe stood still. "He is my child. I shall keep him."

The tall woman looked at her narrowly. "As you like. Now, come with us. We will take you to Dolla, our Director. No one has passed this way in a long time, and you are the first woman I can remember."

Ahroe looked at the spears. The three seemed relaxed, though. "All right. I shall follow." The three set off at a trot, and Ahroe, with Garet and her backsack, walked after them as fast as she could. The three had to wait occasionally, but they showed no impatience. Eventually the turn of a hill showed a low, rambling building, badly put together of logs and stone. Behind it were other farm buildings, and cultivated fields stretched out beyond. At the far end of them stood a stockade wall. A group of women of all ages lounged around the building, but Ahroe's appearance brought them forward.

"We have found a sister," said the tall one.

"Well done, Rabe. You are welcome, sister. Have you come to join us? I am Ambi, the Director."

"Ahroe Dahmen of Pelbarigan, a Pelbar of the Heart River. My son, Garet. We are passing through the country. No, thank you for the proposal, but I am not going to join you, nor, as your Rabe suggested, give up my son. I am merely passing through and am grateful for your welcome."

Ambi drew her breath. "You will keep a male yourself?"

"Yes. It is widely done—among the Pelbar, who are ruled by women, and with the Shumai, Sentani, the Eastern Cities, the Tantal, Rits, the Far Isles, even the Peshtak, so I am told."

A murmur of astonished disapproval followed.

"What do you do with your males?" Ahroe asked.

"They go there for raising by the males." Ambi indicated the far stockade. "This world was unfortunately constituted so that we must endure their presence. And they are useful for heavy work. But we quite naturally preserve what is of value to humanity."

"So said Pell in her writings, more or less. But we live in our families, like the other peoples."

"Perhaps you will stay with us awhile. You seem an intelligent woman. We may alter your views."

"Thank you. I must pass through quickly westward. If it is agreeable, though, I would like a meal in company. Garet and I have been alone since we left the Ozar, and he is not much of a conversationalist yet."

It was agreed. The main meal was due shortly. It was eaten in a central hall, with a high table, at which Ambi sat, with Ahroe by her. There were small babies present, all female, and girls of all sizes, totaling, Ahroe quickly estimated, about seventy-five people. The meal was well cooked, a mixture of vegetables and fowl, and there was plenty. Ahroe enjoyed it, but sensed a distaste in the group at the presence of Garet, whom she fed from her plate, planning to nurse him later. She decided not to refer to her pursuit of Stel, and when questioned, she said she was going west to visit the Commuters, whom Fitzhugh had mentioned. There were possibilities of trade. The Jahv didn't know of any people to their west.

"Perhaps you will spend the night. Your child may stay in the nursery this once," said Ambi.

"Thank you very much, Director. I have never been separate from Garet, though, and I would be uncomfortable without him." She sketched in her encounter with the Roti and saw a deep sense of shock pass across the listeners.

"I have a present for you, Director," said Ahroe. "A

small box my husband made for me." With an inner reluctance, but to prove a point, Ahroe gave the Director the tiny inlaid box Stel had made to hold her hair clasps, which she had carried all the way from Pelbarigan. It was of dark wood, with the fish-and-arrow symbol he was fond of inlaid in three colors of lighter wood. Carved around the sides were the words, "A hold for holders of your hair, when they are working, I hold air."

"Your husband?" asked Ambi. "What is that?"

It was Ahroe's turn to be shocked. "The man to whom I am married. The father of Garet. Stel Dahmen of Pelbarigan."

Ambi stared. "A man made this? This fine work? It is finer than anything I have ever seen. And you are—you are what? Married? You have one man? What does that mean?"

Ahroe felt strong distaste at what she surmised was the system of the Jahv. "You are obviously very isolated here," she began, and patiently explained the marital systems of the Heart River peoples. When she finished, she sensed astonishment and tension.

"I don't know how you stand it," said Rabe.

"It must be demeaning company. We prefer ourselves," said Ambi.

"I must confess I am wholly puzzled," said Ahroe. "I have seen good women and bad ones, good men and bad ones. Some people are sensitive and intelligent, others crass and slobbering. Most lie between. I have never seen that gender made much difference, except as a social system bends the attitudes of its adherents. Stel is much quicker with words than I. I am steadier than he. He is good with tools. He plays the flute. I am a guardsman. I handle weapons better than he. I face facts better, too. But Stel and I mesh like the fingers of two hands."

As she said this, Ahroe knew she was lying in part, talking of the Stel she had married. She also remembered the bones of the Roti. And she suddenly saw what changes had come in her because of Garet.

Ambi fingered the small box thoughtfully. "No male here could have done this. Now supper is finished, come with us. Come to the compound. Show us which male is like this Stel." Those listening grinned. Plainly this was a challenge.

Ahroe was uneasy, but she went with the group across the fields to the stockade and mounted a wide ladder made of pine logs notched and tied lengthwise to two larger logs leaning against the wall. About twenty men were inside, bare to the waist, mostly fat, bent over crude tables. Three chess games were in progress, each one clustered with watchers. Three naked boys sat in the dirt near the one sagging hut in the compound. They were building a structure out of twigs.

The men looked up, and seeing Ahroe, stared.

"Hey, hey, hey," said one. "What is this? Look. A new tomato. Hey, that's nice. Put down the alky, boys."

All eyes turned to Ahroe. Howls and whistles shredded the air. A small crowd sauntered over to the fence.

"Comin' in tonight?" one man asked, holding a mug of some drink.

"Not for him. For me."

"What's the matter, woman? Loosen that collar up."

"Loosen everything."

"Yeah. Corn is no good until it is shucked."

"Hey, Ambi. She's for me, isn't she? Right? Come on, now. Oh, oh. I'm sorry, Rabe. Hey, we were just kidding around."

Turning, Ahroe saw a long whip in Rabe's hand. Then she turned to the fat man who had just spoken. "You shouldn't have moved that bishop," she said.

"What?" He glanced back at the game. "Sure, I should've. Hey, woman, what do you know?" All the men agreed loudly, elbowing to explain.

The man's opponent said, "He'd a better of moved it. It would've been a slit throat if he didn't." He drew his finger across his neck.

"I don't see it. What about the queen?"

"No, no. Yeah, the queen. But what about four moves down? Look, hey, I'd show you, but he will see." He jerked a thumb at his opponent.

A general jeer arose. "Go ahead, we all know anyhow —at least that far," said one.

In a rush, they brought the table to the wall, and with contradiction and argument explained to Ahroe, leaning over, the possibilities of the next four moves. They plainly knew their chess, and they had almost wholly forgotten her except as an audience.

"Where are the rest of you?" she asked.

"Who? Us? This is all of us. Hey, come on in here, and we'll show you enough of us."

"Why don't you take care of your teeth?"

"Teeth?" With slight embarrassment, they all closed their mouths. Then a few grinned widely to show the gaps.

"We have a few fights," said one.

"Yeah. And they go, you know. The alky helps."

"And the stick matches. We lose a few there. Hey, what do you care? Who are you, anyhow?"

"I am Ahroe Dahmen of Pelbarigan, and this is my son, Garet." She held up the baby. He sagged sleepily in her hands, frowning and blinking.

The men stilled and looked nonplussed.

"Your son?" said an older one. "You bringin' him here for us? Another baby?"

"No. I am passing through. I am taking him with me."

"Hey, take me with you," said the fattest one, scratching his belly, then patting it. The others turned on him in silence, though, and he subsided. The men looked at each other awkwardly.

"I am afraid I have disrupted things," said Ahroe. "I must go. I am sorry."

"No need to go, woman," a young man grinned.

"See those boys by the hut?" said Ahroe.

"Hut? That's our house. Yeah, what of them?"

"You ought to wash them. Not only now. Every day."

"Sounds like a woman, all right."

"All right, woman. We'll wash them. Just for you. Then you come and we'll wash you."

Rabe's whip snaked out and caught the man who said that across the shoulder. He howled and ran. The others retreated. Ahroe turned to her, frowning. "I'm sorry. I think we'd better go," she said.

"Which was like your man?"

"None. These are kept in benightedness."

"They have all the opportunities to better themselves they could want. But they do nothing but what you have seen."

Ahroe helped Ambi down from the wide ladder. The old woman was still fingering the box. She looked at Ahroe, and as their eyes met, both felt a tension ease, a communication. Ambi walked in silence. As they neared the building, she said to Ahroe, "Come to my room now, please. I would talk with you."

When they were together, she said, "What are you thinking?"

"They are not the men I know well, but they are a little like some men I have seen. These are grossly underdeveloped. Jestana, our Protector, once said that men are boys all their lives, but women are women from the time they are small."

The Director nodded.

"But then the Protector added, 'I think if we were girls longer, we would see some things that are useful—the play of mind, the free gaming spirit.' But I don't know. The more societies I meet, the less I can tell which things are generic, which matters of custom. The Shumai women are drudges once they marry, but they know every star in the sky and play their star games with the men sometimes nearly all night. I am convinced, though, that the interplay of the genders working together provides a richness otherwise absent. I am sorry if I have offended you."

The Director frowned. "I don't know how I feel about your coming. I have been troubled a long time. This is all we have ever known. And you see how the men are. I fear we have entrapped ourselves in a nonproductive system, but you mustn't tell anyone I said that. I fear I must soon abdicate. There is a feeling for Rabe. She holds to our stated beliefs simply and exclusively."

"Where are the other men?"

"Those are all. They take little care of the young ones, and many die."

The two were quiet a long time. Ahroe said, "Do the mothers not have a feeling for their sons, then?"

The Director shook her head. "When a male is born, they cannot wait for the initial nursing period to end so they can rid themselves of him. They loathe them. I had two sons myself. I had that feeling with the first, so I know it well. He died as a small boy. The other grew up. You saw him in the compound. I will not tell you which he was. I am ashamed to have been connected with him, but a little guilty, too. I have often wondered if perhaps it might have been different. You really are telling me the truth. This box was made by a man?"

"Yes, by Stel."

The Director sighed. "I can see the love he put into it, both for you and for the work itself. In a sense it is the same impracticality the chess players show, but turned to use and delight."

"People with different attitudes speculate endlessly on the superiority of one gender over the other. One can hardly be sure where the facts lie, though I used to be very sure. My present attitude is that men and women do differ, quite obviously, though how seems less certain. So it becomes important for each to consort freely and closely with the other to pick up what the other may more naturally have."

"Which of the men in the compound would you want to start with?"

Ahroe laughed. "That is a hard but a natural question. The long-range answer is any of the three boys."

Ahroe could see the Director thinking that over and slowly turning her mind against the idea. Surely it offered practical difficulties. Finally, the Director said, "Ahroe, I am a little afraid for your safety, and more for his," pointing at Garet, who was sleeping in Ahroe's lap. "It is Rabe and her friends."

"I know."

"You know? I am not sure you can make provision for it. Rabe is a hunter. She is tall and strong, and you have seen her cruelty."

"I will try to defend myself and Garet. But I hope not to hurt her."

"You mean that, don't you?"

"Yes. Now, Director, I wonder if I could leave you with something that will help you all. It is soap."

"Soap?"

Oddly enough, Ahroe had learned from Fitzhugh how the Pelbar made soap. Stel had taught the Ozar. Ahroe produced a small piece and got Ambi to wash with it. The old woman felt her hands and looked at them.

"I will explain how to make it."

"That is something the males would do."

"Then bring one and I will explain it to him."

"They do not come here after dark."

"I will go there."

"That is not done—except in the mating house."

"The— Is there no way then? Must so many of the boys die? They are your boys."

"That is how we have always kept them weaker." But as she said this, and to someone not of the sisterhood of the Jahv, Ambi knew, having pondered it so many times to herself, the weight of what she was saying. "Look at them, how they are," she added.

Ahroe pondered. "Why not bring Rabe in and ask her. She would see the use of soap."

"I don't know. It is irregular."

"So am I. You know I must go. We could go down there with plenty of guards and whips. I could explain."

"Rabe will say to do it tomorrow."

"Of course. But I must leave tomorrow morning. It is prescribed by my religion."

"Is it? Your religion?"

"Not really," Ahroe said, laughing. "We will tell that to Rabe. I am sure that you will not harm Garet, but I feel the animosity of some of the others. I must go tomorrow for his safety."

The Director summoned her chief guard and explained. Rabe frowned deeply.

"Tomorrow night, Rabe," said Ahroe, looking out the window, "the moon swells beyond its half phase, and no journeys are resumed when the moon is in its bent back. It is bad and results in misfortune. I must go tomorrow morning precisely when the sun is halfway to its summit. Thus it gives me the strength of its rising at the start, and the restfulness of its falling when I am tiring. And before it reaches noon, our priests have enjoined me, I must wade in the swift river again to give my feet the strength of the rushing water as the sun swells."

Ambi stared at Ahroe for the ease with which she lied. But Rabe agreed, and a torchlight procession went to the compound, threw back the stockade gate, and roused the men. They began to grumble and joke, but several whips cracked in the air brought a sullen silence.

Ahroe directed them to heat water and bring one of the small boys, still naked in the evening chill. She gave him half her remaining soap and directed an old man to bathe him and scrub his hair with the soap. The child cried and screamed throughout the process.

"Keep it out of his eyes," Ahroe said. "It is strong soap and will make them sting."

When they finished, she explained in detail how soap was made, from the leaching of ashes to the boiling with fat and pouring into molds. The men were amused, and inclined to whisper, but the novelty of the evening, the ring of torches, and the scattering whips, kept them generally quiet.

"Now bring a stool and the man who was whipped," said Ahroe. He came forward reluctantly. The ugly welt across his shoulder and back was crusted with dry blood and purple at the edges. It had not been touched. Ahroe sensed this was a matter of pride. "Sit there," Ahroe commanded. "What is your name?"

"Latz."

"This will hurt, but it will help the healing. You will have to cover it to keep the flies off. Boil a cloth and wrap it. Your friends will help."

"We'll peel the rest of his hide," said a low voice from the back of the group, but Rabe's whip found out the man, licking across the forearm.

"You are gaining on me, Rabe," said Ahroe. Rabe simply coiled her whip carefully.

Latz sat still, looking over his shoulder, until Ahroe applied the warm, soapy water to his back. Then he yelled and winced. She took a handful of his hair and shook him. "Quiet. Where is your backbone?" Rabe smiled in amusement, but Latz endured the washing with no further outcry. Then she tore several strips of her own gray-white cloth, clean and dry, not mentioning it was nearly a third of Garet's diaper supply, and wrapped the wound expertly.

"Stand up," she said. Latz stood. He was about the same height as Ahroe. She looked at the bandage. "Wash that every day. With soap. Now, mouth shut and nose clean. See how that is done? I am sure you can do that."

Latz stared at her. "We're doin' fine, woman. You nearly killed me."

"You see?" said Rabe.

Ahroe didn't turn or reply. "Can you make the soap?"

"Sure. It is simple."

"Will you, then?"

"They will have us. Another job."

"Make some for yourself, too. And use it. I've never seen such an animal pen. Now, Rabe, perhaps we should go. Thank you for all your help."

They left, a stream of torches on silent faces, but as they passed through the field, the hoots and yells swelled behind them. Ahroe knew she had made a nearly empty gesture, but there was the fact of the soap. She had never felt clean in Shumai country without it. At least she would help the women. But perhaps it was hopeless. Latz was much more empty-faced than her own infant. Perhaps he was already tearing the bandage off and dancing around with it. No one would really care. But at least she had given them a glimpse of a different kind of treatment. They might think about it tonight.

Ahroe and Garet were given the Director's workroom to sleep in. The women generally slept together, in one large room, on pallets they hung from pegs during the day. It was Garet's presence that they could not tolerate. Ahroe made a show of preparing for sleep, as Rabe leaned in the doorway talking, but as soon as the door was shut, she dressed, packed, nursed Garet once more, and studied the night out the open window. Was that a shadow? What other way out was there? Behind the fireplace was an ash dump. Shrouding Garet's face with her hand, she crawled through and away. Looking back, she could see a dim figure watching the window, reclining, holding a spear.

In the deep night, Ahroe returned to the river, descending into the gorge and wading in the snowmelt water until she could find a log. She pushed off, poled and groped her way across above the riffle at the head of a rapids. Stumbling and shivering through the undergrowth, she found an overhanging rock near dawn, and slept. Garet stirred, but seemed to understand the need for silence. She laid her finger across his lips. He grasped it and stared at it in near darkness, then puffed a small laugh.

"No, little one. It is not time to play." He wasn't hungry, but she nursed him until he slept. Then she too slept.

Garet's crying awoke her in midmorning. She hoped the rush of the river hid the sound. She fed him, ate some dried meat herself, and listened a long time. She had not set up defenses, but she knew now she would have to resume the practice. Garet's safety outweighed her memory of the sound of Assek's last labored breathing. She sensed danger, the hovering shadow of Rabe, who was not a trained fighter, but still tall, strong, and, above all, intent. Ahroe left the river and traveled into the dry, rough country north of it, then hurried westward.

It was not until the third night that she returned to the river, and then only because she had found no water that day. Somehow the sense of danger hung like the flies over the water. What was it? Would Rabe follow this far, this long? She picked her way through the dusk to a place good for defense, then set up a triple-snare wall in the dark, but without stakes.

Just at dawn, she awakened to the sound of a sapling rushing upward and a shriek. Garet began to cry, but she muffled his mouth with her coat. He struggled, unconsoled. His crying continued, but the pouring river seemed to shroud it. Ahroe had readied her short bow, but she didn't move. Someone had been caught. Were there more? The light came slowly and showed a figure hung by one foot. Rabe. Her spear still held, she saw Ahroe and struggled to cast it. The tree bobbed and she cried out in pain.

Ahroe rushed her, knocked the spear aside, and brought her down by her hair. "Where are the others?"

"The others? All around you, male lover. See them? They will get you sooner or later, and your brat. Let me down, bather of men. Men's spit licker. Men's—"

Ahroe hit her across the face hard, slowly and deliberately, four times. "Where are the others?"

Rabe held her face with her hands. Through them she said, "You would do this to a sister! It is unbelievable."

Ahroe simply stared, then sat down and began to laugh, almost hysterically.

Rabe hung down in front of her. "You are mad. I knew you were mad. You and your males. You and your soap. Dragging a male baby across the wilderness. Cuddling it like it was human."

Ahroe looked at Garet. He was trying to stand, teetering against a rock. She turned to Rabe. "What am I to do with you? If I let you down, you will try to do us harm. If I leave you up there, you will die. The others quit, didn't they."

"I never give up."

Ahroe bound her arms behind her, hauled her downward and cut the cord. Rabe collapsed in a heap, then scrambled up, fell, and tried to stand again, but Ahroe held her down. "How will I be rid of you?" she asked. The other woman only breathed hard. Ahroe forced her forward, sat on her, and fastened her arms behind her, tying each finger separately, arranging the binding so Rabe could not chafe the thongs through on a rock. She was extremely uncomfortable, angry, and silent. Ahroe hummed a Pelbar hymn softly as she worked.

"Now what will—" Ahroe began, but as soon as she started to talk, Rabe yelled, and every time Ahroe tried to resume, she would yell again so as not to hear. Ahroe shucked off one of Rabe's soft-soled shoes and bound it in her mouth. Then she sat down and patted the other woman's shoulder. "You are being very bad," she said. Rabe thrashed around, trying to press one ear against the ground, the other against her shoulder. Ahroe rolled her over and sat on her.

"Now then, Rabe. You will have to walk home with one shoe on. Better go directly. You will not free yourself without help. By then I will be gone, and you will have to be satisfied with that. I wish you no ill. I feel sorry for all of you. If you do manage to follow me, I will have to kill you. You are a female Assek. Know who he was? A man who tried to force me. I had to kill for myself. You I will kill for Garet if I have to. Do you understand?"

Rabe made no sign until Ahroe took the shoe from her mouth and spun it into the stream. Then, panting, Rabe said, "You would really do this to another woman."

"Weren't you trying to kill me?"

"That is different. Only if you defended that male animal."

"Different?"

"Remember this. Somehow I will follow you. I will make you free whether you like it or not."

Ahroe sighed. "You are no match for me, Rabe. I am trained for this sort of thing. But you are welcome to try if you want to." She patted the young Jahv on the shoulder, then packed and walked down the rocky river bank with Garet on her shoulders.

She was relieved but alert. She was also weary, not only with her escape from the Jahv, but with the whole journey. It was beginning to seem endless. The country was so vast, so dry, so empty. Stel seemed nowhere in it. For a moment she wished she had never undertaken this search, but as she thought back, it seemed inevitable. How strange it was. Her feelings of Dahmen pride and justification had faded. How much trouble they had caused her. Were her family as elastic as all the others, Stel and she would never have left home, never gone through this hunger, cold, travel, danger, skulking, and hiding. She would not wonder each day if there would be food, watching a baby's health when his diet was uncertain, his surroundings wild and unpredictable.

As she moved west, the country seemed flatter and drier—sun and tufts of desert plants. Should she turn back to the Shumai, far away as they were? Where was Stel? Would her life dwindle out in the ragged edge of nowhere? High overhead she watched two vultures gathering altitude on the thermals. Surely they saw her. Through their slight thought she passed as a brief consideration. Was she a potential food source? No, she was not, would not be. Where there was discipline, there was defiance of death. But how awful things had become.

XVI

STEL had seen a similar change of landscape to the north, where the stream he followed tumbled westward to join a larger one flowing to the south. He put together a rough raft to cruise down the larger stream, but he soon found it too had rapids. As he waded ashore, watching his raft break up below him, he knew he would have to walk. Increasingly this river moved through canyons, some little higher than the bluffs of home, some much higher. Instead of the gray-white limestone of the Heart, this was a reddish rock, weathered into knobby round promontories with long, rough talus slopes sliding down from towers and buttresses.

Sometimes the walls were sheer, often at the mouths of dry washes, which sometimes made pleasant, flat-floored side valleys raying from the river. As he approached one of these, Stel heard the steady tick, tick, tick of chisel on stone, so familiar from home.

Across the valley he could see someone on a scaffold, crude and rickety, tapping at the rock face. Coming closer, he saw it was a woman, dark-haired, about Ahroe's size. Below her and stretching on either side of the canyon wall were carvings, in shallow relief, all of figures and animals, streaming west in a great migration, still faces in stone imitating the moving flow of life. Some looked back in fear, others ahead in weariness. Some seemed to see promise ahead. Most seemed merely moving.

Stel drew near and stood under, looking up. The sculptor continued working steadily. As the breeze shifted the scaffold, she would occasionally steady her position against the rock with her hands or her bare feet.

"This thing is a menace. You'd better be careful or you'll fall," Stel said. The sculptor jumped and turned, startled, and Stel ran to one set of braces to steady it. "Come down from there before you kill yourself. Let me fix this thing for you."

"You imbecile. Don't you know better than to sneak up on somebody like that? What? Who are you, anyway? I don't know you. You aren't a goatherder, are you?"

"Do they come this far west? No. I am Stel Dahmen. I am, of all strange things, a Pelbar from the Heart. The Heart River, that is. Far to the east. East is best and west is beast, I am beginning to think. Now come down off that and let me put it together right."

"You are rude and presumptuous. Who are you to tell me what to do?"

"I've done a whole lot of stonecutting in my life, and a good deal of it on scaffolds, but none on such a thing of grass as this."

"Go away, please. I am busy and do not want to be distracted. Why are you looking at me like that?"

"You look so much like my wife."

"Who? Where is she—at some mythical river in some other mythical place no one ever heard of? Why do you cut your hair like an inverted bowl?"

"To cook in in the evening, of course."

"As I said, you are distracting me. I didn't come here to be convivial. I came to get some work done."

"You surely are doing that. But you will be killed before you finish unless this scaffold is repaired. What is your name? You didn't tell me."

"I am Elseth. Some call me Crazy Elseth." With that, she turned back to her chiseling, leaving Stel still holding the swaying scaffold. He shook it slightly. Elseth grabbed the rock, then turned. "Get out, get out, get out," she yelled, throwing the chisel at him.

Stel ducked, and as he did, the whole scaffold tilted, swayed, and cracked. He rushed to grab it as Elseth climbed down, stepping on his head and shoulders on the way.

She stamped. "Look what you did. Now you'll have to

fix it." She strode off in the direction of a rough brush hut. Stel was charmed by her. Even her motions seemed like Ahroe's. Now he'd have to fix the scaffold. Isn't that what he had suggested in the first place?

Finding proper material was not easy, but Stel set to work on the scaffold, adding supports, repairing bindings, providing a series of racks for moving the cross seat when necessary. It took him the rest of the day. Then he dressed Elseth's chisel, which was worn and dull. She had not reappeared. He was reluctant to leave without talking to her. He had had no truly good talk since leaving Ozar. Besides, she looked like Ahroe. Finally he went to the brush hut.

"Elseth," he called. "It is fixed."

"Now I have lost the light. It is your fault," came a voice from inside.

"All right. Since you have lost the light, then you can come out and talk to me. You haven't anything to do, do you?"

"I am an artist and I must think. I must think quietly."

"Oh." Stel sat down in the dust. He cleaned his nails with his shortknife. After a time, he said, "Well, I dressed your chisel, too, and if you have any more, I will do them as well and save you time to think."

"What? Are you still here? You ruined my chisel?" She rushed out past him, running to the scaffold. Stel followed, coming up as she examined the tool. She stamped again. "I spent so much time getting this right, and you have ruined it on me."

"Ruined it?"

"Ruined it. I have done nothing to you. Now why don't you go and let me alone?"

Stel sat down again. "I will go if I have to, but look, Elseth, I have traveled a long way, almost all of it alone, and I am weary of it. I have been chased, attacked, imprisoned, threatened by those idiotic goatherds, those raise-a-finger-and-you-die people, and I have been far more alone than I care to be. Here you are the first normal human being I have seen in far too long, with something interesting that you are doing, and you tell me to go instantly. I suppose I will, but it is awfully hard." He looked up and laughed. "In fact, I don't know that I can stand it."

"Normal! You call me normal?"

"Is that an insult, too? Maybe you aren't. But rock-cutting seems normal to me. And not wanting to exploit me seems normal, too. You are intelligent and speak well. Now come on. At least you can spare a few minutes of talk."

"I came here to be alone. And to do this work."

"I won't stop you. I will help you if I can stay awhile and talk."

"I don't need help. I need to be alone."

Stel sighed. He felt both frustrated and whimsical. "Suppose I just stay and watch awhile. I won't even say anything."

"How can I work with somebody watching? And there will be the inevitable suggestions and interferences—such as my scaffold and chisel."

"If you want, I will temper it for you. And make you some more if you have any metal anywhere. What do you use—pieces from old ruins? That looks like a rod from the artificial stone."

"Temper it?"

"Make it harder so it doesn't dull and bend so quickly."

"You can do that?"

"Yes, of course. I am not a metalworker, but I have seen it done enough, and even practiced. I will even show you how. Please?"

"You can make me some chisels if you will go after that."

Stel laughed. "All right. I promise. I have a couple of long-eared rabbits if you would like to share them with me for supper. They are stringy, but they taste all right."

Elseth paused. "I will get some potatoes to put with them." She started, then turned. "You mustn't be here when my brothers come. They would not like it."

"More goatherders—do-this-and-you-die people?"

"No. We are Commuters. You met the goatherders? Had trouble and came away unscathed? You must have more to you than it looks for such a short man. No whip scars?"

Stel briefly told her the story of his encounter with

Catal and Blomi. As he talked, she sat in the dust and drew figures with a twig.

"Well, you were harmless with them. Perhaps you will be harmless with me, too. But you mustn't be here when my brothers come. And you will have to sleep somewhere else."

"Being harmless is what I am best at," said Stel. "I will sleep across the river."

Elseth went for the potatoes, which they cut up together, in their skins, and boiled with the rabbits. As they ate, Stel looked carefully at the young woman, drinking in her resemblance to Ahroe. But she was different. Somewhat short, she was a bit gaunt from self-neglect, but her dark hair, which hung freely past her shoulders, was clean and shiny, her nose finely molded and slightly square at the end. She had large, lustrous eyes and a full shapely mouth. Her cheeks plumped slightly, but her cheekbones rose above them, high but not really prominent. When she smiled, she almost always tossed her head, but a mist of melancholy hung over her. Her shoulders were not wide, and she probably would have had a full figure if she ate well. Her small, strong hands flitted rapidly with fine fingers, but they were netted with cuts and abrasions. Her legs were strong, with small ankles, and fine, high-arched feet. Stel thought she should not be here alone. She was someone who ought to be in a society, and cared for. She was no Catal.

Finally, she said, "You mustn't keep looking at me. It frightens me."

"I'm sorry. You look like Ahroe, my wife, whom I haven't seen for well over a year. It raises all sorts of feelings."

"I trust you will control them."

"Of course I will. She is still my wife. And as I said, I am very good at being harmless."

"I don't understand. Why are you here?"

Stel told her, in summary, the whole story of his exile and journey westward. As he talked, she stared at him more and more thoughtfully. "You must go to the Center of Knowledge and tell them all this—if it is true. Is it, surely? You haven't added anything?"

"No. It is as true as I can render it. What is the Center of Knowledge?"

"To the west—it is a large canyon with overhanging walls, in which the Commuters have gathered all the information they could about history, the time of fire, the small groups of wandering people who survived. As much as possible is chiseled in the rock."

"Chiseled in the rock? Why not simply write it down? On paper?"

"Paper? We have heard of paper. What is it? It is like leaves, isn't it? We never have found how to make it."

"I will show you. Here." Stel rummaged in his backsack and came out with the small compilation of the words of Aven. He handed it to Elseth.

She took it and began turning over the pages, slowly. "This is hard to read. But I can make it out. So this is paper?"

"Yes, it is . . ." But Elseth held up her hand, and soon was lost in the small book, completely absorbed so she didn't notice the sunset, wild with orange cirrus clouds. Shortly after, the moon rose. Stel simply fed the fire, as she sprawled by it, oblivious to all but the small book, her eyes flicking across its pages, then going back. Slight frowns formed and vanished. Stel watched her in fascination, then cleaned up the supper pot, scrubbing it with sand at the river. When he returned and sat down, Elseth suddenly jerked up and saw it was dark.

"Is it night? You must not be here. Take my log and cross the river. You may come back tomorrow." She returned the small book. "All this is bewildering. These are things more strange than dreams." She sighed and looked in the direction of her sculpture. "I don't know if you have ruined it or not."

"Ruined it? I?"

"You have changed the world."

"No. You are showing the world I know. Good night, Elseth. I will come back tomorrow."

As Stel crossed the river, using the log and pole he found on the bank, his emotions were too complex to fathom. A strange sadness fell over him as he found a place among the rocks to sleep. He unrolled his sleepsack and slid into it, but for much of the night simply watched the moon moving slowly across the clear black of the desert night.

He knew he had had enough of being alone. "Ahroe," he said aloud to the rocks. "I think I should have tried to be what the Dahmens wanted. Ah, Ahroe, I am sorry." But even as he said it, he knew he couldn't have. No. He had gone because he had to, and Scule's experience confirmed his understanding of the extent of the family's subterranean side.

Stel didn't cross the river again until well into the morning. He tried to bring his thoughts into focus, calming himself by playing the flute. He knew he could not stay with Elseth very long. He would be in love with her, or her resemblance to Ahroe. And then there were the brothers she referred to. Why had they left her out there all alone anyhow?

When Stel did cross, and walk up to the wall of carvings, Elseth was already on the scaffold chiseling and brushing. Stel didn't disturb her. He found the small supply of steel rod she had, some with the artificial stone still clinging to it, and set to work preparing a crude forge to make and temper chisels for her. He was nearly done by noon when the high sun and driving heat brought her down from the scaffold. She had on a large, floppy, loosely woven hat that shed squares of light across her face.

She looked at Stel and said, "I have some cold potatoes." Smiling slightly, he watched her walking toward her shelter. She even held her shoulders like Ahroe.

As they sat eating in the shade of the cliff, Stel asked, "When will you be done?"

"Done?"

"With your work? You aren't going to cover the whole cliff, are you?"

"Why not? There is much to represent."

"It will take a lifetime."

"Many years. Better to spend them here than chasing cows. This will last."

"But the rock will slough away. It all comes to the same in the end. It is the truth of the doing that counts."

"Perhaps, but it will last a millennium or two anyway, here in the desert."

"A millennium?"

"A thousand years. Don't you know that? We have decades, centuries, and millennia. Tens, hundreds, thousands. One thing the Commuters have is words."

"Where are they from? They make a peculiar combination, herding cattle and gathering knowledge."

"The Commuters were from the far west, by the Pacific Ocean. They were in the mountains at the time of fire, as you called it last night. They were in a town not really devastated, though somewhat burned. They made sure they taught their children these things."

"What were they doing in the mountains?"

"Getting away from the heat of summer. The legend goes that the ancients took time off from work in the summer and went where it was cool."

"What happened? Why didn't they go home?"

"That is one of the ironies. They were people who knew many things, but they didn't know how to do anything much. They could not live in the mountains, so they came west to the desert edge. So today we have fragments of knowledge of the ancients, like you, but we still herd cows. We know there was something called electricity, but we don't know what it was, except that it went through wires to make light and turn motors."

"Motors?"

"I have seen a ruined one. From the time of the burning of everything, a thousand and eighty years ago, by our measure. It simply turned, but with it you could make other things turn. They say you could do all kinds of things with it. But the Commuters had been people who used these things. Other people knew how to make them, and they all died."

"What a great death it must have been."

They fell silent for a time. "I wonder," Stel mused, "if the Commuters were up near the town I saw, below where Scule lived." He elaborated on his visit to the ruined town.

"I don't know. It was many miles to the east."

"Miles?"

Elseth laughed. "Yes. Inches, feet, yards, miles. And centimeters, meters, and kilometers."

"The Ozar have kiloms. In the Heart River country we have fingers, hands, arms, and ayas."

"What a shattering of knowledge. If we could only put it all together."

"There are so few people, and they all scattered, and formed into societies with hostilities and strange attitudes. Why do they call you Crazy Elseth? You are anything but that."

"Because I do this."

"Why do you?"

"It is a long story I don't want to tell."

"When will you finish?"

"Never, I hope. When I am carving, the rock sings, the shapes move, and all things seem in place."

"But all art has an ultimate shape. It fits in some frame, just as when you make a city wall. It goes and turns, proceeds farther, turns again, until it comes back on itself and makes a whole."

"Where is the frame of the sky? And where is the frame of your life? You are simply wandering westward. You may have had a reason to leave, but you have never found another motive."

Stel picked up a handful of pebbles and threw them one by one at a stone. None of them hit. "You are right. I am between lives now. But every song has phrases. Some of them are starting ones, then these develop, and others finish the song. So do poems. So do lives. One proceeds from babyhood to age, rounding oneself out. You will never fill the cliff. You will just have to stop sometime."

Elseth stood up. "I have to go back to work. You didn't ruin the chisel. It is much better. I suppose the shape of my carving will be the length of my life." She looked at him through narrowed eyes, and a sense of hurt crossed both their faces like the shadow of a summer cloud. "You will have to go soon," she added. "My two brothers will be here in a day or two to see how I am surviving, and to bring me some food. I know you mean no harm, but they will not, and they will be furious."

"I will go in the morning."

"Tonight. I will tell you how to find the Commuters."

"Tonight? So soon?" But Stel knew he had to go. And he knew that between them an awareness of why was growing. So he was to be chased off again, this time not by a screaming McCarty, but by someone who feared love. Well, she was right. He would go.

Stel spent the afternoon working on chisels, cutting off the heated steel, shaping it, and tempering the finished pieces. In the heat, he was streaked with trails of dusty sweat, even in the dry air. He had to work with rock hammers, holding the steel with bent-brush tongs. The wood smoked and burnt. It was hard work and the results were not at all pleasing. At one point he paused and called up to Elseth, "I wish your brothers were here so I could show them how to do this."

Before his eyes, a bush seemed to sprout a man, who said, "We are. Who are you? Why are you here?" He had a whip. Stel stepped back and cast his eyes around for another man. There was one, but he stood a good way off, holding two horses. Elseth jumped down and ran between them.

"No, Shay. No. Don't harm him. He hasn't harmed me. No. He is going tonight. Please." The other man rode toward them, leading Shay's horse.

"Who is he? Get out of the way. We will deal with him."

"No. You mustn't. He has a weapon." Shay thrust her aside and advanced on Stel, who stood still with his short bow strung and an arrow nocked. The man on the horse was shaking out a noose in a long rope as he cantered the horse in. Stel surprised him by suddenly running at him, cutting between the two horses, and slicing off the tether with his short-sword as he passed. Shay was after him, and the mounted man turning. Stel wheeled and stood. Shay slowed to swing his whip, and Elseth, who had leaped back up, hit him full force in the back, knocking him down. Stel snapped a quick arrow right between his outstretched hands. Shay looked up with sudden fear.

"Your brother gets the next. Right through the chest." Stel said, nocking.

Shay made a quick decision, jumped up, shouting, "Whoa, Than, whoa. He has some weapon." Than scooped up Elseth under his arm and cantered away. Shay turned and faced Stel.

"I am weary of this," said Stel. "A country full of violent and irrational people. Now, you will go over by your brother while I gather my things, and if either one of you comes anywhere near me, I will at least wound you, at most kill you."

"If you hurt my sister, I will—"

"I didn't. And you won't do anything. You and your brother are like children. More goatherders. More drop-a-pebble-and-you-shall-die people. Now I will count to ten, and if you are not past that fire by then, this arrow will chase you. One, two, three, four . . ." Stel didn't finish. Shay had sprinted off so fast he saw he wouldn't have to. Too bad. Another encounter had turned out badly. After the pleasure of chatting with Elseth, the threatening men. Stel packed deliberately, taking one of the new chisels. He could see an animated discussion between Elseth and her brothers. Stel strung his longbow, and, as they watched, shot an arrow straight up, flashing high, higher, seeming to hang a moment, then turning and rushing downward toward the river. He felt silly, like a child showing off. But it seemed a harmless way of insuring that they would leave him alone.

He walked slowly toward the arrow, picked it up and cleaned it, deliberately sharpened the point against a rock, and walked on down to Elseth's log. He was tired of being victimized, misunderstood, attacked. At the log he stopped, sat down, and played his flute, three full songs. The three watched him across the flat valley. Then he poled the log across the river and beached it. On the shore sand, he wrote with a stick, "Good-bye, Elseth. You are not crazy, but your brothers are. I am sorry not to have finished the chisels. May you fill the whole cliff wall with figures until you are happy and satisfied. And since I have found that there is a shining sea, which you call the Pacific Ocean, I think I may go there. There is another ocean to the east—a thousand ayas east of the Heart. Jestak, a Pelbar of Northwall, has been there."

Laboriously, Stel climbed the cliff. When he reached the top, he could see the three standing on the far shore. Elseth waved to him, but Shay slapped her arm down. Stel waved back and set out westward. The dryness seemed to throb against him like an infection. He would turn south and find the river again. After Elseth, the weight of his loneliness cut into him again.

Nearly two days later, Stel saw five horsemen approach, leading a sixth horse. He strung both bows, setting down the short one and nocking a long arrow. The horsemen halted about two hundred arms off, then one trotted toward Stel. As he approached, Stel could see that it was Shay.

"Stop there."

Shay held up both hands. "I'm unarmed. We want to talk."

"Get off your horse and walk," Shay did so, coming slowly. "That is far enough. I can hear you."

"Elseth says that you can make paper. She says you have some."

Stel said nothing.

"We need to learn how. We will not hurt you. We need to protect our sister."

"Where is Elseth?"

"She is back at her work."

"You have a strange way of protecting her, leaving her out there. I don't trust you. I have trusted too many people—the Dahmens, McCarty, Scule, the goatherders. I am lucky to be alive. Take your horses and go. I will keep my paper. You keep your treachery."

"We will pay you. We will not harm you. This is the truth. You cannot blame us."

"I will count again. Be to your horse by ten. One, two, three . . ." As before, Shay ran, and Stel stopped counting. When he was mounted, Shay trotted back to the others. Stel waited while they talked. Then an older, bearded man detached himself from the others and rode slowly toward Stel. He was thin, almost frail. Stel said nothing until the man was only twenty arms away.

"That's far enough."

"I don't believe you have the paper. Show it to me."

"I don't care what you believe, and have no interest in showing you anything but only in defending myself. I used to be an innocent, but I found it is too costly."

"Young man, failing to trust is as dangerous as trusting."

"Perhaps you are right. I am going to try it awhile, though. Trusting has failed badly enough."

"That is what Elseth feels, and why she chips away at

the mountainside. You made her trust again for a moment, and I am grateful to you. I apologize for Shay and Than. They only thought to protect her."

"I will tell Elseth anything she wants to know about paper. That is, anything I know. But her paper is rock, and mine is sand, it would seem. What do you mean, she carves the rock because she fails to trust?"

"Well, young man, that is my concern. She has been hurt and will not heal. Ah, I see you feel for her. I don't think you will kill me. I am going to dismount and walk to you, then sit down. Please humor an old man. I have carved words in rock until my hands throbbed. I would see your little book."

Stel was alarmed. He backed off as the old man advanced, but when he sat down in the dirt, Stel took the book from his backsack and gave it to him, then backed off again, keeping a watch all around him. The old man felt the pages. He turned the leaves slowly and soon became as absorbed as Elseth had been. The horsemen stood in the heat. So did Stel.

Then the old man looked up solemnly. "It is all so simple—if you know how to do it. We have tried but failed. We have written on cloth and goatskin, as well as rock. Goatskin is all right, but far too expensive to disseminate knowledge. Here is your book, young man. I don't know why you carry it, since you now deny all it seems to say."

"Not all. I am afraid of some. I seem to understand less all the time. It seems a ruthless truth, a right with bite."

"Quite. I am Elseth's father. Cannot you trust me for her sake?"

"They are her brothers."

"They love her, are unwise, a bit foolhardy, but loyal. I apologize for them."

"That would not put my skin back on. A flayed rabbit is good only for stew. I've lost the habit of being a rabbit."

The old man smiled. "If I got that horse, and sent the others away, would you come with me alone to the Center of Knowledge? Are you afraid of me?"

"No. I am not afraid of all of you together on my

terms, though I am a little afraid of the horse. What assurance have I? What need have I to go with you?"

"You know your need as well as we know ours. We need to know about paper, which our ancestors used but never made. We need to know about your Heart River, your Pelbar, the others. You need to know about us. We need to come together again. You are much more valuable to us alive than dead, and vice versa. Besides, we do not kill. We didn't even kill the man who hurt Elseth."

"I would have."

"Then you are like Shay and cannot criticize him. Now come, son, with me alone."

"I have never ridden."

"And that is a very old horse. And I am an old man. My name is Howarth. And you are Stel? Wait. I will get the horse." He rose stiffly, mounted, and returned to the others. A discussion ensued, but eventually the others rode away, and Howarth returned with the horse, showed Stel how to tie down his backsack, and they set out. The sun burned down unmercifully.

"This is a bad year," Howarth remarked. "We have lost the spring rains. Our cattle will be in a bad way by fall. I fear we may have to deal with the Rockpilers again."

Stel looked at him but said nothing. It sounded like more trouble.

☐ XVII

THE river Ahroe had been following joined a larger one and turned west, then more southerly. As it happened, she was not far downriver from the small side valley in which Elseth worked on her cliff. At the time, Stel had already ridden west, leaving the same river behind.

Ahroe continued downstream, increasingly into canyons, and at one point, where the east bank dropped sheer into the water for some distance, she crossed to the west, on which a band of flood plain, sometimes narrow, sometimes wider, lay. Like Stel, Ahroe found she could not float down the river because of the rapids. Occasionally, on a lazier stretch of water, she would ride a log, with Garet straddling it in front of her, dangling his small feet in the water, gurgling with amusement.

On the third evening, she saw lights ahead of her and decided to stop until morning. She wanted to see what it was in daylight.

Before the sun broke the rim of the eastern canyon wall, Ilage, a priest of the Originals, climbed to the parapet with his tambourine and sang his morning song, welcoming and urging the light. He overlooked the northern wall of the small city of Cull, the Original city, a settlement of about five hundred people who supported themselves by agriculture along the river bank, for here the river widened out, affording the only break in the west wall of bluffs for many ayas in either direction. For this time and this region, their population was considerable. Their inclinations were ceremonial, though, rather than dynamic. Satisfied with their way of life, with the endless risings and settings of the desert sun, the unfailing supply of the river, they were content, and lax in many things, except in the rituals of days and seasons.

Ilage was the priest designate of the morning. His reed cape billowed in the light breeze as he made the sun rise with his song, drawing it up into the sky, as the priests of Cull had done daily since time had begun. Ilage shook the tambourine, his eyes supposedly enraptured by the sun. But the song was repetitious, and he knew it many seasons ago, so he checked the river level as well, as he sang. He saw it had again dropped slightly as measured against the Rock of the Great Shoulder on the far bank. He was worried. The spring rains had failed. The Commuters would need water for their cattle. As the branch streams dried, and the washes they dammed lost their last pools into the sand, they would come again as they had when Ilage was a boy, driving their cattle to the river. They would have to come to Cull. But the whole side valley was planted, much more than last time. There would be another fight.

Of course, this time there was a wall, piled according to the direction of the priests, using only rocks unmodified from nature, the great builder. Perhaps the wall would hold. One could never tell with the Commuters, though. They were a wretched lot of impractical people, wild travelers without religion or proper governance, but they were also full of surprises and in love with learning —all of it false, of course, based on the notion of a great time of burning and death in the past, on the concept that there was a time when Cull did not exist, and other cities did, while Ilage knew Cull was the Original city, needed to minister to the sun.

Ilage turned his thought to the sun again, the Great Disk of Life, and this time prayed and chanted sincerely for the Original city's prosperity and safety. As he finished, his eyes fell to the river bank. A woman was standing there, dressed strangely, in a tunic gathered at the waist, worn clothing, carrying something on her back.

"Aaahhhiiieee," Ilage yelled. Boldar, who was lifting

water, came running. "Ah, look, the first of the Commuters. Take your staff. Drive her off."

"She doesn't look like a Commuter to me. She's just a young woman. Thin, too."

"Aaahhhiiieee. Do as I say. Go." Ilage gave the big young man a boost with his foot. Boldar shrugged, took his staff, and trotted down the stairs toward the river as a small crowd of Originals mounted the wall to look on. Ahroe stood her ground, watching Boldar, who towered head and shoulders above her, advancing.

"Go on, now," said Boldar. "I will take this stick to you."

"You so much as try and I'll put an arrow in you."

Boldar stopped, puzzled. "Go on, beat her, beat her," Ilage screamed from above. Boldar looked up, squinting, and turned again to Ahroe.

"I will go," she said, "but don't come near me."

Boldar was nonplussed. Ilage still screamed down at him, but he could see no harm in the woman. What was she? She seemed supremely confident. What was that she held? Now she turned, slowly. A baby sat strapped to her back, squinting in the light.

"Boldar, you sniveling coward, beat her. Send her running," Ilage screeched.

"No you don't, Boldar," came a woman's voice. "You hit that baby and I'll rap your skull." Boldar looked. It was Mati, head of the nursery of the planters.

Ahroe turned and laughed. "You've got problems, Boldar. I suggest you listen to her. Don't worry. I will go."

"You don't have to go for me. I see no harm in you."

"Contamination. She is a Commuter spy," Ilage screamed.

Mati grabbed his tambourine and hit him with it. Ilage was outraged and stared at her openmouthed. "A spy bringing her baby? Has the sun fried your brain? You nanny goat. Sending that big bull after a woman with a baby. Now shut your mouth before I stick this in it."

Ilage drew himself up, took his tambourine, and departed slowly down the winding stairs toward the beehive-shaped sanctuary. He held himself erect and tried to make his face passive. It was another assault on the priesthood. The seculars of Cull would have to be brought into line.

Boldar laughed and turned to Ahroe. "Why don't you come inside and have something to eat? I think it will be all right."

"I'm not sure I want to. I've had experience with this type of person before. I am alone and must be careful."

Boldar gave her the staff. "Don't worry. Mati and I will protect you. The priest is worried because of the drought. He is afraid the Commuters will come for water for their stock. Here is the only place they can get it if we don't get a rain, and this isn't the season for it."

"Then why don't you give them the water?"

"We use the valley for our crops. And we can't carry water for over a thousand cattle, and feed them, until after the fall rains. Last time this happened, I'm told, the cattle broke in and ruined much of the harvest. There was a fight. But come in. My mother is fixing flatcakes. She is called Doray. I am Boldar. There will be plenty for you and her."

"That is a him. Garet. I am Ahroe Dahmen of Pelbarigan, far to the east on the Heart River. I am here—well, on a journey. Have you had any other visitors?"

Boldar frowned and thought. "No. Pelbarigan? Never heard of it. Far from here? Up toward the mountains?"

"Far beyond the mountains and across the Shumai country. Farther than you could dream of distance."

Boldar led Ahroe in, introduced her to the joys of flatcakes, and left to hoe tomatoes. Doray talked with her half the morning, and Mati came and took Garet to the nursery. As Ahroe saw him go, her heart leaped a little, but for the first time since she left Ozar, she felt he was safe in other hands. Garet cried and held out his hands as he passed through the triangular doorway, but Mati hugged him and talked to him, and soon he was studying her ample nose and grasping it firmly.

Doray arranged for Ahroe to stay with her mother, an old, stout woman named Ovi, who wove baskets and mats, slowly but deftly, drinking tea all day. She was a widow, quiet but curious, and fascinated to meet Ahroe, asking her questions with a downturned mouth, as she peered farsightedly at her work. Cull was really a hospitable town, easygoing and relaxed, except for the schedule of ceremonies, each announced from one or another large, squat turret by the booming of a large drum. Ahroe was clearly welcome to stay, but she first arranged an interview with Ilage. She wanted no enemies and told him as much. She found him a fussy man, soon satisfied by her odd accent, and other strange ways, that she was not a Commuter. He even apologized. She could see that he was worried.

"The Commuters are a wild and bestial people," he said. "They have no settled place, except for their silly Center of Knowledge. They come and go, and their talk is abstruse and disorderly. In good years we trade with them some, but this year there will be trouble. It will be worse because of what Dilm did to the young woman."

"What did he do?"

Ilage looked at her and dropped his eyes.

"Did he get away with it?"

"He fled. He is beyond the comforts of Deity now."

"Who is Deity?"

Ilage was shocked. Ahroe held up her hand. "I see. Don't worry. We call Her Aven, Mother of All. The Ozar call her God and think of her in more masculine terms, as you probably do. Every group has Aven, or Deity, under different names. The supernatural and the source of ethics. Right?"

Ilage thought a moment, not wanting to offend, but confident of her woeful ignorance. What could this waif know of the priestly calling, the stately marching of the ceremonies, the chants and drums, the fine-smelling fire and the slow dances with which the true dignity of Deity was celebrated?

"Yes, you are right," he said.

Ahroe smiled. "You are a nice man, Ilage. Excitable, but nice."

"It is the Commuters that have worried me. They are beasts, dressing in rags and holding endless discussions about geometry, mathematics, history—a false history, that is. They cannot make an irrigation trough or prune a peach tree. They know nothing of religious usage. They will be coming here before the summer heat is gone."

"They sound like the Shumai. We have had long experience with marauders at Pelbarigan, though now we are at peace with them."

"What did you do?"

"We lived behind walls. We defended ourselves so well that they seldom harmed even one of us. And we offered them peace and kindness always. That is the first thing you must do. If they need water, you must get it for them if you can."

"There are too many. The grass and plants have failed on the hills. Their cattle need food. Unfortunately, our gardens tempt them."

"Then you must try to help them, and if that does not work, you must have a system of defenses that will prevent them from destroying you."

"We must dance and pray to Deity. We are not experienced in such matters. We have few weapons because we have no need of them."

"I know a good deal about defense. Perhaps I can help. What weapons have they?"

Ilage frowned. "I don't know, praise to Deity. I have never seen them with any except their whips and ropes—and of course their stock knives."

"No spears?"

"Spears?"

Ahroe laughed. "They don't sound very fearsome. Do they throw rocks?"

"Sometimes," said Ilage, nodding seriously. "They throw large ones, and they do use slings sometimes."

"Slings? Do you have these?"

"Only to chase birds."

Ilage arranged a conclave of the priests at which Ahroe was to discuss defense. She clearly knew much more about it than they. As she questioned them and reviewed their knowledge, she found them almost hopelessly lax. And she ran into priestly blockages at every suggestion. As she looked at their walls, too, she found frustrating their theory that one must use stone only as it came from Deity through nature. The builders had become expert in visualizing how rocks from their piles would fit together, but still the result was not strong.

"At Pelbarigan," she told them, "we cut and fit our stone, interlocking it so it makes a single unit. Were my husband here, he could show you how to do it. I see you have no true arches, either, but simply edge the stones out until they meet at the top."

"How else can it be done?" asked Furme, an Original priest, skeptically.

"I wish I had paid closer attention. The result is a round arch, like a bent willow twig. We build whole rooms that way."

"What is to keep the rocks overhead from falling in?" Furme said, smirking.

"Stel could tell you. It is the way the rocks are joined. But it is no time for theory. We must set up some defenses for you. Is there any way you could build a corridor so the cattle could reach the river and not enter the gardens?"

The rejection of this idea was universal. Ahroe could see that the Originals were unable to perceive the value of accommodating the Commuters. They simply wanted to stop them. It seemed not only unreasonable to her, but unwise as well. However, she agreed to help.

Viewing their upper wall, which ran across the narrowest part of the upper end of the valley, tying in to outcrops on either side, Ahroe frowned at its flimsiness. Shumai battering logs would have brought it down in a couple of moments. The enemy would hold the higher ground. There was no backup system. If the Commuters were as wily and ruthless as the Originals thought, there would be trouble.

Nonetheless, she set to work, instructing them on wall bracing, preliminary traps, backup positions, a second ditch and wall, and the use of spears. So little wood was available, and so little time for instruction, that this seemed the most useful set of methods.

She also tried to train raiding parties, with slings, to stampede the herds at night as the enemy gathered above. All in all, it was frustrating work. Eventually, she felt that there were cows on the outside of the wall, and also cows inside. So used to their quiet gardening, their round of ceremonies, were the Originals that they could hardly conceive of the strategy of a raid.

Ahroe tried to relate the whole process to games but found that they had almost no sports. The life of the Originals was hedged in not only with the walls, cliffs, and river, but with observances and ceremonies. Several times she had the men she was trying to train simply walk away when the drums from the heavy towers called them.

She got Boldar assigned to be her assistant. She thought his size and strength would help, and he was one of a number of the Originals who were basically practical, tolerating the priests because that was what they were used to, but not awed by their procedures. He was plainly devoted to her and amazed at her abilities, and tried to be of help. But he could not see the use of posting massed guards on the hilltops when there was water to lift for irrigation, fruit to dry, or grain to grind. When the Commuters did come, the Originals would see them.

One day as they were on the upper slopes with Ahroe studying the possibilities of flanking positions on the high rocks, Boldar tapped her arm and pointed. A single horseman stood at the head of the funneling valley.

"There. He is a Commuter."

"Come. I will talk with him."

"No. You mustn't. They are a fierce and wild people."

"And I am a fierce and wild woman, Boldar. They should have called you Timid. What is it you are Boldar than?"

"What?"

"No matter. Come." She held up her hand and advanced toward the distant horseman, but he turned his mount and trotted over the rim of the height and vanished.

"He didn't look fierce and wild to me. He looked scared."

"I think you should have the walls built higher."

"They cannot be higher without being stronger. As it is, they can be battered down."

From down the hill Recha came running. When he recovered himself, he said, "Upriver. Four miles. The grass gatherers found Commuters. They had begun gathering the grass and passing water up the cliff in buckets."

"How many?"

"I don't know. Many. The cliff is high and it takes many hands."

Ahroe scanned the piled walls. It didn't look at all good. Well, she would do what she could.

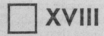 XVIII

STEL stayed with the people at the Center of Knowledge for over three weeks. The paper-making had started poorly, because of the lack of proper materials. But they made progress with cottonwood, once they had learned to make chips and beat the fibers separate. The main problem was water. The process took it in quantity, and there was almost none.

Finally they succeeded in pouring out a quantity of water-laden pulp onto a cloth on a flat rock, spreading it with a roller, squeezing most of the water out, and letting it bake dry in the sun. It was uneven in thickness and a bit lumpy, but it was undeniably paper. Howarth, especially, was delighted.

The other people at the Center of Knowledge kept Stel busy with questions. He was a new dimension to them. They often laughed at his lack of knowledge of things from the time of fire, things they knew well. They had not suffered quite the blackout of knowledge that the early Pelbar had. But he enlightened them on many things, not only about geography, the present peoples of the landscape, and their cultures, but about the practical things they seemed persistently to know so little of. It was easy for Stel to see why Elseth carved rock in her own private valley. Artistic expression abounded. Even wooden bowls and spoon handles were carved individually and creatively.

Occasionally Stel and the Commuters startled each other by some piece of preserved knowledge that they shared—never so amazingly as when Otta, a thin old man who tended the Center stock, played a melody on a stringed instrument with a sound box, and Stel was immediately able to furnish harmony on his flute. It was the "Song to Aven, Source of Joy." The Commuters called it the "Joy of Man's Desiring," but had no words to it. The experience brought a general hush, as they sat in the sun musing on the strangeness of the past.

A horseman came slowly into the box canyon. It was Shay. He dismounted stiffly. "The Rockpilers are ready for us. They have built walls, high ones, and other defenses. Pross is already near Cull. All the north wells have failed. I met Tad and his brothers with twenty-two head as well, going toward the river."

Howarth sighed. "They must share their water and grass. We cannot perish because they are standing in front of the only water. It will be another battle."

"Perhaps you can arrive at some agreement with them," Stel said.

"We have tried. In good years they sometimes trade with us, but in drought they do not. Perhaps we have been wrong. We have destroyed their gardens in our desperation. But they haven't suffered as we have."

"You have almost no weapons. They will slaughter you."

"They have almost none, either. Neither of our societies fights. We have our studies. They have ceremonies. We keep occupied and stay out of each other's way."

"Except when there is drought," said Shay.

"Yes. Drought brings out the worst in men, in spite of hope, in spite of plan."

Stel smiled. "But after drought there comes a rain, and then the grass grows up again."

"When you two get through riming, maybe we ought to do something."

Howarth stood up and brushed his ragged shorts. "Debba will not like this a bit. It is a bad time."

Debba, Howarth's wife, didn't like it. But it was she

who suggested that Stel might help. He knew a great deal about warfare that neither the Commuters nor the Rockpilers had dreamed of. Stel wondered about it. Things were growing more desperate all the time. Eis soon rode in from someplace called North Navaho Sink. They too were running out of water and feed.

Before long, separate groups of Commuters were moving toward the river. The dryness of their grazing lands meant that they lived apart, in small groups, and the entire Commuter society did not total more than four hundred, with about sixteen hundred head of cattle and horses. As Stel was caught up with the gathering migration to water, he noted how poor they were, and how gaunt the stock. In this heat and drought, the Commuters were trying to survive. As he questioned them, he found little overall organization, except educative, largely in history and the arts, and little ability at a concerted military effort.

When Howarth's family arrived above the river cliffs, many others were already there. Lines of people handed buckets and skins of water up the cliffs in relay fashion, but it was much work for little result, and there was nothing much for the stock to eat.

"We will appeal to the Rockpilers for enough feed and water for a trip north. But it is a good sixty miles until we can reach the river ford, then cross and try to get to the mountains. If we even can. Then there are the goatherders, but they will not be all that much trouble."

"Perhaps you can negotiate with the Rockpilers. Offer them some of your livestock in return for what you need."

"I doubt it, but we can try. But make no mistake, Stel, we mean to survive, even if that means a fight, and messing up their precious gardens. We don't like it, but nobody here is going to simply pass out of existence because they have blocked off the only access to water."

Howarth's attitude left Stel musing. The old man normally was quiet and noncombative. The Rockpilers, it would seem, had created a viable mode of life for themselves, denying it to others, while the less provident but more interesting Commuters had not. There was a certain justice in what Howarth said. But as a Pelbar he had long been a defender, and he knew how the others felt. He then gave Howarth a short account of his own experience with the outside tribes before the peace.

"The difference," Howarth mused, "is that they needed you and you them. The Rockpilers need us for nothing. We have offered them education, which we have far beyond theirs, but they see little in it. They are ceremonially inclined. They are woefully ignorant of history. Some of them actually think the sun would not rise if they did not sing it into the sky. Come. Ride with me to Cull and look at it. See what you think."

The two walked their horses with Shay to the crest of the hill above the funnel mouth leading down to the valley of the Rockpilers. Stel suddenly reined and held Howarth's bridle. The old man frowned at this.

"Look," Stel said. "A ground trap. Three more steps and you'd be in it."

"I don't see anything."

"Here," said Stel, handing the old man his bridle. He dismounted, ducked under the horses' heads, and brushed dust away with his hands, then lifted off a framework of light twigs. Beneath was a pit perhaps an arm's length deep with pointed stakes driven into its floor. Stel stood up again, then put it all back together. "If I didn't know better, I'd be sure that was Pelbar work," he said.

"They've never done that before," said Shay. "And look at those walls. They've worked on them a good deal lately."

"See the guard posts? I think I see men in them. Now. Look down there. I think they have ditch traps as well as these pits. This will not be easy. But those walls are flimsy. They will not be much trouble to breach, if it comes to that. Ladders would be easiest, behind a cover of cattle. You will need slings and staves. I can at least give you all a short staff lesson. What will happen when the wall is breached and the cattle pour through to the river? It could get very deadly."

"They will run."

"Are you sure? They outnumber you. Neither side seems heavily armed. There could be a lot of bruising and killing."

"Stel, you don't like this. Neither do I. What alternative

have I? They always have run. I have checked the
records. This has happened four times that we have recorded. Each time there was a fight, then they ran and
hid. We watered the stock well, and fed them, loaded
them down with water, and left for the mountains. Each
time was a hard one. There were always fatalities, and
once it was really bad. But there is no record of any of
these defenses."

"They are all familiar to me. Always remember—when
you have circumvented one set, you will be tempted to
think you have made it. There will always be another
trap for the unwary. I don't like this. They have had
some advice. Look—are those spears I see down there?
Down by the wall?"

"Spears? My old eyes don't see that well."

"Yes," said Shay. "They are spears."

"What is it like by the river? Could we climb down by
the cliff and approach them from the rear?"

"They have walls there, too," said Shay. "So Dres said.
They were gathering grass upriver from Cull."

"Apparently they are ready for us, Howarth."

"What do you recommend?"

"Talk to them. If that doesn't work, nullify the traps at
night, but so they don't know it. Then attack the walls directly behind the cattle, using ladders and crooks to bring
it down. It is an awful wall. They ought to be ashamed of
it."

"Fortunately, they are not. We had better get organ-
ized. Stel, you ought to be there when we talk, but we
will do the talking. It is our problem. You are unknown
to them."

By sundown the family heads had gathered and talked.
They agreed to Stel's plan, having none of their own. He
drew it roughly in the dirt.

"We ought to send some men by the river," said one
man.

"Shay says there are walls. With so few," Stel replied,
"you need a mass assault to break through the wall. The
only real chance is that they will run, as they have in the
past, and leave you the place. Once you are inside, they
will fight as well as you, I assume. After all, it is their

home. I know I would fight. You may well lose a lot of stock, but the stock may confuse them, too.

"They made one very bad mistake—building that silly wall down from the summit in the narrow part. Here we have the height advantage, and they have to look up at us. With missiles, especially, that is important. If you divide your forces, and send some down to the river, the Rockpilers will also have that same height advantage. We mustn't hurry, either. We need at least another day."

"They will have that day, too."

"Yes, but that is time to talk to them, get supplies, coordinate, and most of all to study the trap systems so they can be nullified at night. If that is done quietly, so they don't know it, they will be stunned when the whole force moves over their defenses to the wall."

"Can that be done?"

"Yes, with a lot of people, and a lot of care. Ditch traps you dismantle and fill in, then cover over again. Spring traps you disarm. Trips you tie off so they look untouched. And we need some logs for rams. Are you used to stealth?"

"I can catch long-eared rabbits bare-handed," said one woman.

"Is that a general skill?" Stel asked.

"We are pretty good sneakers, as you may remember," said Shay.

Stel laughed, and, glancing up, saw Elseth. "And so are you, Elseth. Hello. What are you doing here?"

"I knew it would come to this. The cliff will wait, and if I don't come back, it will be the same."

That brought a pause. "By all means talk first," said Stel. "There is a lot of Elseth's cliff that needs to be carved."

At that time, Ahroe was also advising the circle of priests to talk.

Teleg, the chief priest, a portly old man who thought himself wise, said, with his fingertips pressed together, "You have told us that you came from a walled city. Suppose this people came to your wall and demanded more resources than you could give and threatened you if you did not give them."

"They did many times."

"And did you talk with them?"

"Always. We had a message stone where all talk was held. We gave to our own limits, and when further giving would threaten us, we defended ourselves."

Teleg pursed his lips. "And for us, how much would that be?"

"That could be over half your resources if needed. You have plenty. Your water is unlimited. Remember, in a fight, people would die."

"Not with our walls."

"Those walls? They would not hold a wild turkey, let alone a herd of thirsty cattle. They aren't yet braced properly, intertied, locked in any way."

Teleg paused. "We have made the walls in accordance with Deity, using natural materials in a natural way, just like these solid cliffs. We will rely on Deity to help us."

"We always did that, too. But our feeling has been that Aven, or Deity, did not excuse anyone from trying to help himself according to his intelligence."

"Ahroe, the priest has spoken," Ilage whispered, horrified.

"Oh. Yes. I am sorry," said Ahroe. "I will help you if I can. But the best way, if it is possible, is not to fight."

Teleg clapped his hands, ending the conference.

The wind rose with the sun, and piled clouds. Noting them, Stel asked if there might be rain in them. "Yes, for the mountains there might," said Shay. "Not here."

The Commuters brought a delegation down near the edge of the trap field—six men and six women, all family heads. Their flag, showing the great beast on white, with a red base and star, flapped stiffly in the rising wind. Stel stood to one side. At last, five priests of Deity, in reed robes, climbed down the wall and walked through the trap system to face the Commuters.

"Greetings," said Howarth. "We have come because we need water and river bank feed. We wish access to it. We see you have the valley securely walled off. We will offer to trade you stock for our needs. Or work. We have agreed that we will work for you in exchange as well."

Ilage was offended by the abruptness of this statement. Were any people less decorous? And look at them, dressed in rags and skins. A glance to his side showed him the others felt similarly.

He raised himself up. "We have lived here since time began. We have cultivated this valley and made it to fruit in accordance with the wishes of Deity. You have ruined it before. We do not have enough for you, and we have no need for your stock. What animals we need, we have."

"Is that a clear refusal, then?"

"A refusal? No. It is an explanation. You must give us time to confer. We will return after the recital call of half-morning. Then we will give you a reply. In the meanwhile, our greetings to you, and our good wishes for a prosperous future under our father, the sun, given us by the Deity and praised daily by the priests of Cull."

"Confer? You grass-covered goat, you well know that you have already decided. So it is a refusal, then? May I remind you that we have taken food and water before, and we will take them again if we have to. We do not wish to but are driven to that necessity."

Stel winced. "Howarth, perhaps there might be some exchange they will be willing to consider."

Ilage was already turning away, but here was a new voice, in a strange tone. Who was he, a short young man, thin but squarely built, with massive shoulders, bearded, with piercing gray eyes.

"What exchange to you propose?" Ilage asked.

"I am not sure. What needs do you have? What skills do you lack? Perhaps education. I am not a Commuter, but I have seen they are people of wisdom. I have learned much from them. Perhaps you could as well. Or there are building skills. Yours are, by the standards of many groups, just slightly archaic, to put it kindly. I mean no offense."

Shay, who was holding horses, laughed. "He said last night that a wild turkey could tear that wall down."

Ilage gasped and turned white. Those were Ahroe's words. So she was some kind of spy, after all. He didn't know what a wild turkey was, either. Perhaps some kind of cow. Ilage bowed. "We will have to confer, and we will return as we said, and let you know if there are needs you can fulfill for us."

"Something is wrong," said Howarth.

"You were about as diplomatic as an axe," said Stel. "You certainly knew better how to appeal to me when you wanted to know how to make paper."

"We had wronged you. Besides, that was important, a matter of knowledge. They would have put us off in the end anyway. It makes little difference. Did you see the way that gnome talked?"

At the central council of the priests, when Ilage reported the encounter, Ahroe was outside, talking to Boldar. "They aren't a fierce and wild people at all. I saw them from the wall. They are thin and ragged. Only one was bearded, and he looked different. It is wrong not to negotiate."

Boldar smiled and said, "The priests will decide." He was surprised when Ren parted the robe and called him in. He was not gone long. Ahroe was worried. Had she helped these people, who were comparatively rich and well situated, to refuse the destitute? That was not only uncharitable. It was also unwise. Desperate people do desperate things.

Boldar was not long. He came out slowly, reached down and plucked a couple of weeds, then, before Ahroe wondered what had been wanted, he pinioned her arms. She kicked and thrust, but he held her as three others wrapped rope around her flailing legs, then slipped loops around her wrists and bound her.

Ilage came out and looked down where she panted at his feet. "I knew you were a spy when I first saw you. I told them."

"A spy?"

"A spy. But the bearded one gave you away."

"The bearded one? Who?"

"He said a wild turkey could knock down the wall. Just as you did. It was unwise. But Deity will protect his people, and it was revealed to us in due time."

"What is a wild turkey?" said Boldar.

"That is it. No one knows. But they both know. That proves it. And here you have taken our hospitality while you have been just a snake in the garden." He shuddered and then spat at her.

Ahroe was bewildered. She struggled and pleaded, but to no avail. She was put in a large root cellar with a guard by the door. He was young and pimply. He sneered at her and picked his nose. She needn't worry. Her friends would be defeated, he told her. Then she would be alone and guess what he would do with her.

"Ask Ilage who helped him with his defense system," she said, ignoring the threat. "Would a spy do that?"

The adolescent laughed. "There was some trick to that, too. Ilage said you set up a good system to lull us into thinking we were safe. Then you would get word to your friends exactly what the defense was so they could avoid it. They are studying it now to see what weaknesses you put in the system."

"Then you had better abandon the whole system. After all, it was the concept of a spy."

"It is too good."

"You make no sense at all." As she talked, Ahroe thought she finally made a little headway with the cords on her wrists. No. It was impossible.

On the hill above Cull, the Commuters came at the appointed time. The wind still increased, blowing around the legs of the waiting men and women. No one came from Cull.

"It is just as I thought. We ought to take them now."

"There are still the traps. It is odd. I don't understand it at all. Perhaps there was another western Pelbar beside Scule. It is all so familiar."

"Maybe it is a classic method, like the identity of our songs," said Howarth.

"Perhaps. But it is so characteristically Pelbar."

"Well, what do you suggest?"

"Wait until night and nullify the traps. Meanwhile go away so they have no sight of us. Listen, isn't that man shouting at us from the wall?"

"I can't make it out. I thought he said they captured our spy. Cano, do you know of a spy we have sent?"

"No," she said simply. "I know of none. Does anyone?"

All looked puzzled. Turning their horses, they rode back over the crest of the hill, meeting a blast of hot air as they reached it. Howarth squinted up. "If I didn't know better, I'd swear that was rain in those clouds."

"For the mountains," said Shay.

In her prison, Ahroe heard a sound at the door. It was Mati, bringing Garet to be nursed. The heavy woman sat in front of Ahroe, holding the baby to her breast. Ilage came in after her. Ahroe reddened at her exposure, but the priest had changed, and he and the guard seemed to enoy it.

Ahroe bowed her head, saying, "Garet must eat, but they must go." Mati said nothing. "Mati, I am not any spy. I don't understand. A wild turkey is a big bird in the east. It lives in the woods. Somebody among them must have been there."

"He even talked like you," said Ilage, "a degraded accent."

Ahroe started. "What color were his eyes?"

"His eyes? I don't recall. I was busy. I didn't have to notice details to see his strangeness. He was odd, with his beard and his hair cut like a bowl."

"He wanted to negotiate, didn't he, not to fight," said Ahroe, feeling faint.

"Yes, of course. You agree in that, too, thinking to gain from us that way what you were unable to with our wall. See? You still give yourself away."

So it was Stel. Her Stel. After all this way, she had actually seen him, without knowing it, from the wall. She had helped prepare defenses against Stel, and tomorrow he would come through the trap field, never dreaming that it was there, to meet spears she had helped sharpen against him. She looked up at Mati, with tears. "Mati, you must protect me from him tonight," she said.

"And who will protect us from you?"

"Please leave Garet with me."

"He has done nothing. We will keep him even when they execute you. We will do you that kindness, but for the sake of the child. He shall be properly raised."

"Good Aven, the child of Stel raised to grub roots in the desert and believe that songs push up the sun. He must be returned to the Heart River."

"If there is such a place. I doubt it."

"Please send Boldar to guard me tonight."

"Why? So you can convince him to let you go?"

"I can trust him. This one is another Dilm." The young man stood and spat at her, but the glob of mucus slapped down on Mati's ear. She screamed and made for him. He ducked out the door as she threw a rock after him. Garet lay on the floor, kicking and crying. Mati returned and picked him up. She was still furious. Her eyes blazed as she looked at Ahroe. Then, taking Garet, she stamped out. Ilage stood smiling down at her.

"Like your plot, you are uncovered."

Ahroe leaned forward. "What can I do about it?"

"Nothing, apparently." He turned and left.

Before long, Boldar came, grim-faced. "So now I have to stay here. Don't worry. You won't get away from me."

"Boldar, cover me up."

He looked and turned his head away.

"I can't sit here like this." She laughed almost hysterically. "I guess I have lost all my Dahmen pride now, haven't I. But you are at least decent, Boldar. Cover me up. Surely you see this is immoral."

The big man turned, sat on his heels, and with clumsy fingers drew her shirt and deep-cut tunic over her and tied the cord. Both were embarrassed.

"Boldar, do you know people are going to die? Can't the priests make some agreement?"

"Be quiet," he said, going to sit in the doorway. "I have nothing to say to you." When the adolescent returned, Boldar gave him a look, and he left.

Night crossed the canyons and deepened. Ahroe asked for a drink. Without speaking, Boldar gave her some water and returned to his place. Did he sleep? No. Every time she stirred, he looked. She had worked on the cords that held her, slowly and quietly, for some time before she felt the first one begin to give. Fortunately it was dark. Boldar still sat impassively in the doorway. Even down in this valley the wind gusted now, occasionally blowing dust in his face.

At this time, Stel and a group of about thirty moved forward through the trap field, disarming it. Everything was done by hand signals and touches, as Stel had worked it out. Behind them, an ever larger group brought sand forward and poured it into the ditches, smoothing them over as they were before. Stel seemed to know exactly where to go to find them. Shay grew suspicious. It was too neat. He watched Stel more closely.

Eventually they were right under the wall and could hear Rockpilers talking. They spoke of the spy, the crops, and the difficulties of irrigation. At least forty men were there, but most slept.

Shay touched Stel's shoulder and whispered, "We could take them now."

"They outnumber us. We need the momentum of the cattle. We have to be here in full strength and strike deep into the valley before they all gather. Sunrise."

It seemed to make enough sense. Back at the fire, Stel was as openly puzzled as the others. The trap field had been finely executed. "It is as if Oet designed it. She is the guard chief of Pelbarigan. This makes no sense at all."

"Well, the traps are all gone now, aren't they?"

"I think so. We really covered the hill. And we have posted guards to see they do nothing more."

"Then let it go. We will find out eventually. Let us have some music."

"Softly. We don't want them to hear."

"In this wind, no one could hear."

They played a number of songs with a group of stringed instruments and Stel's flute. Finally he stuck it in his belt, saying, "If I'm going to get myself killed tomorrow morning, I think I'd like to sleep a little now. Sleep a little and then leap a lot." He walked into the shadows to his sleepsack, unrolled it, and crawled in.

Shay watched him, standing with Elseth. "I don't trust him. Something is odd about those traps."

"You trust none of my friends, Shay."

"Your friend?"

Elseth put her arm around him. "Brother, he did something for me—just by talking to me. He wanted nothing from me but thoughts, but company."

"Don't fool yourself again, sister."

"Oh, I know. He is a normal man, but he was so wholly free. He came along and said, 'Here I am. I will help. Come down and I will fix your scaffold.' It was in pretty bad shape, you know."

"He didn't do much."

"He showed me another model of behavior. There is nothing wrong with him. He has been through a lot. He has become self-contained. He is as independent as a cactus, needing only a little rain once in a great while."

"I don't understand about the traps."

"Neither do I. Perhaps we will."

In the pitch-black cellar at Cull, Ahroe finally heard Boldar's even snoring, light but sure. Taking a chance, she rubbed the cords hard on the rock wall. After what seemed a terribly long time, they gave. She worked on the ankle cords for a maddening length of time. Then she stood and nearly fell with stiffness. She stepped over Boldar with precise silence and groped along the wall in the direction of the nursery.

As she slipped inside the door, she could dimly see rows of beds. A tentative hand showed her all were empty, even Garet's. She would try Mati's home.

Was that the first faint wave of light in the east? Ahroe slipped through the street and into Mati's courtyard. Inside the doorway she could see the dim outline of the older woman in a side room. Two babies slept in a large basket by her. Quickly, Ahroe ran a finger over the two tiny chins. Garet's was cleft—like Stel's. She gathered him up and stole out into the night. Yes, that was dawn coming.

Once in the fields, she walked rapidly toward the upper wall. The four guard stations she herself had placed—too well, she thought now— loomed ahead. Light was growing. So was the wind. Surely there was rain in that wind. Garet began to cry. Ahroe stuffed the corner of his blanket into his mouth and winced at her own child's discomfort. Better to be gagged than an Original, she thought.

Behind her, lights and shouts showed that her escape had been discovered. She had to move fast. Soon they could see her. Was that a drop of rain? No. It couldn't be.

The easiest vantage for her would be the south station, by the outcrop. It should have at least ten guards in it. Behind her the shouts grew louder. Now surely they could see her. It was true dawn. Yet she had to pause here, kneeling in the gravelly dirt. Were the guards awake? No. True to their complacent nature, they all reclined in sleep. The Deity would protect them. They were needed to push up the sun.

Ahroe heard footsteps behind her. It was Boldar, coming fast. She scrambled up the wall and started across the trap field. A gust of wind blew the blanket, and Garet started to scream.

"Get back," Ahroe yelled. "It is a trap. Get back." At the ridge crest a line of figures appeared. Ahroe yelled again, her legs driving. Above a figure detached itself from the line.

Boldar was nearly on her. Ahroe strained ahead, and as she did, the figure from above flashed by her. She saw him reach for a stick in his belt. A stick? He slammed into Boldar with a solid thud. The big man went down with a yell.

Ahroe shouted again, "Get back, back. They are waiting. There are traps." She gasped. A woman was coming forward, and Ahroe impulsively thrust Garet into her arms so she could run on. The cattle were already milling and lowing. Again she screamed, "Get back," at the advancing line of stock and men, waving her arms. A new gust of wind almost blew her down, and with it came a patter of rain, then a rush. A man took her shoulders. "What is this?" he shouted against the roaring rain. "Who are you? Not one of them."

"Stop. The whole field is full of traps. You will not make it to the wall."

"Stel told us how to dismantle them last night."

"Stel? Stel? Where?" She wheeled around to where a man stood over Boldar, now far down the slope. Blown rain almost obscured them.

The big man sat in the rain, crying, "You've stabbed me in the eye. You destroyed my eye."

Stel looked at his flute, which he had grabbed from his belt, impulsively thinking it was his short-sword as he drove into the man chasing that woman.

Elseth advanced and handed Garet to Stel. "Don't just stand there, Stel. He is hurt." She went to Boldar and knelt by him. "Sit still. It was only his flute. You have been blinded by the power of his art. Lie down and let me look at it."

Stel had taken the baby in puzzlement and now looked at the face, screwed up with its crying. Garet opened his eyes for a fresh breath. Gray. A new gust of rain lashed the baby's face, and Stel held him against his shoulder. Then he frowned, paused, looked again. Cattle were all over the slope, milling and lowing in fear. Something was familiar in that face.

The full fury of the rain fell on them, and the terrified cattle could not be driven, but turned and ran off, with men and women chasing them.

"My eye. He put it out," Boldar yelled.

"Lie down and open it. It is not so bad. Let me see."

"It is all muddy here."

Shay ran down the slope. "Elseth, come away. You will be trampled. He will hurt you."

"He is a child. He hurt his eye." She took the big man's head in her arms and held him so she could see the wound.

A small party of men with spears started from the wall to rescue Boldar, but Stel advanced on them, now with his longbow ready—as ready as he could make it with this unaccountable baby. Someone was beside him.

"Get away. We only want Boldar."

"My eye," Boldar yelled.

"Stop, you baby. It is all right. Here, it is only bleeding."

"Elseth, come away. You are down in the mud."

"Is that you, Ahroe?"

"No. I am Elseth."

"All right, you four. Get down that hill before I put an arrow in each of you," Stel shouted. "Will somebody come and take this baby?"

"It is your baby, Stel."

"It's the bearded man. And the woman, Ahroc." Five gaunt cattle dashed across the slope, and the four Originals retreated.

"See? Your eye is all right. It will be black."

"You are not Ahroe. Who are you?"

"Elseth. I told you."

A cow bumped Stel, jolting him. What? "Your baby, Stel"? Had he heard someone say, "Ahroe"? He turned to the figure by him, running with the torrent. She was laughing, her hair plastered to her cheeks, her face streaming with rain, keeping one eye on the figures down the slope. Stel felt weak. Ahroe? His Ahroe? What? How was it possible? And the child? His baby. It was his own face he saw. He looked again, holding Garet's face out in the rain. Did he ever cry like that? Well, he had been kept out of the rain.

"Give me the longbow." He did.

"Ahroe? My Ahroe? I don't understand. But the traps. You set them up."

"Yes. For the wild and bestial Commuters, according to them. It was my mistake."

"What? The rain is too loud."

Ahroe shouted in his ear, "It doesn't matter. Nothing matters. We are all together. Look. It is your boy, Garet. See his face?"

"Garet?"

Stel hitched him up on a shoulder and put his arms around Ahroe, holding her in the rain. She held his longbow still strung, with an arrow nocked. The swirl of people and animals had left the hill, except for Boldar and Elseth, and Shay standing near. Boldar's eye was clearing slowly. He couldn't understand the two still figures standing together in all the whirl of rain and wind.

"It is Stel with some woman and a baby," said Elseth, her face glistening. She blew some drops off her nose. More streamed down.

"Who are you?"

"I am Elseth. I am a Commuter. Are you frightened?"

"Oh. No. What is going on?"

"We are out in the rain. It is only late August, and it is raining. Did you notice?"

"My eye. How it hurts."

"Yes. Would you like to go home? It is that way."

"No. I will soon enough. There is no work in the rain. I guess we won't have a fight today. I want to find out what is going on."

"Wouldn't we all. Shay, what is going on? Why aren't you helping with the stock?"

"I am watching this Rockpiler. I don't trust him."

"Stel is here."

"He appears to be occupied. Somehow. Unaccountably."

Elseth laughed again. "It must be Ahroe. His wife. A miracle. He told me about her. She has come all the way from the Heart. You know, she does look a little like me.

Older. And thinner, maybe. And not so beautiful. But it is hard to tell in this rain." She laughed again, leaning against Boldar. Then she patted him on the shoulder and said, "We have a lot of cattle to gather up. You will have to go home by yourself. Come along, Shay. I don't think Stel has heard a thing we have said." They started up the slope, Shay looking back.

"Damn him," Shay said.

"Who? Stel?"

"Who else? I thought he loved you."

Elseth laughed again. "He did, I think. I thought you didn't like that. Look at him. See what he loved? No. He really loved me, too, a little. But I will take the big Rockpiler."

Shay looked back at Boldar, who still stood there looking at Stel and Ahroe. They paid no attention to him, and finally, holding his eye still, he walked down the hill through the mud. Elseth dragged Shay away from Stel and Ahroe. Her grip on his arm was astonishingly tight.

"We had better put this baby under something," Stel said. "I know where there is a nice rock outcrop. All my gear is soaked by now."

"Mine is back there in Cull. I suppose they may give it to me sometime."

"None of that matters to me. I don't understand, though. It is a miracle. You are really here. I am dizzy. And our own boy."

"We will talk about it." They set off up the hill, slipping in the streaming mud, and as the rain continued to beat down on the deserted wall, a section of it crumbled and rolled into a growing gully, and the dim outlines of the trap system slowly appeared as sunken earth, filled with rain.

XIX

IT rained hard most of the day under a driving wind. Stel and Ahroe eventually moved from their high outcrop to a large overhang down near the river, downstream from Cull. There was wood on the slope, and they could cut into the dry part and start a fire. Stel stripped to his pants and caught a little wood in the river, which had risen from the rain. He also rigged a hook and line for catfish in a side riffle, and, walking in the rain along the river bank and up into the deserted gardens of the Originals, he picked some tomatoes, cucumbers, and a melon.

But they spent most of the day drying, talking, and looking at each other. Stel held Garet much of the time, studying him in fascination. Finally the rain slowed, and, toward evening, ceased altogether.

"Ahroe, I am running like this river. It is all too full and is rising out of me. How many times I have wondered about you and yearned to have you with me. The most amazing thing is that you would do this for me—and that you actually got all the way out here. It is a rare Dahmen who would do that for her husband."

"What had I left, especially when I knew I was pregnant?"

"I'm sorry I ever put you through all that. I should have gone to Northwall."

"Look what we would have missed. We have been farther west than Jestak. If they sing songs in Pelbarigan a hundred years from now, they will sing one about us."

Eventually they fell silent, watching the water run from

the edge of the rock overhang. After the rain, Stel checked the line and, in spite of the rain, found a medium-size catfish. Setting the line again, he returned, and they baked the fish stretched on a flat stone.

"I will be glad to settle down and have a good meal now and again."

"Yes. Do you like it out here, Stel?"

He looked at her. "Anywhere you are is all right with me. But if you were at Northwall, that would be excellent."

"Not home, then? Perhaps we might find a place."

"What if we started a separate family?"

"Some wouldn't like that. But I am willing. Before I left, I knew that they really had tried to kill you, Stel. But that was a long time ago, and we aren't the same people. They will never fit us in again."

"When I saw you and the Shumai, Ahroe, I came very close to calling to you. How different things would have been."

"All this has changed me. I don't know if that would have been better or not."

"It didn't happen, anyway. We cannot prefer what didn't occur."

"I fully concur. I'll never demur."

"Garet's demure, not very mature."

"A true connoisseur in miniature."

"I am unsure how to procure an appropriate answur."

"Well, Stel, what do we do now? About the Originals and the Commuters?"

"We have to get them to talk. Then we'll take a walk."

"Who can you trust? I think I can trust Boldar—the big man you hit in the eye with your flute."

"Don't laugh. It worked."

"I'm certainly glad it wasn't a sword. You struck the one blow in the whole war. Boldar has no authority, of course. But I will never agree to talk with that Ilage again."

"Then it is Boldar—and Howarth for the Commuters. But we will need more. And we will need to teach them some things. Ahroe, I fear we may need to stay here awhile."

"In a house."

"In a house. I'll be your spouse."

"We'll have a mouse and dine on grouse. It will not be easy. The Originals are all caught up in a series of ceremonies. And most of them, like Boldar, are unthinking. But he is decent."

"Well, now that it is dark, and my sleepsack is dry, and Garet is fed, I suggest that we work that out in the morning." Stel grinned at her.

She smiled back. Their orientations had changed. She would never be a Dahmen again—and Stel never really had been. "I am the guardsman," she said. "You take the sack. We could never both fit into it."

"We could try."

Next morning Stel and Ahroe walked back to the hilltop. Below, the Originals were working on the damage caused by the rain. They were skilled in directing water, but this storm was both untimely and massive, and had dug gullies and toppled walls.

Eventually both Shay and Elseth rode along the ridge top looking for them.

"How are the lovers?" Shay asked.

"Everything is fine. Where is everyone?"

"Now the pools are full, and the wash dams, there is water enough to drive the cattle to the west slope of the mountains where there is grass. So we are mostly going. Well, Stel, I guess you won't be going to the shining sea."

"I have it here. Two of them. See? But we need to talk to the Originals before you go. Where is your father? And Cano? Aren't there any of the others? This is the time to form an agreement for regular trade, exchange of labor, access to water, raising of grass, education."

"Whoa. Now there is no need. There may not be another drought like this in my lifetime."

"And there may be one next year. The point is that you ought not to allow yourself to get into such a position. There should be regular exchange among neighbors. You should be intermarrying and diversifying your activities. We know how to bring the water up the hill to here. It would take a little work to set it up, but wind and the river will supply the power. Raising water will help you both. And there is no reason a walled corridor could not be built to get your cattle to the river. There need be no more encounters at all, ever."

Shay and Elseth sat on their horses looking skeptical. Stel added, "I will teach you how to build wagons, too. Then you can move feed. And you ought to build a road to the mountains. Then you could move aspens for paper and set up a paper-making building by the river. You could move the Center of Knowledge there and build a town. You might lift the Originals out of their—"

"Whoa, Stel," said Elseth. "One thing at a time. Here comes Boldar, whose eye you played upon with your flute. We will see what he has to say. Then perhaps we will get Father."

The big man toiled up the still slippery hill. He had a large bandage on his eye. Elseth and Shay dismounted.

"See, Boldar? It didn't even take a wild turkey. The rain brought down the wall. How is your eye?"

"It is all right, Ahroe. I was sent by the priests to ask if we are going to have peace. Well, what is it?"

"We need to have a conference," said Ahroe. "There are many things to decide. We will be here at noon. Can you bring your people? Ilage must not be one of them. We will not talk to Ilage."

"What? Oh. No. Of course. Mati wants to know how the baby is. She was mad as a snake when you stole him."

"Indeed. I thought it was my baby. By the way, when you come back at noon, bring my things. We would prefer that you talk for your side."

"Me? For all of Cull?" Boldar laughed. "I can see the priests buying that." Then he turned to Elseth. "You are the person who helped me with my eye. Your name was Elseth?"

"It still is."

"Well, thank you. I will bring you something when we return at noon." Without an explanation, he held out his hand to Ahroe, grasping hers. Then he turned and walked back down the hill waving his arms for balance in the mud.

Elseth smiled at her brother. "You see? He likes me."

"Yeah, well, we'd better find Father."

The noon meeting was very tentative, but Stel and Ahroe were able to reveal enough possibilities and new ideas to interest both sides. It became clear that the priests governed Cull only by default, and a sizable portion of the people thought more secularly. One was Boldar, who slowly emerged as a spokesman for the Originals, much to the distress of a number of the priests.

As a start, it was agreed that Ahroe and Stel would live at Cull and work on setting up a waterwheel for lifting the river water to the fields, then a pair of windwheels to lift it farther. Stel would instruct the Originals in wallbuilding on the condition that they left a corridor for the cattle. When the Commuters returned in the fall, the Pelbar would help find other access to the river, even if this meant much construction by both sides. They also broached other ideas that spun the heads of both fairly static groups.

One of the more interesting developments of the next few weeks was the emergence of the genuine love between Elseth and Boldar. She was like a dog around a horse with him, her quick mind and tongue leaping ahead of him, he steadily walking behind. Their relationship continued to develop because Ahroe and Stel held the group talking, day after day, for some time until agreements could be reached.

Stel worked through the winter on his first projects. The spring rains had ended before the first waterwheel was completed, lifting water by a system of buckets to a high flume that led it out over the shoulder of the north hill to a pool in the gardens, where a windwheel lifted it higher still. Opposition to the system as unnatural came from the priests, but the people who had raised the water by hand were overjoyed.

Soon after, Elseth and Boldar were married and went to settle in Elseth's valley. She called her cliff-carving complete, except for an occasional touch on it. They set up a farmstead near the river and kept stock. People from both communities regularly met there, and the Originals gradually lost the notion that they had been in Cull since time began.

The stonecutting took longer, but Stel vindicated Ahroe by demonstrating to the Originals how to construct a true arch, then a vault, tight and strong. Ilage could not believe it. Ahroe still had not talked to him. In fact, she never did while they lived at Cull. After a while she didn't much care, but she saw that it kept him off balance, because he knew he had shamed her grossly, and when the priests elevated him to the chief priest's chair, it helped to control him.

By the time Ahroe and Stel left for home, the following spring, Garet was running and chattering—nearly two and a half years old. They tried to prepare him for the sights of their long trip.

"Ahroe," he said. "Big trees?"

"As high as that rock."

"As that rock? That high? Why?"

"You spend too much time with Stel."

"Why?"

"Sigh. Just wait. You will see the big trees."

Howarth and Debba went with the Pelbar as far as the shattered city in the mountains. With no sister to watch, Shay came, too. From their talk, Howarth and Stel decided that might be the place the ancestors of the Commuters were when the catastrophe of the time of fire occurred. The Pelbar left the Commuters with full instructions on the route eastward to the Heart, should they ever want to come. After staying in the house of Scule, Ahroe and Stel ascended the high pass, which was still deep in snow, in its earliest spring thaw. Then they picked their way down the eastern side, with Garet still staring at the tall trees. They followed a rushing stream down into the basin, and headed across and up the next range to drop down and pick up Hagen at Ozar.

Ozar was deserted. Two graves showed them that Finkelstein and Taglio were dead. Stel crossed the fields to the room of records and found a note inside. Hagen had taken Fitzhugh back to Shumai country.

Rather than risk the Roti, the three walked all the way around the two great empty places and crossed Emeri country, using the north end, where the scattered farmsteads lay. They were quiet and careful, and no one saw them. They felt much relieved to come down out of the last hills onto the vast grasslands of Shumai country. By this time it was nearing midsummer. Rather than walking all the way east, they made a long raft and poled it down a lazy, broad river as Stel worked on a narrow boat. When it was ready, covered and pitched, they paddled much faster.

At last they passed into the great river of the west, the Issou, and down it to Black Bull Island, where they were told that Hagen had already been with a small, dark woman. They had gone on to Pelbarigan. Clearly the two were looking for Ahroe. As the river turned south, they abandoned the boat and walked east through the high grass. The sumac already blushed red. The dry grass stood so high that Garet rode on either Stel or Ahroe so he could see.

"Find black cow," he would call.

"You are scaring them all away with your big voice."

"No, no. Find cow."

"Shut your eyes. There, that is as black a cow as you'll ever see."

"No, no, Stel. Eyes."

At last they topped a rise and saw the mass of trees that filled the bottomland of the Heart River. As they reached the bank, Ahroe said, "I know this place. We are not twenty ayas north of home." They camped a little ways downstream, fished, and swam in the brown water. Silent and massive, the great river steadily drew all the waters of the midcontinent down to the southern sea, impassively, appearing still until you could see the current rolling and burling around the head of an island.

Garet looked at it, his stomach out. "Big?" he said.

"Yes, Garet. It is big. This is your river. We are almost home."

"My river?"

"Yours. And mine and Stel's. Stel, it is as if we've drawn a circle with a compass. It swung out away, and before it was all drawn, it had two ends. Now it has all but closed and has none."

The next evening, as the mist steamed off the river into the cooling air, Hagen stood on Rive Tower at Pelbarigan, looking west. Fitzhugh was with him.

"It is a long walk. Give them time. I never dreamed I would walk so far."

"I think I may go back and look for them."

"I couldn't walk that far, Hagen."

"No. I wouldn't be long. I'd come back. Who is that?"

Sagan and Rutch came up the steps. The first fall gulls were arriving, settling on the river in the deepening dusk. They heard a distant sound from out on the river and upstream.

"What is that?"

"It sounds like a flute."

"A flute?"

"Look, out on the water. What is that in the mist?"

"I don't see anything."

Erasse was the guard on the tower. "It is three people on a log, two adults and a small child." He sounded the guardhorn in three long blasts, which echoed down the bluffs, magnified as it bounced back from the fifth promontory. Then there was a renewal of silence. From far out, thin as an insect song, came three return notes on a flute.

"Well," said Sagan, turning, "that is Stel. That is no one on earth but Stel. Rutch, you are a grandfather surely. Well, don't just stand there. Come down to the river and meet them."

"And Ahroe? And Ahroe?" said Hagen.

"Of course. Ahroe has retrieved him," said Erasse, and he sounded the five clear, ascending notes of the guardsman's salute, which Gagen Tower took up, the echoes mingling as the two calls reverberated from the rows of bluffs and out across the dark stream.

A native of New Jersey, Paul O. Williams holds a Ph.D. in English from the University of Pennsylvania. Following three years of teaching at Duke University, he settled at the tiny Mississippi River town of Elsah, Illinois, where he is currently a Professor of English at Principia College, teaching American literature and creative writing. He and his wife, Nancy, have two children.

His response to his small community has been varied, including helping to found Historic Elsah Foundation and direct its small museum, and serving as the president of the local volunteer firefighters. His poems, essays, reviews, and articles on literary subjects and Midwestern history have been widely published. While he has written largely on nineteenth-century America, and served as a president of The Thoreau Society, he has also developed a deep interest in science fiction and fantasy.

The Breaking of Northwall, his first novel, is set against the same background as *The Ends of the Circle.*